W9-AAQ-779

Also by Jocelyn Davies

A Beautiful Dark

A Fractured Light

JOCELYN DAVIES

An Imprint of HarperCollinsPublishers

To my parents: for teaching me how to dream, and for always believing I'd find a way to turn those dreams into reality.

And for Grandpa, in memory.

HarperTeen is an imprint of HarperCollins Publishers.

A Radiant Sky
Copyright © 2013 by HarperCollins Publishers
www.epicreads.com

Library of Congress Cataloging-in-Publication Data
Davies, Jocelyn, 1983–
   A radiant sky / Jocelyn Davies.
      pages   cm
   Sequel to: Fractured light.
   Summary: "As the leader of the Rogues, Skye must fight to maintain the balance between order and chaos—and for a way for her and Asher to be together"— Provided by publisher.
   ISBN 978-0-06-199069-4 (hardback)
   [1. Angels—Fiction.   2. Supernatural—Fiction.   3. Good and evil—Fiction.   4. Colorado—Fiction.]   I. Title.
PZ7.D28392Rad   2013   2013008065
[Fic]—dc23   CIP
                                                                       AC

Typography by Erin Fitzsimmons
13 14 15 16 17   CG/RRDH   10 9 8 7 6 5 4 3 2 1
❖
First Edition

There are certain things they never tell you about love.

Fairy tales and campfire legends make it sound easy.

A Guardian falls in love with a Rebel, and their love tears the heavens apart. Their daughter isn't light and isn't dark, but both. Undeniably, painfully both. And no transformation from mermaid to girl, no glass slipper, no prince charming or enchanted beast can help her figure out where she truly belongs.

They'll tell you what it's like to fall in love. All the wonderful, terrible things. That it hurts when you're together, and when you're not. It hurts when you know, and the not-knowing hurts even more. They'll tell you that no matter how strong you are, no matter how much you fight or steel yourself against it, it hurts to have your heart broken.

But what no one ever tells you is that to break your own heart—that feels even worse.

I always believed that love could only shatter you. Make you believe the impossible until the impossible is all you know. And then when the impossible is real, when you've forgotten who you are, forgotten everything that makes you you, only when the world is different and you are different and things are shining the way you never knew they could—that's when love rips you open from the inside out.

I always thought I could live without it.

"Love," Asher had once said. "The great destroyer of worlds."

But I was wrong.

1

"I can't go with you."

The minute I said those words, there was no going back. There was no changing my mind. A few months ago, I might not have been so sure. Ever since that icy night in January when I turned seventeen, life as I knew it had boiled down to this: I had to choose.

Between light and dark.

Between the Order and the Rebellion.

Between Devin and Asher.

Tonight, in these woods, everything changed.

Because I chose neither.

I could no longer pretend that I belonged on one side or the other. I wasn't a Guardian, and I wasn't a Rebel. I knew that now, with more clarity than I'd known anything in my life.

"Skye," Asher said. His eyes were pleading. "Don't do this." He looked between me and the group standing behind me, and then to Ardith, as if for help. "We need you." He paused. "I—"

He didn't finish the sentence, but he didn't have to. I knew what he was going to say.

The unsaid words twisted around my heart and squeezed tightly.

I need you.

And maybe he did. Maybe he needed me for my powers, so the Rebellion could win—or maybe to fight beside him, as we'd been planning.

But did I need Asher? My powers had surpassed his, as Raven had predicted they would. I didn't need his help anymore.

And did I need love? It was a new choice, a different choice. Between following my heart and starting on the path I finally knew I was supposed to take. It wasn't easy, but I knew the answer. I had always known.

The silence twisting around my heart snapped, and the pain flooded through me as I realized it.

I had to let him go.

Dusk was settling in the woods around us. To my left, Aunt Jo stood with her arms crossed next to my two oldest friends, Cassie and Dan. On my right, my friend Ian looked defiant next to fallen angel Raven, my former enemy, now linked to me in a way I didn't yet fully understand. And standing in front of me, facing me down, were the Rebels: Ardith and Gideon, Asher—and now Devin. All of them on the same side, for the first time. I couldn't see any Guardians, but that didn't mean they weren't there, lurking in the shadows.

Guardians stalk these woods.

"Skye, you don't have to do this." Asher's hands hung at his sides, where they'd fallen when I told him I was leaving the Rebellion. "Let's talk. We can figure this out."

"She made up her mind," Ian said, stepping forward. He had never trusted Asher, and disdain radiated off him. A light shone in his eyes. He had won. "We're starting a new group."

"Ian," I hissed. I put my hand on his shoulder and pulled him back.

Next to Asher, Devin looked up sharply. His blue eyes pierced mine, but he said nothing.

"I'm sorry if I made you think something else," I said. "But this is who I am. And this is what I have to do."

"You're just as cold-blooded as the Order," Ardith spat,

anger and betrayal clouding her eyes. "I knew we couldn't trust you."

"She's not. You know that," Devin said. "She's doing what's right. Doesn't the Rebellion believe in that? Even if they disagree with her cause?" It was the first time he had spoken since jumping from the Order. Ardith whirled on him, the starlight catching her long chestnut hair.

"Oh, look who feels right at home speaking up," she growled. "A Rebel for a whole minute and you've already found some *rules* to follow. You can take the Guardian out of the Order, I suppose—"

"Don't make me cut you, Ardith," Raven said icily. She ruffled her silver feathers, which glinted sharply in the fading light.

"It's no use arguing." Gideon had been silent, too. Even though his voice was low, we all heard him perfectly. "Whether it's now or on the battlefield. We're enemies now." His eyes grew cold and distant—the look of someone retreating into his horrible memories—memories he spent every day trying to forget. "We're going to war. Against each other."

Silence echoed across the woods as his words sunk in.

"Then that is how it has to be." Everyone turned to look at me, and I felt my hands balling into fists at my sides. All I could think was that I had to get home. To start figuring out what all this meant. What my future held now.

I swept past the group and toward the cabin, where the last remaining pieces of my childhood sat in a box in the attic, waiting for me to bring them home. I knew the Rebels were questioning my decision, but I didn't care. My friends would support me, even if the Rebels didn't. The reality was that I knew I never had a choice to begin with. This was *always* how it had to be—it's just that I hadn't realized it until now.

I tore through the woods to the place where my parents had set up camp once upon a time. The house was exactly as we'd left it that morning, but I saw everything differently now. It was like looking at a jigsaw puzzle that's been taunting you for months, watching the image suddenly snap into place and wondering how you never saw it there before.

I climbed the stairs to the attic, and would have taken them two at a time if I thought the rickety wood could handle it. There, in the corner, was the rumpled sleeping bag that Asher and I had shared the night before. He had been so patient with me while I figured out my powers, given me so much strength. His confidence in me alone made me feel like I could become as powerful as everyone said. Like I really could be the key to saving the universe.

But I couldn't give that same confidence back to him. I

couldn't fight by his side if it meant denying who I really was, my mother's daughter, with my mother's powers—a part of me that was just as much alive as my powers of the dark. He had to understand. He had to have known this day would come.

On the other side of the room, by the stairs, was the stack of boxes that I'd knocked into the night before, spilling their contents everywhere. In the darkness, I hadn't had a chance to go through them. But I knew who they belonged to.

My parents.

Last night, a small metal object had gone rolling across the floor. When I'd bent to pick it up, the ball of fire Asher held in his hands showed that I was holding a baby's rattle. The silver was dented and old, tarnished from disuse. But in the dim glow of the fire, I could just make out that it had once been engraved with something significant.

The letters *Sk*.

And beneath them, a string of numbers. My birthday.

As the rattle jangled softly in my hands, I realized that it wasn't just a childhood toy. It was a message. A *sign*.

Little silver bells, my parents used to sing me to sleep at night, as light from the moon cast shadows of branches and leaves on the walls. *When they ring, we'll know.*

I used to think it was just an old folk song, its gentle rhythm lulling me to sleep. But as I listened to the faint silver jangle in the dead of night, something clicked.

Silver, for my eyes. For the strange mix of powers that surged within me, stronger by the day. For the flashing wings that had finally grown in fits of stabbing pain from beneath my shoulder blades.

I always wondered what, exactly, the lyrics meant. *When they ring, we'll know.*

But last night I figured it out, as sharp and clear as the rattle's bell. When all the silver forces in my life converged, we'll know it's time. To fight.

It was the final sign I needed to have the courage to reject both the Order and the Rebellion. To start off on my own. Since turning seventeen, everyone in my life had tried to control me. But now it was time to take matters into my own hands.

I wrapped the rattle carefully in a T-shirt and packed it in my backpack. I opened the flaps of the box that had fallen on its side and began to sift through what was left. There had to be more clues. Something to tell me what I was supposed to do now.

The sun was beginning to set. As it aligned with the window, it cast an orange beam of light in my eyes. I stood and raised an arm to shield them from the glare. Motes of dust swirled around me as I struggled to slide the window open, letting the fresh mountain air gust into the tiny room.

The sky was a pale, crisp blue, fading to a pinkish glow as the sun hovered above the jagged outline of the mountains on the horizon. I closed my eyes and the light swept across my nose and eyelids, touched the tops of the trees below. The world glowed on the other side. The light shone brightest at the center, seeping into darkness as I squeezed my eyes tighter. Dark and light. I was neither. I was both. I was all of it.

The sun was setting on one chapter of my life. But it was rising on the next. The world was waking up, and I felt like I was waking up with it.

2

"Planning on jumping?"

My eyes flew open.

I didn't have to turn around to know who was behind me. I'd heard his voice so often that it had become a living, breathing part of me, as real as the cells in my skin and the oxygen in my blood. He was repeating the very same words I'd said to him that moment on the roof of Northwood School, when I'd learned who I really was.

The child of a member of the Order and a Rebel angel who had broken away. The daughter of dark and light.

Except now I knew that there was more to this story than I'd ever dreamed possible. My mother wasn't just a Guardian, but a Gifted One who possessed the Sight. Now

I finally understood the visions I'd been having. They were glimpses of the future.

The breeze coming through the open window smelled like spring. Spring meant renewal. Well, maybe I could bring renewal to the world. For too long, two groups had vied for power over the world and the people who walked it: the Order, responsible for controlling human fate; and the Rebellion, who believed in the passion and chaos of a life messy and lived to the fullest. But neither group was perfect. Neither was right. I couldn't let the Order control human life forever, but a world controlled by the Rebellion would mean chaos and anarchy. I stood between them now. Maybe I did have the fate of the universe in my hands.

"You've been waiting for a chance to say that back to me, haven't you?" I asked, gathering the courage to turn around.

"You sort of gave it to me on a silver platter this time." I could hear the smirk in his voice, and I turned to face him.

"I'm not going to jump," I said. "Don't worry." He wasn't smiling. His lips didn't even twitch. "Even if I did, I could catch myself now. Wings and all."

In the fading light, his dark features began to blur, to fade along with the sun into the corners of the attic already cast with twilight shadows. He grabbed at an invisible speck of dust in the air, crushed it in his fist, looked away.

"Asher—"

"Don't."

"I'm sorry."

"You're sorry?" So many things burned in his coal-black eyes. Anger. Betrayal. If I looked deep enough, maybe even pain. Instead, I let my gaze drop to the warped planks of the wooden floor.

"I have to do this."

"I protected you, Skye. I devoted myself, every waking second, to keeping you safe from the Order."

"I know—"

"I gave you a family with the Rebels. I was ready to commit my life to fighting with you. Side by side."

"I—"

"A *team*."

"Me too, but—"

He looked up then, and that look sent lightning crashing through my heart.

"I loved you."

What was I doing? Not for the first time, I wondered if I was making the right decision. It was too hard. Shouldn't it be easier to follow your own star?

"I loved you, too," I said. I walked up to him, took his hands. They uncurled from fists, shaking ever so slightly in mine. "I still do."

"Then how," he said through clenched teeth, "can you leave me?"

The mountain wind blew between us. The sun sparkled through my eyelashes.

"Because I have to do this. It's who I am. Can't I love you but not believe in what you believe in?"

"It'd be a whole lot better if you believed."

The corner of his mouth twitched, and I smiled, despite myself. "That's not funny."

"I know." He sighed, grabbed my hands in his, and pulled me closer. I let him wrap his arms around me, and I rested my cheek on his chest. "It's just that I really did think you were a Rebel. I thought we were in this together. For always."

I felt tears prick the backs of my eyes, and was glad he couldn't see. I forced them down.

"I wish that we could be," I said. "But it's impossible."

"Skye, you know I have to do the right thing, too—don't you? I have to go back to the Rebellion. We've fought so hard for this; I can't turn my back on them now. Ardith and Gideon are counting on me. I let them down once, I can't do it again. It's not about the rules. It's not like the Order. It's about honor. It's about loyalty. I thought you understood that."

"Don't talk to me about loyalty," I said, my face growing hot with frustration. "I'm loyal to my family. To my friends. To my own blood." I took a deep breath. "So, I guess that means we're against each other now."

"Maybe." He looked thoughtful. "Maybe not. Looks can be deceiving. You of all people should know that." He took a step back, and lifted my chin so he could look into my eyes. He raised an eyebrow.

"Do you believe in us, Skye? That there could be a happy ending for us if we wish for it hard enough?"

I swallowed. Did I believe? My life was fine before Asher and Devin came into the picture. I had Aunt Jo and my friends and won ski races and got straight As, and that was enough. It wasn't exciting, it didn't make me *feel* anything, but it was safe, and it was mine. Now, I felt too much. And all it did was make things confusing. All I felt was the pain I'd been trying so hard to escape since my parents died.

It was the kind of life the Rebellion believed in.

But forming this new group, stopping this collision of Chaos and Order—that was a fight I couldn't afford to lose. No matter what I had to give up in order to win.

I closed my eyes, and when I opened them again I was crying.

"No," I said. "I don't."

Asher let go of me. He opened his mouth to say something, then closed it again just as quickly.

"I'm sorry," I whispered.

"I don't believe you."

"You have to."

He took my hands in his and gripped them tight. "Skye," he said fiercely. "Listen to me. When this is all over, when we've found a way to end this, we will be together."

I raised my eyes to meet his. "Then prove it."

It was a challenge. It was the very thing he'd yelled to me above the wind, the first time we'd raced each other.

I'll win!

Prove it.

He pulled me into him so fast I didn't see it coming, and I threw my arms around his neck and kissed him. He held on to me, tightly, as the sun dipped quietly below the mountains and the darkness rose to meet us and the wind blew in through the open window, gusting up under my wings, which had unfurled in Asher's arms, and lifting us both off the ground. It was the kind of kiss you read about in books, the kind they write songs about. A kiss that told the story of us. The whole messy, complicated story.

He let go of me, letting me fall, gently, to the ground.

"I will. And if you think I'm giving up on *that*," he said, brushing the hair out of my face, "you're crazy."

"That's no good-bye," I whispered, pushing down the lump welling in my throat.

"Nope. It's a promise."

Asher gave me one last look, a millennia of history contained within that one gaze. "See you on the other side," he said.

In a rustle of black feathers, he moved to the window.

Then he was gone. And everything went still. The bottom of my life fell out from beneath me. Just like that.

On shaky legs, I walked to the window and leaned my hands against the weathered sill. The night unfolded before me, a dark expanse of stars.

What have I done?

The floor creaked, and soon Cassie had walked up beside me.

"You okay, babe?" she said softly, putting a reassuring hand on my back.

"No," I said, wiping away a tear. "But I will be." I let my head fall onto her shoulder, and she wrapped her arms around me.

"I think what you're doing is incredibly brave," she said.

"That's not why I'm doing it."

"I know." She pulled away and looked at me, her green eyes sparkling. "You're doing it because it's right. And you won't have to go through it alone. I know your secret now, and nothing could make me leave your side."

"Not even Dan?" I asked hopefully.

"Not even Dan. Come on, he's not as important as my best friend!"

"You know, you really need to start making sure I'm not in the room before you talk about me," Dan said, coming up behind her. "I always hear you."

"You need to stop sneaking up on us then," Cassie replied blithely, waving him off.

"You guys have to get the bickering under control," Ian cut in, clapping a hand on Dan's back as he approached. "If we're going to work as a team now." His brown eyes found mine, searching. Ian, always comforting, always a friend, even when neither of us deserved it. "And Skye, Cassie's right. We're here for you. We're going to help you, whatever you need. We're in this together."

For a moment, I couldn't find the words to say what I was feeling. I looked around at my friends, my family, the only people I knew I could always count on. They were so loyal, dependable. As long as we were all together, I would never be alone. I'd questioned it once, but I knew I would never have to question it again.

"You guys are the best," I said, standing up. "I can't believe how far we've come since the night of my birthday. It seems like yesterday, but I feel like a different person now."

"You kind of are," said Cassie.

"But we still love you." Dan smirked. "Weird silver wings and all."

"Come on, Skye," Ian said. "Pack up. Let's go home."

I looked around at my friends and nodded.

"I'm ready," I said.

"For whatever's coming," said Dan.

"For the road ahead," Ian added.

"For a nap!" Cassie laughed.

"For all those things," I said. "And whatever else we're about to face."

3

*R*aven's fork scraped against her plate. I flinched involuntarily, and noticed I wasn't the only one. Everyone around the table—Cassie, Dan, Ian, and Aunt Jo—was looking at her.

"Sor-*ry*," she snapped.

"It's okay," I said next to her, trying to convey both reassurance and thankfulness in my voice. She just glared at me. I'd been really nice to her since learning she had saved my life, but the nicer I was, the more it seemed to get on her nerves. Raven may have joined our group, but I had a feeling it was going to take a while before it really sank in. For all of us.

We'd returned from the camping trip on Friday. Now it

was Sunday. *It had better sink in soon*, I thought, *or one of us might not make it to Monday.*

"Go ahead, continue talking," she said. "By all means, don't stop on my account."

I cleared my throat.

"Thank you, guys, for coming over for dinner tonight. You've stuck by me throughout this whole journey, and I can't tell you how much it means to me. Because it's only going to get harder from here, and I just want to make sure you know that. If you want to leave, I understand. I'm not going to force anyone to help me. This is a battle I have to fight myself." I paused, and looked around the table hopefully. "Not that I wouldn't really, *really* love some company."

I held my breath. No one moved.

"Can you pass the mashed potatoes?" Dan whispered to Cassie. She obliged.

"No one?" I asked.

"Oh, I thought you were being rhetorical," Cassie said. "Are you insane? Of course we're not leaving."

"Seriously," said Ian. "If I was going to bolt, it would have been in the woods with the vengeful angels staring us down."

"They're only going to get *more* vengeful," I pointed out.

"But we can prepare for that, right?" said Dan.

"And I'm pretty sure I'm obligated by law to help you," Aunt Jo grinned.

"There's no angel clause in those adoption papers, though," I said.

"A legal oversight."

"She's not joking," Raven said suddenly, putting down her fork and looking up. "You people are always joking. This is serious, and it's going to get worse. Much worse. Those *vengeful angels* you're laughing about won't have any qualms about hunting you down and killing you in the night."

Dan gulped as Raven turned to look at me. "I know you think they're your friends, Skye. Ardith and Gideon, and even Asher. But they're not. You're just a prize to them. Both sides were fighting over you, vying for control of your oh-so-special custom blend of powers. You've angered the Order by siding with the Rebellion, and now you've betrayed the Rebels, too. They're going to use force if necessary. Capture you, control you—or kill you, whichever serves to benefit them the most. They have a lot to gain from using you, but if they can't, you're safer dead—where they know you can't harm them—than alive."

"Well, that will only give me nightmares for about a million years," Cassie muttered under her breath.

"You don't mince words, Raven, do you?" I said. "But thanks. I need honesty right now." I looked around the group. "There can't be any secrets. No sugarcoating. It's for our own safety."

Raven's eyes bored into mine. "I'm with you. I'll be with you, to the end. Let's take this as far as it will go."

The look in her eyes told me her reasons were complicated. I shuddered as I pictured Devin, standing over her with his sword dripping blood, her mangled wings lying on the ground beside her. She had saved my life to spare him the pain of losing me, but when he'd deliberately defied the Order, her only option was to obey their commands and kill him. Her plan had been to get to him first, but instead, he'd struck the first blow. The Rebellion had offered her a place alongside me and Asher, but when I'd healed her, something shifted. We both had grown beautiful, silver wings. Wings not of the Order—and not of the Rebellion, either. Wings that only made it clearer I belonged to neither side. And that Raven and I were bonded together, a strange, celestial magic flowing between us. We had to join forces, whether we wanted to or not.

"Just stop being so *nice* to me," she muttered.

And now, Devin was a Rebel, free to choose what he wanted, love who he wanted. She hadn't heard from him since.

I didn't blame Raven for having mixed feelings about all this. I understood it all too well.

Aunt Jo drained her iced tea.

"First of all," she said. "There are some things you need to know up front. If you're going to try to succeed where your parents failed, you should know everything about what they were trying to do." The room fell silent, and Aunt Jo straightened. "As angels who had been cast out, humans living on earth, they had some, let's say, unresolved feelings of anger and resentment toward the Order and the Rebellion. They had lived, one as a Rebel, and one as a Gifted, and they decided that neither side was right. So they were forming a splinter group. Their goal was to preserve the balance of the universe."

"Whoa," I said. "So they were big-picture people, huh?"

Aunt Jo looked stern. "I don't want to send you off into this with unrealistic expectations, Skye. There's a reason they failed. Their mission was massive."

We all chewed thoughtfully for a bit, in silence, as we processed this.

"So what was their plan?" Ian asked.

"Plan?"

"Yeah," I said, "how were they doing this?"

Aunt Jo sighed. "It didn't work. Why would you want to do the same thing?"

"Well, we need a jumping-off point," I said. "If we know what didn't work, maybe it will help us figure out what will."

Aunt Jo looked down at her plate and stabbed a slab of meatloaf with her fork. Cassie and I exchanged looks. Why was she being so evasive? *What doesn't she want to tell us?* I wondered.

"Does anyone want more iced tea?" Aunt Jo said suddenly. She didn't wait for an answer before going to the kitchen.

"That was weird," I said. "She is *definitely* hiding something."

"Maybe something terrible happened." Cassie's eyes were growing wide, the way they did when some grand idea had captured her imagination. "And that's why the mission failed. Like, her own powers let everyone down, and it's her fault they didn't succeed. Or she and your mom got into a huge fight! Or—ooh!—a lost love, or—"

"Aliens!" Dan cried. Cassie shot him a look. "What?" he said. "Six months ago you would have given me the same look if I'd said *fallen angels*."

The door swung open and Aunt Jo returned with the

iced tea pitcher. We all went silent. She arched an eyebrow.

"Done speculating?"

"What?" Cassie asked innocently. I kicked her under the table.

Aunt Jo poured herself some iced tea and took a sip.

"Okay," she said. "Here's what happened. Skye's mom still found herself having visions, even after she was cast to earth. In these sudden bursts of Sight, she was able to pick out faces, and later, names. It turned out she was seeing Rogues—children of Rebels and humans—who showed extraordinarily angelic powers and gifts. The thing about Rogues is that they usually don't know what they are or what they're capable of. Only that they're a little bit different, that they don't quite belong, and that sometimes, strange things happen when they're around. What tied these specific Rogues—the ones she was seeing—together was that they all knew. And they were all dealing with it. Some in good ways, some in bad."

She paused to take another sip of tea. It looked like she was only getting more nervous. Ian glanced at me, but when I caught his eye he looked away.

"Who did she see, Aunt Jo?" I asked carefully.

"She saw three Rogues. One," she said with a shaky breath, "was a man named Aaron Ward. The second was a man named James Harrison."

Out of the corner of my eye, I saw Ian's gaze flick back to me, but I was too wrapped up in my own thoughts to look at him this time.

"Wait a minute," I said. "Was the third . . . ?"

She glanced up from her plate for the first time and nodded. "It was me."

Cassie gasped, her eyes growing wide again. "You're a Rogue?"

"I guess I didn't have a chance to tell you that part," I said.

"Look," Aunt Jo said. "In the visions, your mom saw the three of us engaged in some powerful ritual that we could use to call all the Rogues to our side. We would be able to call them to their true angelic selves and—like us—they would finally know who and what they were. The idea was that with strength in numbers, we could overtake the Order and the Rebellion and create a third group that would forever keep the peace—hold the two sides at bay, and keep them from ever gaining power over the other. The irony of course is that control of you, Skye, would give one side ultimate power, for all time. After you were born, we worked harder than ever to make our powers strong enough to create that third group."

I swallowed hard. Again, it seemed to come down to me.

"What happened?" I asked. "Why didn't it work?"

"I don't know. At first, we were frustrated. The three of us were together, and we were strong. We should have been able to do it, and we didn't know why it wasn't working. That's when Mer saw the vision of the fourth."

"The fourth?"

"In the days right before your parents were killed, she began to have a new vision. One in which there was a fourth member of our group. But the fourth was a mystery, surrounded by shadows. Your mom couldn't tell who she was seeing—gender, age, powers, nothing. Mer died before she could ever find out who would complete our circle."

"What happened after my parents died?" I asked. "Did you just give up?"

Aunt Jo put her hand on my arm. "Oh, hon," she said. "After they died, there was no point. You came to live with me, and my whole life changed so suddenly. We had no way of finding out who the fourth could be. Without Mer's visions to guide us, I'm afraid to say we were a bit lost. We disagreed on how to proceed, of course. Aaron wanted to keep going. He thought there was surely a way. James was a new father too, but his wife didn't know his true lineage, and the secrets he was keeping from her were beginning to tear them apart. I was caught in the middle. All I knew was that I had to raise you right, as I promised your parents I would. And I had to hide you from the truth about yourself and your family. One morning, we woke up to find James gone. Aaron begged me to reconsider, but I had made up my mind. We weren't going to continue on our mission. And so he packed his bags and left, too." Aunt Jo's voice broke suddenly, and I reached out to squeeze her hand.

"Oh my god," said Cassie. "He was your boyfriend, wasn't he?"

"Cassie! That is so not the point."

"No," Aunt Jo said. "It's true. I've never loved anyone like I loved Aaron. I doubt I ever will. He's been impossible to replace, even all these years later. The only one who's ever truly understood." It made sense. Aunt Jo had been alone for as long as I could remember. I always figured she was just too independent to settle down. She was always out on some trip to the back country with her outdoor adventure company, fending off bears and sucking the venom out of rattlesnake bites. She could kill a massive spider with her bare hands and bake a mean batch of cookies to boot. I couldn't imagine her actually *needing* somebody.

"He's the one in the picture," I realized. "The photo I found in the shoebox."

Aunt Jo nodded. Neither of us mentioned the other thing in the shoebox—the diamond ring—or the dress that she'd given me to wear to prom, the one she said had at one point been intended to be a wedding dress. I shook my head in wonder at Cassie. She was right. It was lost love, all these years. I always laughed at Cassie's ability to jump to the most tragically romantic conclusion, without fail. But you kind of had to hand it to her, the girl knew her stuff.

"So that's what we have to do," I said. "We have to reunite the three of you. And we have to find the fourth."

"Skye, how—"

"I'll use my visions. I'll find a way." I was my mother's daughter, with my mother's blood. She was dead, and now it was up to me. Maybe I was stronger. Maybe I'd find something she couldn't.

"I don't know. . . ." Aunt Jo's eyebrows knitted together. "There has to be some other way." Without looking at me, she began clearing up the plates and silverware.

"What way?" I asked, standing up and helping her. "I can't think of any other way. And I don't have time to. It has to be this. The Order and the Rebellion aren't going to waste any time now that I've gone off on my own. If they're not hunting me already, they're going to start soon." I shuddered as I remembered the flashes of white feather I'd catch glimpses of between the trees. I would never get used to the chilling sight, but I had a feeling my days of being stalked by angels weren't nearly over.

Aunt Jo brought a stack of plates into the kitchen, and I followed her.

"Is it because of Aaron? Don't you want to see him again?"

"That was another life, Skye," she said, setting the plates just a bit too heavily on the counter and turning to me. "Another time. I was a different person then." She opened the dishwasher and began to load each fork, spoon, and knife, one by one. "I don't want to be reminded of it."

I took the rest of the silverware and shoved it into the dishwasher all at once.

"Skye!"

"What is wrong with you? Since when are you afraid of anything?" I knew my eyes were flashing silver in frustration.

"You couldn't understand."

"Try me," I said through gritted teeth.

She crossed her arms and turned to face me. I had never seen this side of her before.

Aunt Jo smoothed a hand over her graying blond ponytail. Then she walked to the refrigerator and pulled a bottle of bourbon down from the cabinet above it. Without saying a word, she took a tumbler from a different cabinet and poured herself a generous glass. She downed it in one gulp.

When she turned around, there was fire in her eyes. It looked so familiar, I flinched. She reminded me of Asher—when he was serious, determined, on a mission to protect me. When he let his intensity show instead of masking it behind jokes. *It's the Rebel blood in her*, I realized.

"When I was your age," she said, as if she was reciting a speech she'd practiced in her head for a long time, "I was mad at the world. I knew that I was different, and I knew why. I never knew my father, and my mother didn't know what to do with a problem kid like me. I felt like there was no real place for me. I distrusted a lot of people—and *strongly* distrusted the rest. I picked a lot of fights. Did some things I would *kill* you for doing." She narrowed her eyes at me.

I didn't say anything. A lot of things were clicking into place for me tonight. Aunt Jo's famous wrath made a lot more sense now, for one.

"It isn't fun for me to tell you this. But if you're going to go digging up the past, you may as well hear it from me.

I'm telling you this because I think it's important that you know. What things were like for me, before." She paused and tucked a strand of hair behind my ear. "And what they're like now. What *I'm* like. What's changed me."

I gulped and nodded.

"Everyone has a past," she said. "So did I. But with Aaron, I didn't have to carry the whole world alone anymore. I could lean on someone, finally, who understood. And then he just . . . left. When things got hard. Or maybe it was my own fault, I don't know. I didn't ever really figure it out because you came into my life, and from then on it wasn't about me anymore. I finally knew what it was like to take care of someone else. Your parents gave me an unimaginable gift, Skye. You changed me. I grew up."

"What was it like," I said carefully, "when you met them?"

Aunt Jo closed her eyes.

"Like I belonged. I got an instant hair-prickling when I saw them. I knew them, but I didn't know from where, or how I possibly could." *The same feeling I got when I met Asher and Devin*, I thought. Angel blood recognizing angel blood. "They explained everything to me," Aunt Jo continued. "They gave me a mission, a life. They were my family. And they gave me you. The best gift anyone could have given me. Even if it came out of the worst tragedy."

"What about the legend Ardith told me? What about your distrust?" If Aunt Jo was in the mood to share, I was going to get as much out of her as I could.

"Parts of the legend are right. Rogues have an inexplicable distrust of Rebels, for one thing. I understand, now, that initially I trusted Mer and Sam not because they were kind to me, but because they were human. But I had the strange, vague sense that something was off—they had a tinge of angel blood, after all, and I guess the Rogue in me picked up on that. From what I understand, most Rogues can't distinguish other Rogues, but they get a sort of sixth sense about full angels. Mostly Rebels, but Guardians a little bit too. I don't know why I know who, and what, I am. But I always have. Anyway, there are millions of us. Scattered across the earth. If every Rogue *knew* they were a Rogue, I wonder if there wouldn't be some kind of uprising."

"Is that why you never trusted Asher?" I asked. "Because he's a Rebel?" Aunt Jo grinned and raised an eyebrow at me.

"That's *one* of the reasons."

I smiled sheepishly. "Do you trust him now?"

She hesitated.

"He's a Rebel, Skye. First and foremost. He's part of a

group that wants to use your powers to control the universe. You think I'm going to *trust* him?"

For once, I didn't have a response.

Aunt Jo's eyebrows formed the same worry crease that mine did. Asher had pointed it out to me once, on the roof, as we stared at the night sky.

"I want to, Skye," she said softly. "Just as much as you do. Let's leave it at that, for now."

I nodded. "Do you trust *me*?"

"Of course I do," she said.

"Then let me find Aaron and James. It's our only chance."

The door to the kitchen burst open, and Cassie, Dan, Ian, and Raven came in with the rest of the dishes.

"So," Raven said, putting a stack of plates on the counter and turning to face us. Her blond hair flashed in the harsh light of the kitchen. Her eyes were fierce. "Do we have a plan?"

I glanced at Aunt Jo. She set her jaw, and then she nodded, imperceptibly. A silent signal meant just for me.

We were a motley crew. Who would think we had it in us to keep two powerful angelic forces from colliding and destroying the world? But if the feeling I had was right, it wouldn't be just the six of us by the time we were done. We would be an entire army of Rogues, hundreds of thousands of us—with me at the helm. It didn't make sense for me to question what I was about to do. I just had to leap.

I met Raven's cool, blue eyes.

"We have a plan," I said. My parents may have failed, but now it was up to me to finish the fight. "Let's get to work."

4

"Attention, Northwood juniors and seniors. The countdown to prom has begun!"

Student body president Maria Fouler's voice bounced off the lockers and echoed down the halls. We all glared up at the speaker.

The five of us were standing around my locker before first period. Unfortunately, just because we were forming a plan to save the world, didn't mean we were exempt from school.

"No!" Dan cried in mock protest, holding his arms up to shield his eyes. "Not the P-word!" Cassie shot him a look.

Maria's too-chipper voice continued: "The sign-up sheet for the planning committee is posted outside of the caf-eteria. I hope as many of you as possible come on down to sign up and make this year's junior-senior prom our best yet!"

Cassie shot a sideways glance at me, and grinned. *"Dress shopping,"* she mouthed. I rolled my eyes and laughed.

"The nomination period is also open for the prom court, beginning today. You can nominate someone for the court, prince and princess, or king and queen. A candidate must have at least two separate people nominate them in order to be considered eligible."

Cassie's eyebrows shot up. "I know a perfect couple for prince and princess."

"You do?" said Dan. "Who?"

"I'll nominate you," I mouthed reassuringly. One of my favorite things about Cassie was her unfailing optimism in the face of crisis—and yet, something told me she didn't fully understand that come June, there might not *be* a prom. There may no longer be a River Springs, Colorado, or even a United States, or even, for that matter, a planet earth. Everything might be gone. Or, on the other hand, they might still be here—but *we* might not. If Cassie did somehow realize this and still managed to be so optimistic, then I had to give her a lot more credit.

The buzz of conversation resumed again in the hall. I could hear people discussing who they would nominate, where they would buy their perfect dress. But our conversation was more serious than that.

"I just want to make sure I understand what's at stake," Ian said, glancing uneasily at the rest of the students brushing past us, all of whom were vibrating with prom excitement. "If the Order wins, all of our lives will be controlled, down to the tiniest detail, forever. Our destiny will never really be in our own hands, and we'll be at the mercy of some fierce and ruthless angels."

I nodded grimly.

"Uplifting," Cassie mumbled, taking a sip of her Mountain Dew. She never drank coffee—she claimed it was bad for her singing voice. But that didn't stop her from consuming upwards of three caffeinated sodas a day, and at least two of those before lunch.

"But if the Rebellion wins," said Raven, bristling a little at the description of the Order, "the world will erupt into chaos. Anarchy. And there won't be any way to stop them."

"Yup," I said. "That's about it."

"Kind of puts prom in perspective, huh?" Cassie said, chucking her empty soda bottle in the recycling bin at the end of the hall. "Ooh," she said. "Three-pointer. Maybe I should try out for the basketball team—what do you think, Dan?"

Dan booped Cassie on the nose. "Sure," he said. "And I saw this awesome baby blue tux in the window of the vintage store in Darien. I think it was velvet. Or maybe polyester? What's the difference again?"

"Dan!" She swatted him. "You promised! Don't," she said through gritted teeth, "take this single joy away from me. Or it may be the only thing you *take* from me for a while, got it?" She looked at him pointedly. Dan's face turned pale.

"Wait," he said, his voice rising in panic. "I didn't mean—"

"Maybe I'll just go looking for another prom date," Cassie huffed, and stormed off down the hall toward homeroom. "One who will take his attire seriously. I hear Trey is single again," she threw back over her shoulder. Trey was the drummer in Cassie's band, the Mysterious Ellipses.

"Trey?" Dan called, hurrying after her. "He hasn't changed out of that plaid shirt since September!"

I couldn't help but smile as I watched him follow her down the hall. I secretly dreamed of one day having a relationship as fun and supportive as theirs. They fought constantly, but they were happy. I'd even settle for *normal*, to start.

"Well, I was planning to be the one to break up this

party, but it looks like I didn't have to," Raven said. "I'm off to class." She turned to leave, but hesitated. "Be careful, Skye," she said. "Watch your back." I flinched. The last time Raven had said that to me, she'd meant *she* was the one I should be watching out for. It was still so surreal that we were now on the same side. "If you need anything, let me know."

"I will," I said. "Thanks."

It was just me and Ian in the hall as the crowds thinned out, heading to the next class.

"Skye," he said, "I—"

He hesitated. I noticed suddenly that he didn't look good. His eyes were bloodshot, and even his freckles were sort of drooping. I knew things weren't easy for any of us right now, but it seemed like Ian was taking it especially hard.

"Are you okay?" I asked. "You look a little pale."

He glanced nervously down at his hands, then back at me.

"I'll see you later," he said. Unsettled, I watched him walk down the hall and turn the corner into class.

I thought we said no secrets, I thought to myself. I guess it was going to take some getting used to for everyone.

I had a free period, so I went to the library. If my goal

was now to reunite Aunt Jo with Aaron Ward and James Harrison, I had to embark on the somewhat daunting task of figuring out where they might be.

I sat down at a computer and pulled up the white pages online. The girl next to me glanced at the screen, and I felt the hair at the nape of my neck prickle. She had short blond hair cut in a pixie style, and ice blue eyes. A Guardian, for sure. It reminded me that I had to be careful—that I was being watched, dogged, followed, all the time. They were waiting, holding their breath for the perfect time to strike.

It wouldn't be at school, Asher had advised me.

If not school, then where? I didn't want to think about the fact that the answer could have been "anywhere else."

As inconspicuously as possible, I angled my screen away, pretending to avoid a glare from the window. In my periphery, I saw her eyes narrow.

As I entered Aaron Ward's name into the search engine, I let my mind wander to the shoebox I'd found in Aunt Jo's closet. In the faded picture, she'd been leaning up against a tree, wind whipping strands of her blond hair (there were no hints of gray in it then) loose from her signature ponytail. Aaron was leaning into her, his arm resting against the tree, a mischievous gleam in his eye—a touch of Rebel energy radiating from him. Whoever was taking the picture had caught them in the most private of moments. The moment right before a kiss, when the world is brighter and sprawling out before you, and anything is possible. She was smiling up at him, a full-body smile.

I knew Aunt Jo wasn't ready to be reunited with Aaron. She would rather we did this another way, and part of me—the reluctant romantic—couldn't blame her. I tried to put myself in her shoes, to wonder how I might feel if Asher and I had parted on worse terms. What if Cassie was trying to reunite us against my will? Would I be angry? Or would I be excited, and hiding that excitement to protect myself?

I held within my own secretly fragile heart the deepest and most unwavering hope that Asher and I would be together again. It was a hope I would carry with me always, and no one, not the staunchest skeptic, could take it away from me. How could Aunt Jo not want to find Aaron? What if in trying to bring together this blend of powers and celestial magic, I could also find a way for her to be happy again? I couldn't think of anything more noble than reuniting two lost loves. Aunt Jo had done so much for me over the years, and given up even more. It was time I gave something back to her.

The search turned up eleven Aaron Wards in Colorado, which seemed like the best and most likely place to start. But how to narrow it down?

I'd been getting better at controlling my visions, when they struck. Could I make one happen on purpose? What if I could use one to figure out where in Colorado Aaron Ward was living?

I printed out the page and folded it into the pocket of my jeans. I still had half an hour until the bell and needed to go someplace private, someplace where I could have complete concentration and focus. Someplace where I could use my angelic powers, and still be back in time for class.

Out of the corner of my eye, I could see Blond Pixie still watching me. I couldn't let her think I was up to something. I walked slowly to the library door—but once I was through it, I ran like lightning to the staircase that led to the roof.

The air was heavy; it was about to rain some serious spring showers if I didn't act soon.

Did you forget you can control the weather? I reminded myself.

That bought me a little more time. I propped the door open with a brick and walked around to the side of the entrance. The ledge where Asher stood with his back to me, the place where Devin first showed me his wings, the water tower that I accidentally burst in a fit of uncontrollable power—everything about this roof held a special, supernatural memory for me.

If anyplace had the right energy to help me see the future, this was it.

I dropped my bag to the ground and sat cross-legged under the water tower.

Putting my hands in my lap, I closed my eyes and concentrated on an image—the photograph of Aunt Jo and Aaron. A stolen moment captured on film.

Thunder rumbled above me, but I didn't want to break concentration to stop it. I let the mercurial silver slip through me, filling me with a bright, glowing energy. On the backs of my eyelids, my vision went cloudy. And then, as the edges of my sight began to take shape, to shift into clarity, I began to see things. A house. It looked a little unkempt, with paint chipping off the railings on the porch, window frames that looked like they needed replacing. It was shabby and worn, and not in the cozy, homey way. In a way that signified neglect. That made me think the owner no longer cared.

The image in front of me shifted, and I saw a girl sitting on the bottom step. She looked about six or seven, with light brown hair that was pulled up in two messy pigtails. Her chin rested in her hand, her elbow propped up on her knee, and she sighed a bored, comically dramatic sigh. I had an urge to toss her a book or something.

I heard the noise at the same time she did. The bushes along the side of the yard rustled. The girl's head snapped up, scared. And my own heart pounded. Because I had seen what the girl hadn't. A flash of white, between the leaves.

The wing of a Guardian.

"Look out!" I tried to yell to her, before realizing it was pointless to call out to a vision of the future. Besides, my visions never worked like that. I couldn't interact with them. I could never change what was happening. All I could do was watch. Helplessly.

An engine roared in the driveway and the girl jumped to her feet.

"Dad!" she called. And then a man swooped into my sight. He put a brown paper takeout bag down on the porch steps, and lifted her up in his arms. She looked a tad too heavy and a bit too old to be held like that, but the way the man's eyes darted protectively around the yard—lingering on the bushes where I'd seen the white wings—made me think he'd do anything to keep his daughter safe.

He turned to face me, and I caught my breath. His hair

was dark, a perfect tangle of waves that fell into his slate gray eyes. Eyes that were locked directly with mine. For a brief moment, my heart stopped. *Can he see me?*

But as quickly as the thought popped into my head, I realized it was impossible. There was no way. His gaze shot straight through me, to something moving through the trees. He tracked it with his eyes until he must have felt satisfied that it was moving away.

"What did I tell you about waiting outside?" he said. I could tell he was trying to sound tough, mask the fear in his voice. "Come on, let's go in." When they got to the front door, he looked behind him one more time.

Something was out there.

Then he and the little girl disappeared into the house.

The edges of the picture dissolved into static, and I opened my eyes to find myself back on the roof of the school. Thunder cracked, but I held up my hand to silence it, and the sky went quiet. The clouds whispered away into nothingness.

That was him—Aaron Ward. It was the same guy from the picture. He had the same dark hair, the same Rebel attitude gleaming from his eyes. And he was definitely being watched by the Order.

I tried to pick out distinguishing features, to figure out which of the Aaron Wards I'd found on the white pages matched this one. The house and the neighborhood looked run-down, but they could have been from any number of run-down neighborhoods in the area. The number on the mailbox was obscured by bushes. There weren't too many clues, other than the man, the little girl, and . . .

The takeout bag! It had writing on the side, and I closed my eyes again and tried to pull back the memory of what it said. He'd been carrying it, put it down on the front steps. I'd been more focused on the two of them than I'd been on the brown paper bag, but I focused hard and tried to remember what the writing had said. The letters were small, but a T and an R jumped out at me.

Could it be *Tabula Rasa*? That was the name of a café that Aunt Jo and I had stopped into once on our way home from Denver. It was about two hours west of River Springs, in a town called Rocky Pines.

My heart in my throat, I took the folded-up printout from the white pages out of my pocket and opened it.

Third from the top:

Aaron Ward, 144 Sycamore Street, Rocky Pines, CO.

There was a phone number listed next to it. I took out my cell phone and dialed. The phone rang a couple of times, and then a little girl's voice picked up.

"Hi, you've reached the Wards. We're not here right

now . . ." In background, I heard a man's voice prompt:

"But if you leave a message . . ."

"Oh, right. But if you leave a message," she continued, "we'll call you back!"

I opened my mouth to leave a message, but thought better of it and hung up quickly. What exactly was I planning to say?

As I stood up and slung my bag over my shoulder, a thought suddenly occurred to me. What if the girl had a mom? How could I not have thought of it before? What if Aaron Ward had a whole new family out in Rocky Pines, and was perfectly happy to never see Aunt Jo again?

What if he didn't want to come back?

Below me, the bell rang for the end of the period. That meant I had ten minutes until the next one began. I had the whole rest of the day to figure out what to do about Aaron. I didn't have to have an answer right now.

I kicked the brick aside and let the door close behind me, then snuck back down the stairs and into the crowded hallway.

Someone grabbed me from behind.

By instinct, I elbowed them in the stomach and turned around.

"Jeez," Ian panted. "I was going to tell you to watch your

back, but it looks like I didn't need to warn you after all."

"Sorry!" I cried. "Are you okay?"

"You might have broken a rib. Other than that, some wounded pride maybe. Nothing a little flattery won't fix."

"Your freckles are looking especially handsome today, Ian."

"That's a good start."

"How about this? I think I know where Aaron Ward is. Will you come with me to find him?"

Ian batted his eyelashes. "Li'l old me?"

"I haven't asked anyone else. Not even Cassie."

Ian grinned. "Okay, my pride has totally healed. I'll definitely come."

"You're the best!"

"Hey," Ian said, his face growing serious. "Speaking of that, can I talk to you for a second?"

I glanced at the clock. "I'm going to be late for—"

"Just a minute."

"Okay," I said. "What's up?"

"It was driving me crazy all night. The name James Harrison—it sounded so familiar. I thought he was a politician. A president or something."

"I think you're thinking of James Madison," I said.

"Yeah, I realized that. I was racking my brain. Finally

when I got home, I asked my mom if maybe he was an old doctor or a family friend or something."

I paused. Suddenly, my heart was pounding.

"What did she say?" I asked.

Ian took a deep breath and met my gaze.

"He was my dad."

"hat?"

The white noise of the hallway was ringing in my ears.

"That was my dad's name," Ian said. "He left, you know. I don't know if I ever told you. I had just turned seven. The timing works." No, he had never told me. And he knew it.

"How come you never said anything?"

"Look, the third Rogue you're looking for—that could be my dad."

Ian never talked about his family. I knew he lived with his mom, but he never talked about her. We hadn't been friends since kindergarten like me, Cassie, and Dan. We'd all started at Northwood freshman year, and he and Dan had become buddies through track. We'd been to his house a couple of times, but mostly we all congregated at mine.

"I—I didn't know that," I said. "I guess I—"

"Don't worry about it," Ian cut me off quickly. "I just thought you would want to know, in case it helps."

I hesitated before asking the next question. "Ian," I said. "You know this means . . . that you could be part . . ." I wasn't sure how to finish the sentence. How do you just blurt out to someone who has spent his whole life thinking he was just a normal human that he . . . well . . . might *not* be?

Asher and Devin did the same to you, I reminded myself. *And look how it changed your life forever.*

"I know what it means," he said quietly. He looked up at me and smiled grimly. "I gotta get to class."

Before I could say anything else, he started to walk away.

"Ian!"

"What?" He turned around.

"You'd be okay if . . . we looked for him? If we found your dad?"

The look on his face was hard to read. "I kind of have to be, huh?" he said. "I'm not going to get in the way of your plan."

I caught up to him and threw my arm around his neck. "Thank you. You really have no idea how much this means to me."

"No problem, Skye. It's cool."

I narrowed my eyes, again wondering if he was telling the truth. But he just patted me on the back and dashed off down the hall.

"So, after school?" I called.

"I'm working at the Bean," he shot over his shoulder. "Tomorrow?"

I nodded as he ran off, but I couldn't help feeling uncomfortable.

First Aunt Jo's ex-fiancé, then Ian's dad. Two guys with a *lot* of unfinished business back in River Springs. And why River Springs? What was it about this place that drew my parents, that seemed to draw so much angelic activity? My heart fell into my stomach. I had my work cut out for me—getting these guys back to town was going to be harder than I realized.

What if the universe didn't want me to bring these three powerful Rogues back together, after all?

I was so lost in thought that I didn't pay attention to where I was going, and knocked into someone on my way to class. When I looked up, I was staring right at Devin.

"Oh," I said. He looked down, and our eyes met. His were blue pools of light. Like Raven, the frosted layer of ice that usually shut him off from me, from the world, had all but melted. And when he looked at me, I could see the confusion that he felt, too.

"Skye," he said. "Hey."

He seemed so uncharacteristically at ease, so comfortable in his own skin. He looked radiant, his face glowing and warm, his hair even blonder. He wore a plaid button-down flannel and khaki-colored work pants that hung off his hips. Such a contrast to Asher's olive skin and dark hair, thermals and jeans, boots and beat-up army jackets. Everything about Devin now exuded light.

So that's what happens when you give someone the ability to feel.

I glanced down, grasped the handle of my book bag so tight that my knuckles turned white.

Since my seventeenth birthday, Devin and I had been through more than I had with anyone else in my life. I'd gone from bristling at his unrelenting pressure for me to manifest my powers to near-death when those very powers inspired the command for him to kill me. He had to follow it, was programmed that way. He didn't mean it and never could. He had taught me how to embrace who I was, to feel proud of what I could do. He showed me how to use my powers of the light, and he was the one who figured out what my visions meant—that my mother was a Gifted One. But ever since his betrayal, he held me at arm's length. Who knew what he was capable of under the Order's ruthless thumb?

The last time I had seen him, he had told me how much he loved me. But his words, so perfect, seemed so empty. Telling someone you loved them didn't make it true. Showing me—proving it—that's what would make me believe. Even when Devin jumped from the Order and became a Rebel, Asher had been holding a sword to his throat, threatening to kill him if he didn't.

But whether or not he did it for me, Devin *had* jumped. Things would be different now. He was a Rebel, and anything was possible. Especially if we were enemies. Again.

The bell rang to signal the beginning of class, snapping me out of my reverie.

"I'm late."

"Skye," he touched my arm, and it sent goose bumps shooting across my skin. I pulled away. The look in his eyes the last time I saw him was too imploring, too hopeful that there was some kind of future for us. "Can we talk? Not here, but later. At our spot, on the trail?"

The hall had emptied out, and we were the only two people left. He looked harmless enough, but as Asher had pointed out, I knew better than anyone that looks could be deceiving.

"I don't think that's such a good idea."

"Please. I want—" He paused, and swallowed. "There are some things I need to get off my chest."

Did I want to hear them? Something told me it would only make things harder.

"I have to go," I said. When I got to the classroom door, I turned around. He was still standing there, watching me. He lifted his hand in a wave. I took a breath and went inside, leaving him behind. But I could still feel the weight of his gaze, even when I closed my eyes.

There's some law of nature that says when you don't want to see someone, you suddenly see them everywhere. After that moment in the hall, everywhere I went I saw Devin. Sometimes he was alone. Sometimes he was flanked by Ardith and Gideon. The three of them must have been assigned to stake out the school. They formed an imposing unit, one I didn't want to cross. And I didn't know if it was just in my head or if the barometric pressure was changing, but when I passed them and they turned to look at me, the air around me grew darker, heavier.

At lunch they sat at a table in the corner of the cafeteria, and it was impossible to forget that Asher used to sit with them. I could still feel his absence acutely, like a splinter in my heart that I couldn't get out.

"Skye," Cassie leaned over the table to get my attention.

"Don't be mad, but I kinda sorta joined the prom committee." She winced and ducked.

"I don't even have anything to throw at you," I said. "This apple?" She straightened.

"I know we have kind of bigger fish to fry right now. Angel Fish, and everything—"

"Really? Angel Fish?"

"At least they're not Clown Fish," Dan said, sliding in next to Cassie and planting a kiss on her cheek. "I hate clowns."

"But I've *always* wanted to be on the prom committee! Besides, it seems like we could all use a little levity now more than ever, and I am happy to fill that role."

I grinned at her. "You are the queen of levity."

"If the gray suede bootie fits." She winked, then her face clouded over as she caught me glancing at the table in the corner. "Don't let them intimidate you, Skye," she said. "You've got a posse, too. We've got your back."

I looked back at them. "I know," I sighed. But knowing the angels were there, watching, waiting to attack, just made me want to find the remaining two Rogues even faster.

"I'm not hungry," I said, standing up. Cassie looked worried, but she didn't argue. A few months ago, she wouldn't have let me leave this table until she'd exhausted all possible angles of interrogation about why. The fact that she let me go meant she was really growing.

"Call me later?"

"'Course."

A vague, uneasy feeling had been following me since my vision that morning. There were Guardians stalking Aaron Ward. That meant they knew something—but what? That he had been working with my parents before they died to thwart the Order, and that made him a target? Or was it possible they knew we were trying to find him again? To reunite the powerful three?

If the latter was true, that meant *all* of the former team were being watched. Not just Aaron, but Ian's father, too. And Aunt Jo.

Instinctively, I ducked into an empty classroom, whipped out my cell phone, and called the number for Into the Woods Outdoor Co.

"Skye," Aunt Jo said breathlessly, as if she'd run to pick up the phone. "Are you okay? Why are you calling me in the middle of the day? Did something happen?"

"No," I said quickly. "No, no everything's fine. I just . . . how are you?"

"I'm fine, Skye. I'm just holding down the fort at the

store." She paused. "You're sure everything's okay?"

I took a deep breath. "I had a vision," I said. "On purpose. I think—I mean, I know where Aaron Ward is. In Rocky Pines."

Aunt Jo was silent on the other end of the line.

"You saw him?" she said softly.

I nodded, then remembered that she couldn't see me. "Yeah."

"What did he—I mean, how did he . . . ?"

"He looked good, Aunt Jo." *Should I tell her about the little girl?* I wondered. How could I begin to start that conversation?

"Is he okay?"

"He's being watched," I said. "You might be, too. By the Order. I need to go to him soon, before anything . . . happens."

She sucked in her breath. "They know."

It made me think of what Aunt Jo had written in her journal when she worked with my parents at the cabin.

Guardians stalk these woods. They know.

I shivered. "So you agree," I said. "We need to find him, no matter what? He's safer with us than out there in Rocky Pines, right? At the very least we need to let him know what's happening. I have to warn him."

I could almost see the worry crease between her brows.

"Of course," she said. "Do whatever you can. Bring him here, if you need to." Was it me or did she almost sound excited? "Hey, Skye? Be careful, okay? You're all I have left."

"I will, Aunt Jo," I said. "I promise."

I hung up the phone. I would go after school today, whether Ian could go with me or not. I would find him before they did. I only hoped I was doing the right thing, bringing him back to Aunt Jo again. Was heartbreak worth the price of saving his life—of saving the world from a clash of powers that would certainly destroy it?

A door slammed, and suddenly Ardith was standing in front of me.

"I just want you to know," she said, "that this works both ways. You really betrayed us, Skye. And so here we are, enemies now."

"It's not personal," I said. Before I could think twice, I willed the silver power to my hands in case I needed to defend myself—or attack. "We were friends. Maybe we still could be."

"We weren't friends. Please, everything is personal. Making friends, falling in love, breaking hearts, becoming enemies—we take risks and we make mistakes and we mess up and it is *all personal*. You betrayed us."

"I swear I don't want to hurt you. I'm not against you. I just have to do whatever I can to keep the balance of power."

"If you're not with us, you're against us."

"I'm not. Listen—"

"No, you listen. Once Gideon risked everything in the world to save my life. And it scarred him. He will never be free of that darkness the Order put in him, how they tortured him. It will follow him wherever he goes. And I have to do whatever it takes to destroy the Order and anyone who stands in my way. That, Skye, is personal. And that is why we're enemies now, you and I."

Her words stung, like a slap across the face. "I didn't mean for any of this to happen."

"No," she said. "No one ever does."

She turned on her heel, her patterned maxi skirt billowing around her ankles, bangles jingling on her tanned arm. I got up and followed her out the door, but she was already halfway down the hall as the bell rang and students began to filter in around us.

She caught up to Gideon and said something in his ear.

Gideon turned slightly and looked at me.

If you didn't know his past, had no idea he was a Rebel

angel who had been brutally tortured by the Order, that his mind had been manipulated and infiltrated, and that he had learned, with every bit of strength he had, how to protect himself from it—had held out, kept his secrets, saved Ardith's life—if you knew none of these things, you would think Gideon was just a normal seventeen-year-old guy. He had a mop of curly hair, and even today, was wearing his signature band T-shirt under a blazer, wire-rimmed glasses. He could have been in Cassie's band.

But I knew who he was. I knew about his past. His eyes usually looked tormented and haunted. But from across the hall, at that moment, they smoldered and glowed. They *burned*. I had never seen anything like it.

He looked away quickly, and before I could do anything, he and Ardith had turned the corner and were out of sight.

6

Gideon's eyes haunted me all day. I knew that Ardith meant business. This was going to be war.

It also meant that I didn't have any time to waste when it came to finding Aaron. As soon as the last bell of the day rang, I booked it out the door and to my car. The sky was so dark it was almost black—a heavy storm was brewing.

"Hey!" A girl's voice called as I neared the car. "Where are you going?" I whipped around to find Raven rushing after me, a sheet of silky blond hair flying behind her in the wind.

I hesitated. I knew Raven was on my side now, but some small part of me still wasn't used to trusting her. "I have to go find Aaron Ward," I said.

"Alone? In this weather? Are you crazy?" She looked scornfully up at the sky. "Those Rebels are so obvious. No subtlety whatsoever."

"If you're so worried, here." I tossed her my keys. "I'll handle the storm."

Raven met my gaze coolly. A two-hour drive alone in my car would be the most one-on-one time we'd spent, like, ever. I wasn't thrilled about the idea, but I needed to go to Rocky Pines, tonight.

"I have a better idea," she said. "Come with me." She took off, back through the parking lot, winding her way between the cars toward the school.

"Hey!" I cried, following her. "Where are you going?"

Everyone was leaving school, flooding past us in the opposite direction. But for whatever reason, Raven led me back inside, through the halls and up the stairs.

At last I stumbled past her through the fire door and onto the wide, white cement of the roof.

"Okay," I said. "What's going on?"

"There's a faster way to get to Rocky Pines." She raised a challenging eyebrow. "I know you haven't had them that long, but have you already forgotten?"

"Had wha—" But before I could finish my question, a

tumble of glossy silver feathers spilled from her back.

"Your wings," she said triumphantly, as hers rose above her, massive, bright against the gathering storm clouds. "We can fly there."

The wings were a part of my body that had been added on, foreign and strange, and using them still took some getting used to. I guess that's what Raven was trying to do—help me.

"I can trust you, Raven," I said. "Right?"

"You don't have to question my loyalty," she said, her smile small and slightly shy. "It's not like I have anywhere else to go. We belong together, Skye. For better or for worse."

That would have to count as reassuring.

I closed my eyes.

You can do this. You were born to.

When I opened them, I could feel my pupils burning brightly silver. I let my powers sweep across the sky, changing the colors underneath the darkening clouds from a light pink and gold to dusty mauve, burnt orange. The feathery silver liquid took hold of me, hot, then cold, fire and ice. I grimaced and clenched my fists. It wasn't as painful as it had been at first, but I felt the sharp feathers of my wings slice through my back nonetheless. The massive vibrations echoed in the hollows of my bones.

And as the colors in the sky shifted and sharpened, I could see the shadow of my wings on the concrete before me.

Here we go, I thought.

Raven smiled—a genuine, impressed smile.

"Ready?" she said, her hands resting on her hipbones.

Let's do this.

I nodded.

I aligned my toes with the roof's ledge. I bounced once, twice, on the balls of my feet. And then, I took a leap.

At first I fell, plummeting through the air like a skydiver before pulling the string on the parachute. The wind roared around me, and for a split second I waited for Asher's arms to wrap around me, for his wings to catch the wind and glide us toward the sky. But I remembered just in time. He wasn't here, he wasn't coming for me. I was going to do this on my own.

I spread the massive wingspan wide behind me, catching the wind in my silver feathers, feeling the drag and then the pull. And then, as if caught by the strongest and most delicate of threads, I halted in midair. I began to soar upward.

One morning, months ago, in the darkest dead of winter,

I woke up floating. And now I knew why. My body had been preparing itself for this.

Raven flew up alongside me.

"They're beautiful," she whispered, yet somehow I could hear her perfectly above the rushing clouds. "I hate to admit it, but they are."

I nodded. "I could never have imagined what it would feel like to have wings."

"Sometimes I imagine what it's like to not." She looked serious. "I envy the way you grew up. Your friends. People, really. They don't have to live by the rules I was bound to. They're free."

"You were a Guardian," I said. "The Order has always controlled our fate. So are my friends really as free as they think?"

She seemed to contemplate this, as thunder rumbled around us. "I guess not. But they're freer than I was."

"Well, you don't have to follow commands anymore," I said. "You're free now." We dipped together, then rose again, as the sky churned angrily around us.

It struck me how strongly our lives were tied to each other. We'd been through a trauma together, we shared a strange, unspoken bond. She'd saved my life. I'd saved hers.

"Look out!" she called as lightning forked across the sky. "Can't you control that?"

The Rebellion doesn't want to see us make it to Rocky Pines.

"You're going to do something about this storm, right?" Raven called, panic rising in her voice. Her silver wings shone like lightning against the churning sky, as the real thing flashed behind us.

I spread my arms wide and let energy burst through my fingertips. The sky seemed to grow brighter, but not because the clouds were thinning. All of the electricity in the sky was gathering, hurtling toward me.

"Skye, look out!"

But I didn't need to—because I was making it happen. The light zapped into my fingers, and as the storm came crashing down, I pulled it inside of me.

Almost at once, the clouds vanished, and a ray of late-afternoon light broke through the mountains. Raven stared at me, her jaw hanging open.

"Come on," I said. "Let's go."

I flew with reckless abandon above the mountains and valleys below. Raven stayed by my side. The higher we rose, the deeper the color of the sky grew. The moon rose high above us, waiting for the sun to set. It was such a different feeling from skiing, where the speed picked up beneath my feet, pulling the very breath from my lungs, leaving me panting. Now, I embraced the wind instead of fighting against it. I embraced the feeling of letting go, and gave in to the swoop of flight.

My wings caught me. They would catch me again. I could leap, I could let myself fall. I could catch myself. The world spread out below me, the rocks and trees, houses and tiny cars. Life went on without me, the world continued to spin. And I was flying.

"Do you miss Asher?" Raven asked suddenly as we flew through a wisp of cloud.

I opened my mouth, then closed it again, a little taken aback. My instinct was to lie, to say no, to act tougher than I was. But when I opened my mouth again, what came out, simply, was "Yes."

She looked contemplative.

"I'm beginning to think I know what it feels like," she said softly.

"What?"

"Love."

I stared at her, so surprised I almost stopped flying.

"You do? *You* do?"

"Don't look so shocked," she said, ruffling her feathers. "You know, I didn't think it would be this hard. I knew Devin and I were meant to be, I knew we were fated to belong to each other." She drew a shaky breath. "But I don't even know what that means anymore. Now that our fate has dissolved before our very eyes, I don't know who we are to each other." She looked at me, and a tear slid down her cheek. "Now that I can feel, I don't know how to."

"Okay," I said slowly. "Well, how do you think you feel?"

"I think I love him," she said. "But I don't have anything to compare it to. It's like . . . I feel warm inside when I think of him, like I have this secret, even despite what he did to me. But it's a secret that I shouldn't have, or want to have. I had been ready to kill him, and he hurt me, too—I mean, he cut my wings right off my back, for god's sake. And still, after all that, my heart feels all twisty, and I think that must be what love feels like, right? But it doesn't make sense. How can you love someone who's hurt you?"

I didn't know what to say, and the wind rushed between us.

"I thought love was supposed to make you feel happy," Raven said at last.

"I think it is in theory," I said. "But the only people I know who feel that way are Cassie and Dan. Everyone else is pretty miserable. So maybe they're the exception, not the rule."

We flew silently for a couple of seconds, both lost in thought.

"It's very confusing," she said. "He's a Rebel now—something I was born to hate. I still do. I think I may finally understand how you feel." She sighed. "You love Asher, but to become a Rebel would mean turning your back on your destiny. I love Devin, but . . ." She trailed off, looking away. "I think he fell in love with someone else."

A heavy silence hung in the air between us, full of unsaid things.

Finally, she spoke. "Anyway, I get it now."

"I don't love him back," I said quietly.

"Please," she smirked at me knowingly. Not in a malicious way, but more like we were confidants. "Like I'm afraid of a little competition." The smirk turned into a full-blown smile. "I'm free now, after all. I can fight as hard as I want."

"The question is," I said, "with all that's standing between you, What are you going to do if you get him?"

The ground was rushing up beneath us. We were reaching our destination.

Raven didn't answer right away.

"You know," she said. "Devin never looked at me the way Asher looked at you. As if the whole world was bottled up within him, and only you understood what it meant." She paused, twisted in the air to face the sky above her. "I think the universe has a way of finding loopholes when you want something badly enough."

7

The sun hung low in the sky, and the hazy orange light cast a sepia feel over the flat, cracked streets and run-down houses. Somewhere, I thought I heard the sound of a truck backfiring—at least I hoped that's what it was—and a chorus of dogs began to bark, followed by a siren. We weren't in River Springs anymore.

We touched down outside of 144 Sycamore Street.

"Nice," Raven said, raising her eyebrows.

It looked exactly like it did in my vision: a gray house, shabby, showing neglect, with a dilapidated porch, and a metal chain-link fence around the front yard. A russet colored pit bull was tied to a tether in the ground. And standing next to him, scratching his ears, was the girl from my vision.

She had the same straight-but-messy light brown hair, tied up in the same lopsided pigtails. When Raven and I pushed open the gate, she looked up quickly.

Her eyes darted between the two of us in confusion.

"Hi," I said. "We're friends of your dad." I cringed as I realized that's what creepy stalkers and kidnappers might have said. "I'm Skye." The little girl squinted at me appraisingly, then nodded her chin at Raven.

"Who's she?"

Raven stiffened. "I'm Raven," she said.

"I don't understand." The girl had backed herself up onto the porch, one hand behind her on the doorknob. "Why would one of *you*"—she pointed at me—"be with one of *them*?" And she pointed at Raven. "Why would you be *together*?"

Raven and I glanced at each other.

"What do you mean?" I asked slowly. "One of who?"

"A light-haired one and a dark-haired one."

"You know about that?" I said in surprise.

She nodded.

"You don't have to worry," I said. "She and I are on the *same* side." The girl withdrew even farther, panic flashing across her face. "A different side!" I added quickly. "Not dark or light. Something new."

"New?"

I nodded. "We want to stop both sides. Keep them from hurting each other, or anyone else."

"Oh." She looked confused.

"I'll explain more, if you want."

The girl twisted one of her ponytails around her finger. "Your name's Skye?" she asked.

"Yep. What's your name?"

She looked at me quizzically.

"Earth," she said at last.

"What?" said Raven, just a tad too aggressively, perhaps forgetting we were talking to a small child and taking a step forward. "Are you trying to be cute or something?"

"I've heard of you," Earth said quietly. Raven stopped in her tracks, and I stared.

"You've heard of *me*?" I asked hoarsely.

At the sound of a pickup truck rumbling into the driveway, Earth's eyes grew wide. The door opened and slammed closed, and Aaron Ward came hurtling forward.

"Hey!" he shouted, bounding past us and taking the rickety porch steps three at a time—which, judging from the state of them, maybe he shouldn't have done. "Hey! Get away from my daughter. What the hell are you thinking, coming here, out in the open where anyone can see you? Are you crazy?"

There was no mistaking Aaron Ward. He looked the same as in the picture—but older, like in my vision. His dark hair was wavy and shot through with gray, and there were lines on his face from too much time weathering the sun. The only difference was his eyes. All trace of mischief, of conspiratorial smile, was gone. It had been replaced by something gruff and surly. "Get off my porch and leave us alone," he spat. "And you can take your spies . . ." he said, motioning toward the trees and bushes along the side of the property, "with you."

"Dad!" Earth said, rolling her eyes dramatically. "It's *Skye*."

Aaron shut his mouth and stared at me, hard. He squinted, as if trying to place me, to determine if what his daughter said was true.

"What's she doing here?" He nodded toward Raven, his voice so low it was practically a growl.

"Please." Raven put a hand on her hip. "Nobody mask their disdain on *my* account."

"She's with me. Don't worry, she's cool. She's not a . . . Guardian."

"Can they stay for dinner?" Earth asked, looking up at her dad with big, brown eyes. "Please?" Aaron stared at us a little longer, then seemed to come to some kind of decision.

"I hope you like takeout," he grumbled, opening the door.

Earth made a face at me as we walked inside.

"We *always* get takeout," she whispered.

The four of us sat around a white metal table in the kitchen.

"Water?" Aaron said gruffly, holding out a glass pitcher.

I nodded politely. "Thank you."

He took a bite of apple pie, chewing thoughtfully. He'd gotten two slices, and we'd cut them into four. Earth insisted.

"We don't have guests a lot," she said earnestly. Aaron glanced at her, almost amused. I could tell that this kid was a handful. I already liked her.

I studied her. If she was Aaron's daughter, then she had traces of Rebel blood in her. And possibly some of the special Rogue powers her father had. She clearly knew about the Order and the Rebellion. Maybe even knew about her own heritage.

"Who was that out in the yard?" I asked. "He's cute. I always wanted a dog, but Aunt Jo said if we got one I had to feed it and walk it, and I was always too busy skiing."

"*I* get to walk him," she said proudly. "That's Milo. He's our attack dog."

"Scary," Raven said, sounding like she meant the opposite.

"We got him to scare away the light-haireds."

I glanced at Aaron. He was watching me.

"We saw you race once," Earth said.

"Okay, Trouble, that's enough sugar for you," Aaron said brusquely, whisking her plate to the sink.

"He calls me Trouble," Earth stage-whispered to me and Raven. "Because I talk a lot."

"Not a lot," Aaron corrected, sitting back down and mussing her hair. "*Too* much."

"Right, *too* much. Dad says one day I'm going to say the wrong thing to the wrong person and get in BIG trouble. Do you know what that's called?"

"No." I smiled. "Tell me."

"It's called eating your shoe." She crossed her arms and beamed, impressed with this knowledge.

"I think you might want to check again," Raven said, and I elbowed her in the rib.

"Ow!"

"Raven knows *all* about eating your shoe," I said to Earth.

"It's not a good habit." She shook her head, as if to confirm this fact.

"No," I said. "It's not." I looked up at Aaron to find him watching me again. "Your attack dog," I said. "The Order. They're watching you."

"Every damn day," he said.

"They come to my school, too," Earth piped up. "Every damn day." Aaron glanced at her sideways. "I can see them out the window during class. And sometimes if you sit in the kitchen at night with the lights off, you can see their wings moving outside the window. Like pale butterflies."

"When do you do that?" Aaron asked, surprised.

"When you get home late," she said. "Don't worry. Milo sits with me."

Suddenly, all the windows in the kitchen slammed closed—on their own—and the curtains drew themselves in tightly. I flinched.

"Just in case," Aaron said through gritted teeth. "They could be watching us right now."

I wondered what kind of powers he had, as a Rogue. Some kind of control over wind or energy, to be able to pull off a trick like that?

I forced myself back to the conversation, and the little girl sitting next to me.

"Do you spend a lot of time alone?" I asked her. Earth nodded vigorously. "So do I," I said. "You should come to

River Springs sometime. Hang out with me."

She perked up. "Dad used to live in River Springs! I saw pictures in his album. And then we visited to watch you ski. It's so pretty."

"When did you come watch me ski?" I asked. "I don't remember—"

"Okay, Trouble. I think it's bedtime, wouldn't you say?"

"Do I have to?" Earth puffed out her bottom lip.

"Yes, you do, missy," he said, giving her a nudge to get her moving. "Go brush those teeth while I talk to Skye and Raven."

Earth got up. Suddenly, I felt a tiny pair of arms wrap around my waist, and looked down to find her hugging me good-bye.

"Hi there," I said, and patted her head awkwardly.

"Will you come back and visit us again?" She looked up at me with big brown eyes.

I glanced at Aaron, who stiffened.

"Well, that's up to your dad," I said.

"I'll talk to him later," she whispered behind her hand.

"Okay, it's a deal."

"Bye, Raven!" she called over her shoulder on her way out the door.

"Hey! Don't I get a hug?" Raven yelled after her. But the

little girl was already gone.

"I bet you get a lot of sleep," I said.

"You don't even know the half of it." Aaron paused, as if trying to figure out what to say next. "I've thought about this day." He looked down at the water glass in his hand. "Seeing you all grown up. What I would say to you. The last time I saw you, you were her age." He glanced at the stairs. "Earth!" he shouted. "Let's hear that water running!"

"I'm going!" she called back. We heard a skitter of small feet climb the rest of the staircase.

Raven rolled her eyes. "I think somebody could use some help," she said, and stood up. "I'll let the two of you talk."

We sat in silence, the only sound the hum of the refrigerator.

"Why don't I remember?" I asked softly. "You, the cabin, the Uprising. If I was six when all this took place, how come I remember none of it?"

Something flickered in his eyes, but I could sense him beating the flicker back.

"Look," he said awkwardly. "I don't know if I should be the one to tell you all this. Shouldn't Josephine do it?"

"She's told me things. She told me about you. What you meant to each other. What my parents were trying to do.

But I know she hasn't told me everything, and I don't know if she will. Please," I said to him. "There's still so much about myself and my family that I don't know."

He took a thoughtful sip of water. "Your mom was very powerful, Skye. She could . . . see things. Visions of events that would happen. And she could do this thing . . . mess with your mind a little. One of her powers of the light."

"She used mental manipulation?" I said quietly. "My *mom*?"

"She was pretty good at it," he said. "Even on earth, even as a regular person. I guess the stronger you were as an angel, the longer those powers stay with you, a part of you. She lost her wings, but her powers never really left her."

I stared at him, trying to process what he was saying.

"She messed with my mind," I said. "She made me forget."

Aaron looked away. "I know that's probably hard to hear," he said. "Look, I'm really sorry. Maybe I'm not the best person to talk to about all this."

"No," I said sternly, looking up. "You're the person I *need* to talk to."

"I wanted to keep trying," he said. "After your mom and dad died. But Josephine insisted against it. She had you to look after. She promised your mother she would protect you from all this. That you would grow up like a normal kid." He smiled ruefully. "I guess you know now. Looks like the Order got their way after all."

"Aaron," I said. "You know why my parents were trying to protect me, right? About my powers—the mix of dark and light?"

He nodded. "Yeah," he said. "I know."

"I have powers that I inherited from my father—dark ones. And I also have powers that I inherited from my mother. Gifted powers. I can see things too, just like she could."

"Oh," he said, his eyes softening into awe. "Is that so?"

"Yes, and no matter how much they want me to, I can't join either side, the Rebellion or the Order. I'm starting my own group. I'm going to finish what my parents started."

"Skye," he said seriously. "We failed. Your mom saw a fourth Rogue in those visions of hers, but she couldn't tell us who it was."

"I can use my own visions. I can find out who it is. But we need you, Aaron. And," I added, trying not to smile, "so does Aunt Jo." I hoped I sounded subtle.

He looked up. "She does?"

"Please come back to River Springs with us. We'll figure this out. We'll find a way to keep the Order and the Rebellion in balance, prevent any more lives from being destroyed. We can only do it with your help."

He stood up and stretched, leaned against the kitchen counter with his back to me. I saw his back rise and fall in a sigh.

"It's not that easy. That was my old life. It's taken a lot for me to put it behind me."

"But wouldn't it be worth it?"

"You don't understand," he said, turning around. He had that same fierce look in his eyes as Asher and Aunt Jo. "That life, it follows you. My wife—"

I flinched. What was I thinking? Of course Earth had to have a mother.

"My late wife," he corrected. "She was followed by Guardians, every day. She didn't know it, of course. Didn't know what they were. They tracked her as a threat to me—to keep me in line, to prevent me from ever going back to Josephine and James, finishing what we began. Or from starting some kind of uprising on my own." He looked pained. "I couldn't live like that, with the constant fear anymore. I went back to River Springs, to beg your aunt to think about joining forces again. She said no, and by the time I got back, my wife—" He broke off, his voice going for a moment. "They killed her."

I sucked in a breath. "No," I whispered.

He nodded.

"Earth found her, in the car with the windows up. Those bastards made it look like she did it herself, but I knew it was them. The kid's learned to grow around the pain, push it down. But she's a special one. Strange, but special." He looked at me. "I think you two have quite a bit in common."

"I could teach her," I said. "I know she has powers. She must. I can show her how to use them."

"I told her about the angels at a young age. Didn't want to lie to her about how her mom died, you know?"

"Please come," I said. "It's safe with us. We're protected."

"Are you?" He looked skeptical. "How protected are you, really?"

I felt a chill spread across my skin, prickling it with goose bumps.

"You don't know what they're capable of," he whispered.

I stood up quickly, suddenly scared to be away for too long. "I have to get back," I said. "You'll come, right? Isn't this what you wanted?"

He sighed deeply. "Just give me some time to think,"

he said. "For my daughter."

When I got to the door, I paused. "They killed my parents, too," I said without looking at him. "I don't know about you, but I have to fight."

Raven and I stood on the sidewalk in front of the house. A light still glowed in the kitchen window, but otherwise it was dark. We could see Aaron's silhouette behind the curtains, sitting with his head in his hands.

What are you doing, Skye? I asked myself. *Is this worth it?*

But I knew that it was—that any small pain I caused now would save us all from the greater pain that would be caused when the Order and the Rebellion clashed.

"Well, that was productive," Raven said. "You caught up with Aaron Ward, and I got to read a bedtime story."

I pressed my fingers into my eyes and breathed deep.

"Skye," she said. "Are you okay? I swear I'm not being bitchy when I say this, but you look awful."

"It's been a long day," I said. "Let's just go home."

But even as I said it, the edges of my world began to blur out of focus, into something darker, hotter.

Tiny, dark stars bloomed into life in the air around us. They smoldered like the glowing embers of a fire, igniting the air, causing smoke to unfurl in plumes.

"Skye?" Raven's voice faded into the snap and crackle of flames.

My heart beat faster.

My vision began to swim, to fill with thick, black smoke, as the rest of the street faded away.

Please make her be all right, I found myself thinking.

Who?

Flames exploded around me, shattering glass, filling the air with acrid, heavy smoke so thick it felt solid. Sirens shrieked somewhere off in the distance, and someone was yelling. Wooden beams above me glowed bright with fire, raining sparks and ashes down around me, and glossy papers burned and fluttered to the ground. Panic and smoke filled my throat and lungs. All I could think—the one thought that rang through my every fiber—was *I have to save her.*

"Skye!" Raven's voice pierced my thoughts, and the vision dissolved into wisps of smoke. Sycamore Street was quiet and dark. A dog barked in the distance. "Are you okay? Was it a vision?"

I blinked. "There was a fire. I had to save someone."

"Did you see who?"

I shook my head.

"Well." She paused. "There's no use standing around

here, is there? Can you fly?"

"Yeah," I said, suddenly itching to get back home. Aaron's words burned like those flames in my mind.

You don't know what they're capable of.

"Let's go."

We took to the sky. It was dark now, but clear and scattered with stars. The moon shone a path for us toward the mountains, toward home.

And then, all of a sudden, it was less clear.

"Is that smoke?" Raven asked, coughing.

Smoke.

"Can we get closer?" I urged. The smoke was gathering in the sky in billows of soot. We descended. "It's coming from downtown," I said. "See?"

Through the rising smoke, I could make out the buildings along Main Street, a crowd gathering. And then my heart lurched as I pinpointed exactly where the fire was coming from.

"It's Into the Woods," I said, my voice going hoarse. "It's Aunt Jo's store."

8

he fire raged.

Main Street was clogged with fire trucks and police cars. Raven and I touched down around the corner so that no one could see, and ran down the block toward the commotion. It was impossible not to think of the night of my seventeenth birthday—the night Asher and Devin showed up at Love the Bean, and the boiler had exploded. Shattered glass covered the street, and angry smoke poured from the front windows.

I could feel the heat pressing into me the closer I got to Into the Woods.

"Skye!" I whipped around. Raven pointed across the street—Aunt Jo's pickup truck.

"Oh my god," I yelled. I broke my way into the throng

on the street. Police cordoned off a group of spectators that had gathered to watch as firemen hosed down Into the Woods from the outside. "Let me through!"

"Hey, you have to step back." An officer stepped into my path, blocking me from the front door. "It's not safe." He was young and shockingly attractive, with hair as dark as the soot rising into the night sky.

"My aunt is in there!" I shouted at him. "You have to let me in! Please, you have to get out of my way!"

"I can't let you do that, it's not safe. There's all kinds of structural damage in there. The firemen are inside; they'll find anyone who didn't make it out." He looked me in the eye, and there was something off about him. Familiar—and yet I'd never seen him before. I shivered despite the intense heat.

Raven ran up alongside me. "I have a bad feeling about this," she hissed, grabbing my arm. She noticed the look in my eyes. "Oh, no. No. I know what you're thinking. Do *not* go in there."

"I have to. She needs me."

"Skye, there are trained professionals in fire suits. They have gas masks."

I stared into the flames, looking for the best way in. "But none of them have powers like mine."

"Skye, you really are crazy, aren't you? If you go in there without any kind of protection, they'll come looking for you. What are they going to think if you make it out alive?"

"We'll just have to change the way they think, then, won't we?"

Raven squinted at me. "You know," she said. "I think I may have underestimated you."

We ran together to the nearest police officer. He, too, had a strangely familiar look to him—but in the chaos of smoke and flame I couldn't place it.

"Have you ever done this before?" Raven whispered.

"I'm part Gifted. I'm sure I'll be able to figure it out."

The officer looked down at me, the fire reflected in his black eyes. And I stared right back into them. All I had to do was influence his thoughts. Make him forget he ever saw me—or what he was about to see.

His eyes grew vague, far-off. He whispered something I couldn't hear, and then turned his back to me, walking away in the other direction.

Raven and I looked at each other. I was just as surprised as she was.

"I can't believe you just did that," Raven said. "*I* couldn't even do that. Only the most powerful, the Gifted—"

"Flatter me later," I said. "I have to go." I should have felt panicked, but what I felt instead was a fierce determination to save Aunt Jo. And so I did the only thing I could think to do. I ran straight into the fire.

It was just like in my vision. The tin ceiling had peeled back in an evil grin, revealing a mouthful of smoldering wooden beams. Flames licked the walls hungrily, leaving a trail of char and soot in their wake. The floor beneath my feet was so excruciatingly hot, it felt like the soles of my shoes were melting.

But I was half Rebel. And I'd learned how to handle fire ages ago.

As I stretched my hands out, I could feel the cooling liquid silver pour through me, forming a protective barrier of some sort around my skin. Then before I knew it, the barrier erupted into flame itself, creating a fiery suit of armor that somehow kept me cool and dry.

"Aunt Jo!" I called. My vision began to swim, and my eyes watered. "Where are you?" I could hear glass shattering in the distance, and the sound of someone screaming. I booked it in the direction of the screams.

Amid the snap and crash of falling wood, someone called my name. And I used it like a beacon, homing in. I found her crouched behind the counter, with her arms over her head. The fire was closing in around her, jumping out, licking at her arms and legs and face—but remarkably, it hadn't engulfed her completely. The area behind the counter was untouched by flame. Aunt Jo was okay. If I didn't know any better, I'd have said Aunt Jo was working some similar powers to mine. There were definitely some otherworldly forces in action, keeping the fire from encroaching on the small circle of floor where Aunt Jo sat.

"What are you doing?" I yelled. "You have to get out!"

"I came back here to save some papers!" Her eyes were watering from the smoke, and tears streamed down her face. "But now I can't get out." Through the smoke, she stared at the strange force field of fire I'd surrounded myself with. "How are you . . . ?"

"Come on." I extended a hand to her. "I can get you out."

Aunt Jo eyed it dubiously, then took a deep breath and grabbed it. The minute she made contact the cooling silver snaked up her arm, spreading over her entire body. The fire-armor enveloped both of us.

"Skye," she said hoarsely. "You continue to amaze me."

Together we made our way back through the smoldering store. Firemen were just beginning to pour in, spraying water over the flames. When we came trudging over the doorstep, I focused on the crowd and let my mind penetrate theirs.

Nobody saw us leave.

I took Aunt Jo down the street to her truck, where we knelt on the ground and I grasped her hands in mine—healing her minor scratches and burns with my touch. I couldn't help but flash back, one more time, to the night when the boiler had exploded at Love the Bean during my seventeenth birthday party. Cassie had knelt beside me in the snow behind her car, clasping my mittened hands in hers. And I had tried to explain how I felt. The panic, the fear—knowing something was happening, that I was changing, but not knowing how or why.

The last time I'd knelt in this spot, I had been so lost, helpless. But as I held Aunt Jo's hands in mine and felt the power surge from my fingertips into her wounds, closing them, healing them completely, all I could do was marvel at how far I'd traveled since that freezing January night.

I might not have known everything about myself yet, might not have known every bit of truth about my parents, who they were and what they were trying to do. But I knew who *I* was. I was a force to be reckoned with.

"You saved my life," Aunt Jo wheezed, looking up at me with a shaky smile.

"And I'd do it again, Aunt Jo," I said. I leaned in and kissed her forehead. "I would do anything for you."

"There you are!" Raven's blond hair flew behind her in a sheet of corn silk as she ran to us. "What am I feeling? What is this? It's not good. I feel . . ." She put a hand on her chest and stopped for breath.

"Worried?" Aunt Jo said drily.

"Don't ever scare me like that again," Raven said. "Come on, I'll drive us home." She paused for a second, as if realizing what she'd just said.

Home.

In a way, it was something we were all searching for. I smiled, and then Raven smiled too. She reached out her hands to help us up, and Aunt Jo and I each took one.

"I don't think I've ever seen you smile, Raven," I said as she pulled me to my feet.

"Yeah, well, don't get used to it." But she grinned awkwardly, and I could tell that she was blushing.

Raven got in the driver's seat of Aunt Jo's truck, Aunt Jo squeezed in next, and I followed. The blond fallen angel revved the engine. I leaned my forehead against the window and watched the last glowing embers of the fire float up into the night sky, fade to ash, and float away on the wind.

As we pulled away from the curb, the hair on my arms stood on end, and a shiver went up the back of my neck. I looked out the window. A familiar silhouette stood in the shadows, partly obscured by several police cars. He turned to face us as we drove off, and there was no mistaking those flashing dark eyes, the sense that he wasn't just inhabiting the night—he was a part of it.

Asher.

I slammed my hands against the window, but the sirens wailed and the crowd swallowed him, and we drove away before I could call his name.

The headlights cut a swath through the dark night of our driveway. The house was still and silent when we entered. It was only this morning when I'd been here last, but it felt like I was returning from an epic journey. I'd learned things about my past that changed the way I thought about myself and my life. I saw things differently now.

"I'll make us some tea," Aunt Jo said, padding off to the kitchen.

"Shouldn't I?" I called after her.

"You saved my life," she called back. "It's the least I can do."

Raven and I were alone in the living room, curled up

on the couch. Moonlight spilled through the plate glass windows, and the jagged outline of the mountains cast shadows on the floor.

"How am I going to tell her what we saw?" I wondered aloud, half to myself. "How am I supposed to tell her that Aaron's still in danger? That he was *married*? Oh my god— that he has a daughter?"

"You'll find a way," Raven said. She reached out to place a hand on my back, and patted it awkwardly. "You always do. That's what you do best. Make the people around you feel better." She paused, and took her hand away. "Did that help? I've never understood why people pat each other's backs. It seems so unnatural to me. Just unnecessary physical contact."

I laughed.

"What? What's so funny?"

"Nothing." I paused. "Did you notice anything weird about those police officers? Almost like they were—" And then, in a flash, I realized why they seemed so familiar. "Raven, they were—"

"Girls?" Aunt Jo called from the kitchen. "I think I hear the door. Will you go see who it is?"

Raven raised her eyebrows at me. I got up and crept warily to the front door. Who could it be so late on a weeknight? And on the night of the fire, of all nights. I braced myself.

"Your house is so *big*!" Earth was staring up at me with round eyes. "We got in the car as soon as you left." She brushed past me into the house. "Can I sleep in your room?"

"I— What?" I looked back at the doorstep. Aaron hesitated, a duffel bag in his hands.

"The thing is," he said, "I thought about it, and I guess we're safer here with you than out there in Rocky Pines all alone, so . . ." He looked cautiously behind me. "Is she . . . ?"

"Come in." I smiled. My entire body flooded with relief. I knew he would come. I *knew* it. Maybe Cassie was infecting me with her love of happy endings. I made a mental note to tell her.

"Hey, hon? Who is it?" Aunt Jo came into the hallway, wiping her hands on her jeans. When she and Aaron saw each other, they stopped short. "Oh," she said faintly, one hand moving to rest on her heart.

Aaron let the duffel bag fall to the floor with a soft thud. "Josephine," he whispered.

"I found him," I said, looking back and forth between the two Rogues. They stood there, motionless.

"I see," Aunt Jo said quietly. She looked down suddenly, as if remembering there were other people in the room. Earth was standing by her feet, squinting up at her with her little hands on her hips.

"Boy was he nervous to see *you*," she said.

"Earth!" Aaron said, turning purple with embarrassment.

"What? She doesn't look so scary in person."

"Watch it." Aaron looked like he wanted to crawl into his duffel bag. He smoothed his dark waves back and looked at Aunt Jo sheepishly.

"Oops," said Earth. "Did I eat my shoe?"

"Well, hello to you too." Aunt Jo laughed, a little dazed. "I'm Josephine."

"I'm Earth," Earth said. Aunt Jo looked up at Aaron in wonder.

"And I take it you met Skye."

"Oh, yeah," she said. "We're sharing a room." She waved a hand in my direction. "Don't worry, we're cool."

Aaron laughed uncomfortably. "I guess we have a lot to catch up on."

That seemed to snap Aunt Jo back to reality.

"Yes," she said. "Yes, come in. Can I get you anything to drink? I just brewed some tea." She put her hands on her knees and crouched to Earth's level. "And I could whip up some hot chocolate, easy peasy."

Earth looked apologetic. "I already brushed my teeth," she said with a shrug.

"Good kid," Aunt Jo said, patting her on the head.

Earth giggled. "I'm not a *dog*. Oh, but—Milo is in the car. Can he come in?"

"Milo?" Aunt Jo asked skeptically.

"Our attack dog."

Half an hour later we were all sitting in the living room, mugs of tea (and one hot chocolate) clasped in our hands, Milo snoozing on the rug.

"I was closing up at the store, and all of a sudden I smelled smoke. When I walked out of the office, the whole front of the store was up in flames." She stared out the window and shook her head. "All of it. Gone. My whole life's work."

"It wasn't a cigarette or something, left in the trash?" Aaron looked concerned. He was sitting next to Aunt Jo—a good foot between them—and seemed unsure of what to do with his limbs: his arm was draped along the back of the couch, then it was in his lap; his legs were crossed and then they weren't. Raven seemed oblivious, but Earth caught my eye and rolled hers, like, *parents, what are ya gonna do with them?* She was pretty astute for a seven-year-old.

"No," Aunt Jo said, shooting a sideways glance in my direction. "I gave up smoking years ago. It's bad for you, Skye, don't do it."

I raised my hands in surrender. "No arguments here. So you think it was an attack?"

I was met with an uncomfortable silence.

"Well, I'll say it. I thought the same thing." Raven flung her glossy hair over her shoulder. "That was no accident. Skye and I were off trying to convince a powerful Rogue—who himself, I might add, is watched every day by Guardians—to come back with us? The Order must have taken that opportunity to pounce. It's definitely a warning."

"I think you're right, Raven," Aunt Jo said, leaning forward. "It's starting. The Order has made their position perfectly clear. They're on the offensive."

"I thought we'd be safe here," Aaron muttered.

"Safer than in Rocky Pines!" Aunt Jo countered.

"Wait," I cut in. Something didn't sit right with me. The vision, the fire, the strange police officers . . . and Asher, watching me as we drove off. My heart sank. "It wasn't the Order," I said. Everyone looked up at me. I knew what I was about to say would change everything. "Those police officers looked familiar for a reason—they were Rebels. It was the Rebellion."

"Are you sure, Skye?" Aunt Jo asked, the worry crease returning.

"Definitely. Fire? That's a signature Rebel power—the Order can't do that. And I was able to protect us both against it with my own powers of the dark. It wasn't the Order this time. It was the Rebellion, for sure."

Aaron seemed bewildered. "Even back in the day—" He glanced at Aunt Jo. "It was mostly the Guardians who were after us."

"This is so much bigger than what we were doing then," Aunt Jo said. Her voice was suddenly so small. "Skye is grown now. She has come so fully into her powers. With her at the helm, we really do stand a chance."

"That's what we thought last time, too," said Aaron. His hand moved automatically from his lap to Aunt Jo's knee. Without thinking, she placed her own hand on top of his. Earth and I shared another look, but this time neither of us smiled. "I'm here," he said. "Earth and I are going to help you, however we can."

"I hate to say it," said Raven. "But it feels like—"

"It feels like this is only the beginning." Everyone looked at me again. I was getting used to saying the thing that made the room fall into uncomfortable silence. The thing that made them nervous. "They're not just fighting against each other anymore. Now they're targeting us. Trying to take us out of the equation."

Raven hesitated. Her blue eyes shone with realization.

"Not you, Skye," she said. "Your friends and family. The people you love. You're strong on your own, but what makes you even stronger is how much you love the people in your life—Aunt Jo, Cassie, Dan, Ian. And how much they love you. It's why the Order always tried to isolate you from everyone. The Order may want to kill you, to keep your powers from falling into the Rebellion's hands. But I don't think the Rebellion has the same strategy. I think they want to kill *us*. And *use* you."

I shivered. If that was true, then no one—not a single one of us—was safe.

I turned to Aaron and Aunt Jo.

"You know what we need to do," I said. "We need to find James Harrison. And soon." Aaron and Aunt Jo exchanged glances. Something seemed to pass between the two of them that I couldn't read. Some secret, unspoken language that they'd learned to use a long time ago. They'd picked it up again effortlessly. At the same time, they looked at me. And nodded.

"Good," I continued. "Because once the three of you are back together again—I have a feeling that's when I'll be able to see what my mother couldn't." The moonlight shone through the window. Everyone's face was turned to me. "That's when I'll see the fourth."

I stayed up late.

Eventually we all said good night. Aaron and Aunt Jo brought our mugs into the kitchen and sat down at the table. Instead of going upstairs to bed, I hung out on the stairs, peering through the slats in the railing as Aunt Jo and her old flame talked in hushed tones, their heads bent together. As I strained to hear what the two Rogues in the kitchen were saying to each other, snippets of memory came pushing through to the forefront of my mind.

Rebellion—

Guardians—

Powerful one day—

For her own good—

Keep her safe.

I was six again, watching my parents have another argument about something I didn't understand. They were having more and more of them. Almost every night, it seemed.

Little silver bells. When they ring, we'll know.

If only I had known, if only they hadn't kept me in the dark, I could have been better prepared for what was happening now. I could have spent my whole life preparing. I wouldn't have made the friends I did. I wouldn't have to put the people I love in danger.

If only my mother hadn't forced me to forget.

The Order controls human fate. And she'd been one of them, for so long. Even after she left, their ways stayed with her. And she hadn't thought twice about using her powers on me. Her own daughter.

I wished, right then, that somebody had given me a choice.

"You can see better from up here." A small voice cut into my memories. I glanced up and realized Earth was sitting several steps above me.

"How long have you been there?" I whispered.

She put a finger to her lips. "Shh." Silently, I moved to sit next to her on the top step, and we peered through the slats in the railing together.

"You're right," I whispered. "You can hear better, too."

"It's not my first time spying like this."

I looked at her, surprised.

"No," I said. "Mine either."

I guess no matter how strong or powerful I was, part of me still felt like a kid, no idea what I was doing and making it up as I went along. How the hell was I supposed to save the universe?

But if I gave in to that nagging feeling of doubt, the one that told me there was no way I could pull this off, even for just a second, I knew it would unravel everything I'd worked so hard for. There was no room in my life anymore to question. It was time to act.

Side by side, we listened to Aunt Jo and Aaron talk about the past. It occurred to me that I didn't understand it any more now than I had when I was six.

I opened my eyes just as the first golden reaches of sun were peeking through my window.

Aunt Jo finally let me take the day off of school. It had been a long night, she said, and we could all use time to process what was happening. For once, she even agreed with me that it was safer at home than it was roaming the halls of Northwood.

If the Rebels could attack her store out in the open like that, then maybe Asher had been wrong that cold night on the roof, when he told me the Order wouldn't strike at school. Maybe the rules had changed, and nowhere was safe anymore.

Raven offered to go to school and keep an eye on Cassie, Dan, and Ian. She knew the Order's tactics and methods, and could watch out for the Rebels. She would be able to keep my friends safe, until they could all come over. If all of us cut school on the same day, it was sure to raise some eyebrows and cause more than a few phone calls home. And we couldn't let their parents find out what was going on. Who knew what the Order or the Rebellion would do to them if they did?

I texted Cassie as soon as I woke up.

Big news for all you epic love story fans out there.

Before I could even put my phone down she texted,

Asher's back???

No, I wrote. **Stick with Raven. Come over after school.**

A second later,

Just the 2 of us? Raven = She-Devil.

I typed back:

She's not that bad when you get to know her.

There was a pause while Cassie was either typing or

staring daggers at her phone.

She is the physical embodiment of everything I hate in this world.

I typed back the following:

Get used to her because she is going to be on you all day like frosting on a cupcake.

Another pause.

Thanks, Skye. Now I want a cupcake.

After the drama of the night before, and the night before that—and so many nights before—my body ached to move. I pulled on running clothes, laced up my sneakers, and crept out of the bedroom. I was careful not to wake Earth, who had burrowed into a Hello Kitty sleeping bag and was snoring peacefully. On my way downstairs, I passed Raven, curled into a C-shape on the couch in the den. Her porcelain cheeks were red, and her perfect golden eyebrows were arched menacingly. She must have been dreaming—and man, she looked angry. I was glad not to be on the other end of her wrath.

The rest of the house was silent and still. I quietly opened the front door and jogged outside into the cool, spring morning.

Now that ski season was over, I had to think of ways to keep my powers focused and under control. I could do things I never imagined—that suit of fire-armor was new—but I still felt like I had to keep my mind and body in sync. It was easier now, and getting easier every day. Asher and Devin may have showed me what I was capable of, but I could take it from here. I didn't need them to get stronger. I could do that on my own. What had Raven said to me? *Isn't it always the girls who run the show, anyway?*

I could feel the wind in my hair, the weather in my blood, the clouds in my eyes.

At the top of the trail, I looked out over the clearing as I'd done so many times in my life. It used to be one of the only places in the world where I felt truly at peace. But a lot of things had changed in the past few months; I'd had a lot of important milestones here. Once, I slipped on a patch of ice, and would have fallen off the edge, plummeting to my death in the valley below, if Devin hadn't caught me. After that, it had become our secret, unspoken meeting place. In this peaceful spot, I'd come to terms with a lot of my powers.

"I thought I might find you here," a voice behind me said. I turned around.

"I was just thinking about you."

Devin looked like he didn't know quite how to handle that information. Asher would have said something clever without thinking, like, "I bet you say that to all strange guys you meet in the woods." But Devin thought things through before he said them out loud. You could see the struggle in his eyes, even now. I always thought it was just because as a Guardian, there was so much he couldn't express. Now, in the early morning light, I realized it was as simple as this: that's just how Devin was.

He struggled with things. He said he loved me, but he had betrayed me more times than I could count. Raven's words from the night before came spilling back to me. *How can you love someone who's hurt you?*

In the months that I'd known Devin, I'd felt a range of emotions toward him—a whole spectrum, really. He had been a friend when I'd needed one, and in a moment of shadows and firelight in the woods, I'd questioned my loyalties and let him be something more. We'd been allies, then enemies, and then allies again when he chose to become a Rebel. But Ardith's warning at school and last night's attack on the store made it clear as glass: we were enemies, again, and always would be.

"Why are you here?" I asked him. "If you're coming to warn me, don't worry. Ardith has already done the job for you."

"Skye, that's not—"

"And the Rebellion's pyrotechnical performance last night spoke volumes, too."

"I wasn't a part of that." He looked pained, like there was more he wanted to say, but he wasn't sure how to say it.

"Right," I said. "Just like you never meant to hurt me, and you had no choice about cutting off Raven's wings, and—"

"You're right. I'm sorry."

I stared at him. "You're . . . you're *what*?"

"I'm sorry. I was never able to say that to you, or give you the apology you deserved. Now, I can."

Now *I* was the one who couldn't find the right words.

"Listen, Skye," he continued, as if gathering the momentum he'd built with his apology. "I didn't come here to argue with you. I came to say thank you."

"Wow," I said. "Now I really don't know what to say."

"That's okay." The light radiated from his eyes. He looked so free. "I have a lot to say, if you'll listen." He led me to our rock, and we sat down. Side by side, just like we used to.

Something about being with Devin felt so strange and different, and I couldn't place why. *The tranquility,* I realized. *I don't feel it anymore.* I didn't feel the usual

Zen-like calm radiating from him. Instead, I could feel his nervous energy, matching mine, pulsing underneath his skin as his arm brushed against me. It was true. He really wasn't under the Order's control—or possibly, anyone else's.

He was free. He could do whatever he wanted.

"I know we're fighting against each other now. In some ways, I think we'll always be fighting against each other. But I just want you to know that when you inspired me to jump, it was the best thing that ever happened to me. You showed me that I needed to break away. I couldn't have done that without you." He looked nervous. Maybe as nervous as I felt. "I don't know. Maybe I needed to hurt you like that in order to realize how bad it was. How much I needed to be free."

When I had gone to Devin for help when he was still a Guardian, there was always something holding him back. Something in his eyes that, I knew, meant there was a disconnect between what he said and what he felt. It was why my feelings were always so unresolved after I spent time with him. Who was the *real* Devin? What was really behind those eyes? I wondered if I would soon find out. A light burned in him that I'd never seen before. A different Devin sat next to me.

"Let me get this straight," I said slowly, puzzling it out. "You're saying you're *glad* you hurt me?"

"I'm saying I didn't want to do it. I didn't want to do any of it. And *that's* why I jumped. I was choosing freedom." He looked up, and his deep blue eyes were oceans. "I can finally feel. I can feel everything for the first time. I hate myself for everything I've done. And I'm going to do everything I can, everything that's in my power, to make it up to you."

I swallowed. I had absolutely no idea how to respond. Running into a burning building, I could handle. But this?

"I'm a Rebel now, Skye." He grinned, and it lit up his face in a way I'd never seen. "I can break the rules if I want." The meaning behind his words was clear: *Asher isn't the only one.*

"You talk a big game, Devin," I said when I'd finally found my voice again. "But you never put your money where your mouth is."

"Okay. How's this: That Guardian with the long hair? Lucas? Look out for that one. He's bad news. Ruthless and dangerous."

"What?" I said. "How do you know?"

"He's very highly regarded in the Order. Used to be

trusted, ranked right below me and Raven. And now . . ." He trailed off.

"Now *he's* the one stealing car brakes?"

Devin winced. "Exactly."

While we were talking, the sun rose higher in the sky. I had to get back. The house would be waking up, wondering where I was, and after last night I didn't want them to worry. Besides, we had work to do today.

"I have to go," I said, standing up. "Thank you. For the apology. I'm not sure how I feel about it, but . . ."

"That's okay." He brushed off my excuse. "The important thing is that I got to say it."

I nodded to myself and then made my way back toward the trail.

"Did you know?" he called suddenly as I began to jog away. I stopped and turned back to him. "Tell me the truth."

"Did I know what?"

"What Asher was planning? What the Rebellion wanted to do to me?"

There was something so strange about the moment, so heartbreaking. We were on equal footing now, Devin and I. We had both been betrayed. We both wanted answers. There was a satisfying symmetry to it.

"Just tell me yes or no."

"No," I said finally. "No, I could never let that happen to someone I cared about."

Devin said nothing. I turned and ran the rest of the way down the trail. But I wasn't running away from something. I was running toward it.

10

Aunt Jo stood at the stove, flipping pancakes. She was especially chipper this morning.

"Don't forget to put the smiley face with the chocolate chips," Earth instructed from the table, where she was reading the newspaper. "Dad, what's Wall Street?"

"It's a place that's very far away from here," Aaron said warily. He glanced at Aunt Jo, and Aunt Jo grinned at him over her shoulder.

"Hey, kiddo," she said as I walked in. "You're just in time for breakfast! There's coffee brewing. Extra strong."

"Mmm," I said, grabbing a mug from the cabinet and filling it to the brim. "Did Raven leave already?"

"She left pretty early. She wanted to get there before

everyone else, to scout it out."

I took a sip of coffee and scrunched up my face. "It's too bad Ian can't come over until after school."

Aunt Jo and Aaron exchanged glances, and then looked at me. "Why?" Aunt Jo said cautiously.

"I didn't have a chance to tell you this in all the drama of yesterday," I said. "But Ian thought the name James Harrison sounded familiar. He asked his mom about it."

Aaron stood halfway out of his chair. "And?"

"That was his father's name. He's pretty sure there's a connection. And that would mean . . ."

"I had a feeling about him," Aunt Jo said, stacking the pancakes on a plate and sliding it onto the table. She wiped her hands on her apron and took it off, all the while watching me. "I knew he had angelic lineage. But James . . . his father?" She looked at Aaron. "I suppose that timing makes sense. He was very secretive while we were working together. We knew he had a young family, but we had never met them. He kept us so separate. He led two lives, really."

Aaron nodded. "Part of why we believed he left was that it was too much of a burden on him, lying to them about what he was doing. His wife didn't know, and his son was so young. Must've been around your age, Skye."

"So it makes sense." I took another sip of coffee. "But he left Ian and his mom then, too. If it was a burden on him to lie to them, why would he leave?"

The kitchen was quiet.

"Good job on these pancakes," Earth said from behind the newspaper.

After breakfast, Aaron suggested that Earth go watch TV upstairs.

"But TV rots your brain! Can I go play outside, Dad? Please?"

Aunt Jo stared at Aaron. "Okay, seriously, what parenting manual did you use, and can I have it?"

"Hey," I said, "standing right here!"

Aaron patted Earth on the head. "It's not safe out there right now, Trouble. Go on up and watch some television. I think your brain will be safe for a couple hours this afternoon."

She trudged reluctantly up the stairs.

I brought down everything I'd taken from the box in the cabin, and we spread the loot across the living room floor. There was the rattle, with *Sk* and my birthdate engraved into the tarnished silver. A stuffed dog that looked like it had spent the better part of six years sleeping in the crook of my arm. A series of drawings and amateurish water-colors I'd apparently done as a kid. They were all signed in big blue letters in the corner: SKY.

"It took you a while to figure out that your name had an 'e' at the end of it. That you weren't actually named after the sky." Aunt Jo smiled a little wistfully at me. The drawings depicted several tall people, with large swirls and curlicues in a rainbow of colors surrounding them. I knew exactly what they were. I could almost hear myself at six. . . .

Those are their powers.

It struck me again how unfair it was that I wasn't allowed to remember any of this. And yet, small things, snippets of memory, were seeping back. Maybe the longer I had powers of my own, the more they would counteract the ones my mother had used on me as a child.

I'd also brought down the artifacts I'd found the first time I'd visited. The notebook Aunt Jo had kept during their time in the cabin—and the shoebox that I'd discovered in Aunt Jo's closet, that held the remaining pages she'd ripped out and kept, among other things. When I pulled out my father's old, moth-eaten fisherman's sweater, Aaron's eyes grew wide.

"My sweater!" he cried. "I must have forgotten it when I left."

"This—this is yours?" I asked. My stomach sank. This whole time, I'd been thinking it was my father's. It was the only piece of physical evidence I had to connect me to him. Growing up, I always thought it was so sad and strange that I had nothing that belonged to my parents— no pictures, no evidence that they had ever existed. Now I understood why. If they were being hunted, if they wanted to keep me safe, and if they wanted to protect me from the knowledge of who I really was, of course they could leave nothing behind that might trace me to them. This whole time, I'd thought they were depriving me. In reality, they were protecting me.

"Yeah, I wore that ratty old sweater straight through the winter before Sam and Meredith—" He cut himself off quickly and looked away. "Before we all parted ways. You can keep it, if you want. I'm not sure it will really provide any clues for where to find James, though."

I folded it up and put it aside. Aunt Jo was thumbing through the notebook, and Aaron was going through the shoebox. When he pulled out the photograph of him and Aunt Jo against the tree, I watched something change in his face.

"You kept this?" he asked.

She blushed and nodded. "Yeah, well. You can see I don't throw much out."

He continued sifting through the box and came up with the little black velvet case that held the ring. He glanced at Aunt Jo, but she was suddenly busy examining something she'd written ages ago in her notebook. Aaron slipped the ring into his pocket without a word.

I coughed. "Is there anything here that might give us any idea of where James went? Or even why he left?"

"I know why he left," Aaron said quietly.

"Aaron—" Aunt Jo looked up. "You don't."

"I'm pretty sure I do. If we want to find him, isn't it important to get everything out in the open?"

"Get what out in the open?" My heart began to beat faster. If they had any information about where he could be, then we were one step closer to reuniting the three of them. And then I could focus on using my visions to find the fourth.

"The night he left," Aunt Jo said quietly, "we had a fight. The three of us did. Your parents didn't know about it."

"What was it about?" I asked.

"Aaron and I were spending a lot of time together," she said.

"He was jealous," Aaron said darkly.

"We don't know that," said Aunt Jo. "But he did think we were spending too much time together, that we were losing our focus on the mission and weren't strong enough to call the Rogues. He also said it was throwing off the balance of power between the three of us."

"Do you think that's true?" I asked.

"Who really knows?" said Aaron. "I always suspected . . ."

"Aaron, please."

"What?" I asked. "What did you suspect?"

Aaron looked out the window. "I thought he was in love with your aunt," he muttered. "It got to be too much for him, so he left. Left his family, too. Just went completely off the grid."

"Whoa. That would explain a lot, right?"

The two of them nodded.

"I don't know that's really what it was, though, Skye," Aunt Jo said. "I have no way of knowing if he was." She sighed. "I just know that love can make you do a lot of stupid things."

It can sway the outcome of a war, Ardith had said once. I never put that much stock in the power of love, but I was beginning to think she was right.

"So where does that leave us?" I asked. "Where could James be?"

"Anywhere," said Aaron. "He could be anywhere."

"I'll talk to Ian," I offered. "See if he or his mom knows anything more."

"It's worth a shot," said Aunt Jo. "But if we don't know, it's not very likely that they will. He was such a private person. Kept so much from all of us."

I sighed. "I need to go be alone for a little bit," I said. "Think about some things."

"Go ahead, hon. We'll be here."

I went up to my room and closed the door. I figured if I thought hard enough, I could make something happen, put the rest of the puzzle pieces together. James. The fourth Rogue. I tried not to let the pressure get to me. I tried to forget that I had to figure all this out before these attacks culminated in something bigger, some collision between the Order and the Rebellion that would destroy us all. I didn't have much time left.

Then I noticed something on the floor by the backpack I'd taken on our camping trip: a small box made of polished wood—about the size and shape of an index card. It must have fallen out when I was gathering up my finds to take downstairs. I tucked it into the band of my running shorts and slid out my window onto the roof.

A spring breeze ruffled my hair and kissed my cheeks. I couldn't help but remember how cold and barren the field below me had been all winter. Then, I'd stared out at a bleak white sky and watched as a flock of birds took off from the treetops, the rush of hundreds of wings echoing in my ears. But now the sky was bluer, the treetops greener, and the birds were coming—not going.

I took out the box and studied it. The wood was a dark, rich hue, polished to a shine. It struck me as weird—everything else that I'd salvaged from the cabin was showing signs of age, decay. The wooden box was as polished and shiny as it might have been on the day it was made.

Strangely, the wood appeared to be all one piece—with no grooves or hinges where it might open. There was a keyhole in the front, but no actual key. I shook it and heard something lightweight flutter within.

There was a design etched into the lid—or what should have been the lid. An old-fashioned key, with an elaborate top that swooped out in four intertwining loops—like a four-leaf clover.

The whole box looked like some sort of strange puzzle. If it was left with other personal items in the cabin, then it must have belonged to my parents, or to the Rogues they were working with. It was clear that whoever it had belonged to didn't want just anybody to discover its contents.

I put my hand on the engraving, and it glowed silver beneath my fingers. And then, before my eyes, the silver became solid, real metal—and I found myself holding a key.

Like it was meant for me.

The key fit into the lock perfectly. I held my breath as it clicked, and the top of the box slid sideways.

Resting inside was a single piece of paper folded many times into a tight square. I couldn't stop my fingers from trembling slightly as I unfolded it to reveal a page filled from top to bottom with cramped, tight script. My heart expanded like ink in water when I saw how it began:

Dear Skye,

I'm writing you this letter, my sweet girl, because I don't know what else to do. We are in danger. Your father and I have made a risky mistake, and we are being watched. Followed. If I'm being truthful with you, I don't think we'll make it through another week.

But you will. They won't kill you. You hold the key to breaking them, and they'll do whatever they can to harness that power. You're not ready for it now. I can't put you in the position of having to save the world just yet. I can hardly let you wander off by yourself for two seconds,

Skye, without worrying! But one day, your powers will grow to be stronger than any angel's before you. And the great task—a burden, and an honor—will be asked of you. It was the thing we could never accomplish, because it wasn't time yet. But for you—for you, it will be time.

Of course, you know none of this. I've made certain of that. I hope that one day, when you read this letter, you'll understand that I kept you in the dark out of love, and protection, and for no other reason.

There will be a time when you come looking for answers. Even though I am no longer with you, I promise you, my little silver clover, that I will tell you everything you need to know.

All you have to do is ask.

Love,

Your Mama

Only when I looked up and the colors of the world were blurred around me did I realize I was crying.

After school, everyone came over.

Cassie was, predictably, thrilled that we had found Aaron and Earth, and ecstatic that they'd come to join us after all.

"I'm telling you, Skye," she said with a wink. "Epic love is always reunited."

"What's it like to be in your head?" I asked. "Is it rainbows and puppies, all the time?"

"Mm-hmm." She grinned mischievously. "Labradoodles."

"Well," I said, "just because Aaron is back doesn't mean he and Aunt Jo are, like, back together or anything. And it *definitely* doesn't mean that *all* epic love is reunited."

"No word from Asher, huh?"

My stomach suddenly lurched. It had been him at the fire, hadn't it? It was possible I'd made it up, hallucinated him because I wanted so badly to see him again. But his silhouette was unmistakable against the dancing flames.

Had it been a message for me? A sign?

Or—a more troubling thought occurred to me—had he been involved in starting it? If he was fighting with the Rebellion—no. I put that thought out of my head as soon as it popped in.

"No word yet," I said.

"Don't worry, Skye," she whispered, putting her arm around my neck and pulling me tightly to her. "You guys will find a way. I could never believe anything else."

I wanted to believe it, too, that Asher and I would find

a way to be together. But I'd been hurt and betrayed too many times to believe in love with much certainty. I couldn't believe anything anymore—unless I had proof.

We rejoined the group in the living room. Cassie's hair was woven into an elaborately braided masterpiece, and when she sat down on the floor, Earth, who seemed to have a hair fixation, begged her for something similar.

Cassie braided away, and I filled the group in on what was going on.

"You guys heard about the fire on Main Street last night?" I began. "It was an attack on Into the Woods."

"The Order?" Ian asked sharply.

"No. It was the Rebellion, this time." I took a deep breath. "This is going to be hard to hear, but I have to tell you, so that you stay safe. We think they're trying to pick off my friends and family, to isolate me. Then they can take me away and use my powers to defeat the Order."

"And what about the Order?" Ian asked. "What are they planning?"

I sighed nervously. "I don't really know yet. But they'll do anything to keep the Rebellion from taking me."

Cassie looked equal parts terrified and enthralled. She loved drama, indiscriminately and in all forms.

"That means time is running out," I continued. "Ian, we

have to find James, and soon. Can you talk to your mom, and try to find out where he might be?"

"Of course," Ian said, his voice and expression deadly serious.

"Cassie, Dan, I'll need you guys at school, every day. It's important to keep up the appearance that everything is normal—that we don't know what's going on, and we don't have a plan. I think the element of surprise will work well in our favor here. No one will expect that you two have a plan up your sleeves."

"Hey . . ." Dan said.

"And Raven." I turned to her. "You have to be at school, too. Just like today. Keep an eye on Ardith and Gideon. Make sure Cassie and Dan stay safe."

She mock saluted.

"Great. Aunt Jo, Aaron. I need you guys to try to remember and dig up as much information as you can about James. And I need you working on your powers. Any Rogues you know of who you think we can easily get on our side, reach out to them. Tell them to come to River Springs. I think they'll come if they know I'm at the helm. Explain that we're starting a new faction, and they have a place in it."

They nodded.

"The Rebellion broke away from the Order because they

didn't share the same beliefs," I said. "Well, now, we're breaking away from them both for the same reasons. We," I said, looking around at everyone in the room, "are officially the Uprising."

11

I couldn't sleep.

In the dark, too many questions swirled in my mind. What *had* Asher been doing outside of Into the Woods last night? Where was James—and would my visions lead me, as I hoped, to the shadowy fourth Rogue?

Then there was the question of my mother. Her note said that she knew this day would come for me. That if I had questions, all I had to do was ask.

But what the heck did *that* mean? She was dead, and she wasn't coming back. I wondered if there was some clue in the tiny wooden box, the mysterious etching of the key that became solid when I touched it. Aside from being an apology for keeping my mind a blank slate all those years,

I couldn't shake the feeling that there was some deeper, hidden meaning that I wasn't quite getting.

Perhaps most unnerving of all, though, was this: What was the Order planning?

The Rebellion thought big picture—they could use their elemental powers to cause huge catastrophic events and natural disasters. But the Order worked on a smaller, more calculating scale.

They focus on nuances. A whisper of a breath. A hair out of place. They manipulate each and every small thing on this earth. And every little thing has an effect on something else.

I couldn't help but think of my own life like this, every event, large and small, that had led me to this crossroads, this moment in time.

The Order had driven me here. But what were they planning *now*?

I held the power to blur destiny—their ability to see it, their control of it.

The Order starts small.

And my power, in turn, affected those close to me. Cassie, Dan, and Ian. Aunt Jo. Asher and Devin. Raven. Everyone's fate was intricately intertwined, down to the tiniest of nuances. Could the Order still control me—kill me, even? If they could, they would have done it by now, right? I realized, with a start, that every day that passed it would be that much harder for them to get rid of me. I wasn't the girl who they led into the woods the night I almost died. I was so much stronger now.

Unless . . . they were planning something else.

I shivered. This was not a good train of thought to hop on late at night.

I got out of bed and fished the wooden box out of my sock drawer, where I'd stashed it earlier. Instead of getting back into bed, I climbed out onto the roof again.

It was a gorgeous spring night. The warm air wrapped around me like a blanket, and the stars shone bright above the mountains. Instantly, I felt better, and I began to examine the box again. It was beautiful, with delicate inlaid panels and unique craftsmanship. Whoever had made it was a really skilled woodworker. There was definitely something special about it.

In one fell swoop, dizziness overcame me. It pitched the roof forward at an impossible slant, and black spots bloomed across my vision like inky bloodstains. I grasped at the shingles behind me, trying to keep myself from falling forward, sliding off the roof into the yard below.

What was going on? Was some power within the box doing this? Was it me? But this was more than just exhaustion or confusion—and it didn't feel like a vision either. Instead of the feathery-light liquid silver shooting through me, I felt cold, heavy, like just focusing my eyes was a struggle. I clung frantically to the roof, as the stars dimmed and darkness moved in. And then I heard it.

A voice that had haunted me since it gave the command to Devin, months ago, to have me killed.

"Stay calm, Skye," it said, in that bone-chilling way I remembered. "You're not going to fall. In fact, you're going to be just fine. You don't care about standing your ground, do you? Haven't you always wanted to find a place with no troubles? No anger or betrayal?" I could almost picture his lips curling back in a sinister grin as he said, "A place where the people who love you don't leave you? Join us," it whispered. "Join us."

I felt myself slipping back, to a clearing high atop the mountains, the air thin and cold, the sky dark with menace. Asher was there, with his Rebel elder. And so was Devin—with his Gifted leader.

"No," I said out loud, pressing my hands against my ears, though I knew it wouldn't help. "Get out of my head, Astaroth."

He had trained Devin and Raven in ruthlessness and sliced through Oriax's chest like it was butter before turning Devin on me. He controlled the Order, and the Order controlled the world.

It wasn't just his voice but his very presence that seemed to fill my head.

What am I doing? I thought. *There's no way I'm going to succeed at something where my parents failed. I'll never find James Harrison. I'll never figure out who the fourth is.*

"Now you're catching on, Skye," Astaroth's voice echoed in my brain. "It's so very pointless. Your plan is never going to work."

He's right. I'll never see Asher again, either.

"Asher," Astaroth said. "You don't want to see him again, trust me. After what he's doing to you?"

All the muscles in my body tensed. What was Astaroth talking about?

It's a trap, I forced myself to think. *He's influencing your mind. You have to block him out.*

Mustering all the presence of mind I could, I closed my eyes tight and did exactly as Gideon had taught me. Methodically, slowly, I placed brick upon brick, watching the wall in my mind grow taller. It blocked out the voice, the moon and the wind, it blocked out the clouds and the snowcapped peaks and everything as far as I could see. It blocked out the entire world. I was alone in the darkness of my own mind.

My entire body felt cold, empty. Devoid of all hope and joy.

Shadows danced against deeper shadows. I didn't feel the calm Astaroth wanted me to feel. I didn't hear the voice anymore, I didn't hear anything except the blood in my ears and the beating of my own heart. But I didn't feel relief. What I felt was emptiness.

I am alone.

"The Rebellion may be watching your friends. . . ." Astaroth's voice was fading away.

My family is dead. My friends can't help me. Asher will betray me.

"But I am watching your mind."

Alone. Alone. Alone.

I was floating in space, nothing above me or below me, no—

"No!" I cried. My eyes burst open. I was hanging on to the edge of the roof, my body dangling over the side, legs kicking the air for something to grab onto. Panicked, I scratched at the shingles with my fingernails, trying with every ounce of strength to pull myself back up.

I was about to yell out for help—but then I remembered I had wings.

They unfurled just as my fingers gave out, and I couldn't hold on to the roof any longer. I cried out, but my wings held me aloft in the night air, bringing me back up to the roof, to my window, to safety.

Inside, I crawled under the covers, but I still couldn't stop shaking—both from the near-fall and from Astaroth's words.

You're not alone, I told myself. *Your friends aren't going to leave you. Aunt Jo won't abandon you. Earth looks up to you. You have help.*

A tear of frustration slipped out and trickled down my cheek.

But do I have Asher?

It had taken me so long to get over Devin's betrayal. I didn't know if I could handle Asher betraying me, too. Was the angel who had sworn to fight beside me now the one I had to fear?

Hours later, I still hadn't quite calmed down. And just as I slipped into sleep, the thought came rushing into my head:

Is this the Order's first attack?

"Guys, I figured it out."

It was lunchtime the next day, and the weather was finally warm enough that we could ditch the cafeteria and sit outside on the quad. We picked a sunny spot near a big oak tree—close enough to other people so that it didn't look suspicious, but far enough away so that no one could hear what we were saying. The gentle breeze brushed against my cheeks, urging me to feel hopeful. But I kept replaying my conversation with Astaroth. Picturing Asher as my enemy filled me with dread. I had pushed him away—but I never dreamed I would push him that far.

"What?" Cassie asked between bites of her kale salad. My turkey and Swiss sandwich sat, untouched, on the tray by my feet.

"I had a visit from Astaroth last night."

"What!" Ian's head snapped up protectively.

"Not in person," I said. "He was—this is weird—"

"Not any weirder than most of this stuff," Dan mumbled.

"In my *mind*," I finished, shooting him a look. "Last night, I was having trouble sleeping. I went out onto the roof to clear my head, and suddenly he was *in* my head." Cassie's eyes grew wide and concerned, and even Dan looked tense. Ian remained on high alert, his eyes darting around the quad for any sign of danger. Ellie, my former ski teammate, was sitting with a group of friends several feet away. She caught Ian looking and swept her blond corkscrew curls over her shoulder with a half-smile. Ian remained oblivious.

Cassie nudged him. "She thinks you're looking at her."

"What?" Ian blinked. "Who?"

"Ellie, you nimrod," Dan said.

Ian glanced over at Ellie again.

"And from the looks of it," Dan added, "she doesn't seem too upset about it."

Ian looked panic-stricken. "What should I *do*?"

"You could ask her to prom," Cassie suggested.

"There's that word again," Dan muttered.

"I don't know," I said, trying to suppress a grin. "Ian shouldn't be distracted with all that we have to work on right now."

"That's true," said Cassie. "He has to stay focused."

"What!" Ian protested. "That's bullshit. Skye gets to cozy up to angels and you two can't leave each other's side for five seconds. Why can't I have some fun, too?" And with that, he jumped up and marched over to where Ellie sat with her group of friends. Cassie and I beamed at each other, satisfied.

"That was some of the best reverse psychology I've ever seen," said Dan. "You guys should work for the CIA."

"Who's to say I don't already?" Cassie winked.

We watched Ian talk to Ellie, then shove his hands in his pockets and slink back to us.

"Aw, sorry buddy," said Dan. "Next time, don't listen to these two. They are evil, evil ladies."

"Wow," said Cassie. "I really thought those were come-hither eyes. I'm usually so spot-on about this stuff."

"I am never listening to you guys again," Ian muttered.

"I'm sorry," I said. "But maybe what I have to say will put it in perspective?"

"Right," Ian said gravely. "Tell us more."

"Guys, it was like he controlled how I felt. Like there was no hope for our mission. I blocked him out, but by the time I succeeded I almost fell off the roof. It was scary. It definitely felt like an attack."

Dan's face clouded over. "So that's what the Order is up to?"

I nodded.

"The Rebellion is attacking using their powers over the elements," Ian said. "And the Order plans to shake you up from the *inside out*."

I nodded again, goose bumps trickling up my arms. "I think that's exactly right."

"But how can you protect yourself from that?" Cassie asked.

I looked around at them. "Before you guys knew the truth about all this, Gideon was helping me to steel my mind against mental manipulation from the Order. Mainly, at the time, we were concerned about Devin and Raven and the Guardians at school. But I can use it now. If I practice, I can get better."

Dan raised his hand. "Uh, not to sound slow or anything," he said, "but Gideon's a Rebel. How does he have mental powers?"

"He was kidnapped and tortured during the last war

between the sides. They used their mental manipulation to try to get him to reveal the Rebellion's plans. But he wouldn't cave, and the tactics they used got worse." I grimaced. "Guys, I've felt what it's like to have your mind messed with. It takes something from you, leaves you cold. He'll always carry that darkness around in him. I don't know if you ever shake it." I shook my head, trying to erase the memory of what it felt like to have Astaroth in there. "Anyway, during his capture, he taught himself how to protect his mind against them. He's the only Rebel who's been able to do so."

The group looked at me, the mood subdued.

"So now I'm on the lookout for visions about elemental attacks, and I also have to block my mind from invasions by the Order." I sighed. "Sorry I always have to be such a downer."

"Skye." Cassie put her arm around me. "You're not a downer. You're just doing your job. And we're going to help you, no matter what. Even if it's just making you laugh a little."

I felt a little better knowing Astaroth was wrong about at least one thing. My friends were awesome. And nothing in the world could make me question that.

School was tense during the next few weeks. It seemed like everywhere I went, I stumbled into Ardith, Devin, and Gideon. I couldn't shake the feeling that every time I ran into Gideon, he averted his gaze so we didn't make eye contact. At first I thought it might just be that he felt bad about being on opposing sides. But then he showed up one day with a slight—but noticeable—tweak to his appearance.

Gideon had replaced his usual wire-rimmed glasses with dark aviators. He wore them everywhere—not just outside on the quad or shuffling down Main Street with Ardith by his side—but roaming the halls at school, too. I almost didn't think much of it. But then I remembered the first, and last, time we made eye contact since the Uprising began. The way his eyes burned red when he looked at me.

Like the sun. Like fire.

What was Gideon hiding?

If it was something to do with the attacks the Rebellion was planning, I had to figure out what it was. But it was going to be difficult. Ardith never left his side. And something told me she would be ruthless about protecting him.

Every night, the gang gathered at my house. Even

though we were preparing for battle of some kind, part of me loved that we always had a full house. Aunt Jo was in her cooking element, making all of my favorites—and some new recipes, too. I watched her and Aaron with fascination. She seemed to want to impress him, and he, in turn, appeared to want the same. He'd cleaned up a little since that night Raven and I flew to Rocky Pines. His hair was combed and the stubble was gone. He shaved pretty much every day now, and someone had given his hair a trim. *Maybe people can change*, I thought. Maybe they were both working to undo the mistakes of the past. I watched the way they were with each other. Sometimes, when they thought no one was looking, Aaron would put his hand on the small of her back, and Aunt Jo would lean against him, gently.

"Do you think my dad and your aunt are going to get married?" Earth and I were spread out on the floor of my room. I was going through the journal for the thousandth time, looking for some clue to James's whereabouts. She was lying on her stomach by my feet, studying an astronomy chart.

"You like the stars, huh?" I asked, nudging her.

"You didn't answer my question." She chewed thoughtfully on the end of her colored pencil.

I stared her down, one eyebrow raised. I had a feeling I'd met my match in Earth. Just like the real earth and sky, she kind of kept me grounded. I wondered if her name was a coincidence.

"Do you want them to get married?"

Earth seemed to consider this. "I want a mom again," she said.

"Me too."

"You *have* a mom."

"No, I don't. My mom died. And left me with this." I gestured around me to the sea of papers, childhood artifacts, the little wooden box. "Riddles."

"But you have Aunt Jo," Earth argued. "You're lucky. She makes *such* good cookies."

"I can't argue with that," I said, watching her. "You seem really lucky to have your dad, too."

"He's all right," she rolled her eyes. Then she seemed to grow serious. "I don't think he's happy." It was a shocking thing to hear out of a seven-year-old's mouth.

"How do you know?" I asked.

She looked thoughtful. "I can just tell."

"Are you?" I asked her carefully.

"I want a family." She sighed, studying her star chart.

"Me too, Earth," I said. "Me too."

"Do you think they're in love?"

"They sure look like it." I put the notebook down.

"I don't think that when you love somebody, it ever really goes away," Earth said, looking out the window. "It's like riding a bike. You can decide you don't like bike riding any more, and do soccer for a while, but then when you get back on a bike, it's like your body remembers how to do it without you even having to *think* about it." She looked up at me. "I think love is like that."

I felt surprising tears prick at the backs of my eyes, and swallowed.

"You're a smart kid, Earth," I said. "Don't ever let anyone tell you that you don't know what's up."

"No one ever does." After a beat, she said, "Well, maybe I could give *you* advice."

"What about?"

"Asher."

"How do you know about Asher?"

"Cassie told me," she said casually.

"Of course she did."

"No, really," Earth said, turning to me. She was excited now. "Let me help you. I'm good at this. When Mom and Dad used to fight, I always helped them meditate."

"I think you mean mediate."

"That's what I said." She grinned. "Dad says I have a gift for making people feel better. It's like a special power."

A power. It sounded like Earth had inherited some powers from her father's half-Rebel blood after all. But what kind of power was making people feel better? Was that something the Rebels had control over?

"Well," I said finally, trying to figure out how best to phrase this. "Asher and I have to fight for different sides. And he promised that when this is all over, we'd find a way to be together. He seemed so certain."

Earth frowned at me. "But you're not sure," she said, her eyes glazing over. "And you think there's something wrong with you that you're not as certain as he is."

I looked at her in surprise. "Did Cassie tell you that?"

"No," she said. Her eyes had a faraway look in them. "I just knew."

"It's just that I know how people are. They say one thing and do another. And I know that love can change the outcome of a war. But also . . . I think war can change the outcome of love, too. What if Asher thought he loved me, but it turns out he believes in his cause more than he believes in us?"

"Are you saying that because you think that's how he

feels?" Earth asked. "Or because you're secretly scared that's going to happen to you?"

"Uh . . ." I gaped at her. "Man, you're good."

"I know." She smiled hazily. She was sitting there with me, but her mind was somewhere else entirely. "So am I right?"

I sighed. "My parents were so in love that they gave up everything to be together. They didn't have to question how they felt. How come I can't be that sure? How come Asher can?"

"You're both kind of stubborn," said Earth, wrinkling her nose. "My dad says I am, too. Also, you're proud."

"But what if I never know a hundred percent if he's worth fighting for?"

Earth shrugged.

"That's it? That's your advice?"

She went back to drawing. "Hello, you're never going to just *know*," she said with exasperation. "You have to take a risk."

I paused. "And if I make a huge mistake?"

She put down her colored pencil and looked at me seriously. "You have to trust yourself."

"Are you sure you're only seven?"

"I get that a lot."

And that was it. I'd been schooled by a seven-year-old.

I felt tiny arms wrap around my waist, and looked down to see a messy light brown set of pigtails nestling into the crook of my arm.

"I'm glad we're here," she said softly.

"Me too," I whispered. "Me too."

That night at dinner, I watched Aunt Jo and Aaron carefully. If all this ended well—if the Uprising worked—would Aaron and Earth go back to Rocky Pines? Or would they stay here with us, for good? Was Earth right—were they going to get married? Maybe what I'd always wanted was on the verge of coming true. Maybe I was going to have a complete family again. They could never be a replacement for my parents. But Aunt Jo and I wouldn't be lonely anymore. And that was a start.

Raven excused herself to stalk the perimeters of our property, keeping an eye out for danger. Aaron and Aunt Jo went to assess the damage from the fire at Into the Woods. Earth helped me clear the dishes, trailing behind me with a stack taller than her head.

"Don't drop those," I said over my shoulder.

"I have impeccable balance," she piped back. We rinsed

the dishes and loaded them into the dishwasher.

"Hey, Earth," I said, turning around to face her. "This, um, *power* of yours." I thought for a minute. "Want to see if there's anything else you can do?"

Earth grinned up at me mischievously.

13

It was an idea I'd been brewing for a while.

Earth was an astonishing child, a "special kid" as Aaron had said. There was something almost wise about her, a maturity that was surprising, out of proportion with the number of years she had lived. She had the remarkable ability to understand emotions much more complex than she should. Part of this could have been that she had experienced more in those seven years of life than anyone should have to. But I had another idea.

I had a feeling there was something magical about Earth. And that I was the one who'd be able to bring it out in her.

I slid the door to the deck open onto a clear, warm night. Earth slipped her hand into mine as she followed. We stood, facing the mountains. Fireflies blinked on and off in the space between us, illuminating Earth's face in a soft yellow glow.

"Mountains make me feel so small," she said.

"You *are* small." I knelt down next to her. "Earth, I think you came into my life for a reason. Obviously, you're the smartest kid I know"—at this, Earth grinned—"but you can do things, too. Special things. Things maybe you don't get to do that often because it freaks out your dad—right?"

Instead of answering my question, she looked up.

"Do you think they can really touch the sky, or is it only an optical illusion?"

"I don't think anything can really touch the sky."

"You can," she said simply.

"Oh," I said. "You're right. I guess I can when I'm flying."

"I can too."

"You? Have you been hiding wings from me all this time?"

She rolled her eyes as if that was the dumbest question ever. "*No.* I can touch it with my mind."

"Earth," I said, my heart beating faster. "What are you trying to tell me?"

"I can hear it. Shh," she said. "Watch."

I looked up at the wide, endless sky, inky blue and scattered with stars, and let this strange kid guide me.

"It's kind of like a Ouija board," she whispered.

Before I could ask what she meant, the sky tilted violently. I lost my balance and fell to the deck.

"Ow," I said. "What—?" But I stopped short. It wasn't the sky that had moved—it was the stars. The whole dome had shifted like the ceiling of a planetarium. And then, individual stars began to swerve toward one another. Earth was concentrating hard, her eyes trained on the sky and her hands balled into fists. The stars were forming a pattern. A word.

SAVE

My heart was beating out of my chest. Earth's face and neck had broken out in a sweat, and she was struggling for breath. Still, she focused on the stars even harder as they arranged and rearranged, and another word began to take shape.

HIM

"Huh?" I said out loud.

The sound of my voice seemed to break the spell. Earth collapsed, exhausted, and the stars scattered into the night. I rushed to her and scooped her up in my arms. She was shaking.

"Hey," I said gently. "Hey, shhh. It's okay. You're okay."

I smoothed her hair back and kissed the top of her head. "Earth," I whispered. "Say something."

Her eyes fluttered open.

"That . . ." she panted, "was . . . so . . . *cool!*" Earth looked up at me excitedly. "Did you *see* that?"

"I couldn't look away. It was amazing." I thought for a minute. "What do you think it means?"

Earth scrunched her face up thoughtfully. Then she shrugged.

"You got me," she said. "I've only been able to do it, like, one other time."

"What did it say the last time?"

She gave me a small, sly smile.

"*Help Skye,*" she answered.

As I stood there, I could feel the power rolling off Earth in waves. The fireflies glowed brighter, larger, unblinking in the night. And then they were so bright that they eclipsed everything else, and Earth, the mountains, the deck—it all disappeared.

I squinted my eyes against the sudden, jarring light of day. The sun was shining down on me, but as I stood there, dark clouds rolled in faster than I could count seconds: big, churning storm clouds that threatened to burst at any moment.

Thunder clapped, and lightning backlit the clouds.

A hard rain soaked me before I had a chance to run for cover. But where was there cover? Where was I? Rain ran down my hair in rivulets, into my eyes and mouth. The ground beneath my feet felt wet and spongy, and when I looked down, I saw that I wasn't on the deck anymore— I was on the bank of the river that ran through Foster's Woods.

"Dan!" Cassie's voice cried out from somewhere below me. "It's rising too fast!"

"Hold on to my hand!" Dan yelled back.

"I can't breathe!" she screamed.

"Guys!" I shouted. "Cassie! I'm coming!" I scrambled down the steep side of the bank, trying not to let my footing slip in the rising mud and water. I had to get to my friends in time. I had to save them.

Lightning zigzagged through the trees, and I heard a massive crack, and somebody screamed.

"Skye." Earth tugged on my hand, bringing me back from my vision. I had to blink a few times before the deck and the starry night came into focus. "What did you see?"

What had I seen?

"I saw a flood," I said, still dazed. First a fire, now a flood. Elemental forces at work against the people I loved. "I saw the future."

"Does the future talk to you the way the sky talks to me?"

I nodded.

"Maybe we can make them work together," she said. "We can tell each other what they say."

"It's a deal, Earth," I said. Because I would need all the help I could get to figure out when that flood was going to happen. Another attack was coming. The Rebellion was plotting again. But this time, I refused to be caught off-guard. This time, I would be ready for it.

Suddenly, I got the feeling that being outside at night wasn't very safe.

"Let's go in."

Earth nodded. "I'm scared, too," she said. She took my hand and the two of us slipped through the sliding screen door and into the cozy house.

It had been alive with noise and chatter during dinner, but now it was still. I squeezed Earth's hand tightly. This house had been still for so long. I couldn't let anything stand in the way of it feeling full again.

Earth scampered up the stairs to get ready for bed, but I hung back. Something drew me to the wide window that looked out on our field, the dark sky, the mountains beyond, and I struggled to understand the message from the stars.

Save him.

I waited for the answer to come.

As I lay in bed that night, watching Earth squirm around in her sleeping bag like a burrowing animal, I thought about her strange, quirky powers—intuiting my emotions, "listening to the sky." It had told her to help me.

Suddenly I sat bolt upright.

Was it possible that Earth was the *fourth Rogue*?

Immediately, I rejected this idea. It couldn't be—and more than that, I couldn't *let it*. I couldn't knowingly put Earth in danger like that. She was only a kid. A complicated one, sure. But she had already seen enough violence, enough tragedy in her lifetime. I couldn't let her also go into battle.

But if she was the fourth, and I denied it, then my group would never succeed. We would never win, and the balance of power between the Order and the Rebellion would come crashing down. And I would continue to be the thing I feared I was: a weapon one side could use against the other. Nothing more.

Was there a way to find out? I had been able to make myself have a vision on the roof of the school, when I'd found Aaron. Could I do it again? Could I make myself see if Earth was the one I'd been looking for?

I didn't want to do it. I didn't want to decide anything just then.

But maybe it was better to know, and protect her—than to not know, and risk putting her in even greater danger.

I closed my eyes, and I let the room fall away and the Sight overtake me.

The familiar fog rolled in off the ocean. Thick and white, making it hard for me to see more than a foot in front of me. I had been here before—in my visions, at least. As my eyes adjusted, I realized I was on a huge black-sand beach. The fog misted out with the ocean tide, lapping against the shore. Breathing in. Breathing out.

The beach was lit with candlelight. Where was it coming from?

Three figures stood in front of me. As I squinted in the dim light, their faces sharpened into focus. Aunt Jo. Aaron. And a third man whose face I didn't recognize. *James?* They were holding hands. Aunt Jo and Aaron reached out in front of them—beckoning to a fourth to join their circle.

I struggled to expand my sight, to grasp onto any detail that might give me a clue. But the vision seemed to elude me, and the harder I tried, the more it slipped away. Almost as soon as it started, I was back in my bedroom, in the dark, alone.

Crickets and cicadas chirped in the backyard now. The snowy mountains no longer kept out the sounds of the outside world. Kept the cold air in, the warmth and light out. Now, the weather was warm, and the natural world was reawakening.

And Earth was listening to it.

I slid down in bed, rested my head against the pillow. Why was this vision so hard to grasp? Was my own sight trying to protect her from the truth? She was sent to help me. She was an important key.

Trees from outside cast dark shadows across my walls, and I shivered.

Astaroth's warning came back to me, whispered in the night.

I'll be watching your mind.

If that was true, if I was leaving it unguarded and unprotected during these visions, was it possible that the ancient Gifted One was watching me right now? Could he know how I felt about Earth?

I made a silent promise to myself. I would watch this girl especially closely from now on. And I would protect my mind, keep it safe. Because if Astaroth could see what I was thinking, Earth could be in even more danger. What if the Guardians in the darkness outside her house in Rocky

Pines weren't just there for Aaron, for the powerful Rogue who was her father?

What if they were watching her, too? Waiting for the right time to attack the fourth?

14

onday nights at the Bean were the quietest. The plan was to get there early and study for finals until ten o'clock, when Ian could close and we could really get to work.

I parked my car a block away from the coffee shop and took a detour past Into the Woods. The air was warm, summer was on its way, and it was staying lighter out later. Couples strolled the streets downtown, hand in hand, stopping for ice cream and lounging on benches. Families of tourists popped in and out of stores, dressed in jeans and lightweight fleeces, sandals instead of hiking boots. It could have been any spring night. I was struck so suddenly by how separate I felt from these people, how detached. They seemed so happy and carefree, walking with their families, their girlfriends, boyfriends, wives, and husbands. They knew nothing about the Order, the Rebellion, or Rogues. They were unaware that their lives were controlled right down to the tiniest detail. The brand of toothpaste they use, arriving five minutes late to pick up their kid from soccer practice, the whisper of a breath on someone's cheek; the smallest most insignificant events wound up like a snowball right at the start of an avalanche. One thing happens, which leads to another, and that leads to one more thing, and then before you know it your whole life has been written out for you like some great and ancient book. And every time war broke out, every time a tsunami wiped out half a population or an unexpected earthquake decimated thousands of lives— that was the Rebellion, trying to rewrite the history of the world. Fighting control with chaos.

I practiced putting up mental walls against Astaroth as I walked the rest of the way down Main Street and through the door to the Bean. Ian jumped as the bells on the door jingled, and shot me a look. The place was almost empty. It looked like I wasn't the only one who was tense.

I made my way to the couches in the back where we always hung out. When I unzipped my bag and went to pull out my history textbook, a few others fell out with it. The one on top was a well-worn guide to colleges and universities, the cover ripped from carrying it around in my bag all year, and lots of pages dog-eared and marked with neon Post-it notes. The book fell open easily to the page I'd gone back to the most over the past year. Columbia University.

I traced my finger over the student testimonials, descriptions of the food and housing, tips and tricks for life in New York.

I hadn't looked at this book since I found out who I was—now there was a chance I might not even make it to college after all.

New York. So different from my tiny mountain town in Colorado. I had dreamed about living there one day, going to museums and the theater, discovering more to life than just what was contained on all sides by mountains. I had never left Colorado. Now, I realized, it was because my parents and Aunt Jo were trying to protect me from my destiny.

I knew that one day I needed to escape. My heart would always belong in River Springs, but my life here had never been on my own terms. What I longed for more than anything was to put the past behind me and live out a future that was entirely mine.

The door jangled again, startling me from my thoughts,

as the last customers of the night left, and Ian locked the door behind them.

"All clear!" he called. I made my way over to the counter, where he was already logging in to Love the Bean's computer. "Okay," Ian said. "I've googled him a couple of times since we talked, but I can't seem to find anything that might fit what we're looking for. I mean . . . I don't think my dad is a Welsh politician, do you?"

"Unlikely," I said. "But we know his name, and we know what he looks like now, because I saw him in my most recent vision. Do a Google Image search, and let's see if I recognize him. Then we can cross-reference with the white pages or something, like I did with Aaron Ward."

More typing.

"Okay," said Ian. "Do any of these guys look familiar?" I scanned the faces.

"Not really," I said.

Ian frowned. "Do you think . . . ?" He trailed off.

"What?"

"Nah, never mind."

"Ian," I prodded. "Tell me. What are you thinking?"

"Well . . . there have to be a bunch of different James Harrisons out there, right? What if the guy we're looking for *isn't* my dad? What if we just want him to be?"

I thought about it. Ian did have a point—there were a bunch of Aaron Wards, and I'd used my visions to track him down. When I saw him, I knew. I'd gotten the same feeling when I'd seen James's face in my mind. Besides, he'd kind of looked like Ian.

"I'm pretty sure it's your dad," I said. "It's just a feeling I get. But it looks like . . ." I took over and typed a few more things into the computer, which yielded zero search results. "He doesn't want to be found as badly as we want to find *him*."

Ian pounded his fist against the counter in frustration.

"Is it possible he changed his name?" I asked.

"Well, *yeah*. It's possible he moved to Siberia. *Anything's* possible."

"We'll find him," I said. "Don't give up hope." I tried to recall the mental image of James Harrison in my head, but something was bugging me. "Hey, Ian?"

"Yeah?"

"How come you've never mentioned much about your family before? This whole thing . . . it's the first I'm hearing about your dad."

Ian glanced at me, then busied himself with emptying the cash register.

"No reason. There just hasn't been much to say."

"Yeah, but . . ." I paused, wondering the best way to phrase this. "I'm an only child. You're an only child. My parents died when I was six and I live with my aunt. Your dad left when you were the same age, and you live with your mom. It seems like somewhere down the line, this would have come up."

"Yeah, well, it hasn't."

"Ian!"

"Look, Skye, Aunt Jo loves having us all over for dinner and being like a den mother or whatever. My family's not like that, okay? I guess I'm just a little more private."

I glared at him. "Don't talk to me about private," I said. "I have had to keep *way* too many secrets in my life."

He sighed and tossed the zip-up bag with the money onto the counter.

"Okay, listen. I was kind of ashamed. Your parents died, Skye—all noble and trying to protect you and everything. They would have done anything for you. My dad ran out, just left without a word. I was so little, I don't even remember what he looks like."

"But aren't there pictures? Didn't your mom tell you anything?"

"My mom was so furious she hid everything from me. She refused to tell me anything about him. Who he was, what he did, why he left—until now. And only because I said I was old enough now that I could find him on my own, if I wanted. There's still a lot she won't tell me. But at least I got his name."

I didn't know what to say. I had been so focused on the mission, I'd barely stopped to think what this might be like for Ian. "I'm sorry," I said softly. "I didn't realize."

"Yeah, well. I grew up hating him, thinking he was bad. Determined that I wouldn't end up like him. I never *wanted* to find my dad." We sat in silence for a minute. "You miss your parents every day, Skye. Before this whole thing started, I was pretty content not knowing anything, you know?"

"We don't have to—"

"Yes," he put his hand on my arm gently. "We do."

"I can't believe you would do this for me."

"I would do a lot of things for you, Skye." He winked at me. "*Most* things. But this? I'm doing this for all of us." He finished clearing up, then turned back to me. "You know, maybe it's not too late for me to want to find out the truth."

When I pulled into my driveway, the light was on inside, spilling out in window shapes over the front lawn. It didn't seem like so long ago that I would come home to find Asher leaning against the front door, legs crossed casually in front of him, smiling that slightly wicked smile of his, his eyes sparkling like dark stars. Something sliced through my chest, a pain so sharp and clear I had to put my hand on the car for support.

It seemed to me, all my life, that love was letting someone in, only to have them leave you.

I could hear voices coming from inside—Aunt Jo's, and then Earth's, and then Aaron's deep baritone cutting in above the clinking of pots, the rushing of water in the kitchen sink.

Love was letting someone in, only to have them leave you.

I was getting too attached to Earth and Aaron. We needed him—both of them—to help us with the Uprising. But after that, would they stay? Maybe Earth was wrong, and loving someone wasn't just like riding a bike. Or maybe you realized that riding bikes was fun when you were younger, but you're a different person now.

I didn't want them to leave. I wanted to have family dinners and weekend camping trips and big turkeys at Thanksgiving, and inside jokes that only the four of us would know.

I hesitated in the driveway, and instead of going in right

away, I walked around the side of the house and climbed the trellis up to the roof. The sky was clear, midnight blue and cloudless. The moon shone bright as a lantern over the mountaintops.

Why had I seen Asher the night of the fire? What else was the Rebellion planning—and was he involved? The Rebellion was violent and unpredictable. And whether he wanted to be or not, Asher was one of them.

What if he'd turned his back on me?

What if Astaroth was right?

15

The weekend opened up before us like the little purple flowers that were springing into bloom across the field behind our house.

For me, it couldn't have come soon enough. It had been a rougher week than usual at school. In addition to the finals schedule being announced, and Cassie throwing herself full-force into prom planning, my visions were getting stranger, scarier. And I was having dreams every night now.

In one, Asher was holding a sword to my neck, telling me to jump or he would kill me.

In another, I was walking on that same beach from my visions. But it was covered with broken wings, spattered with blood and jagged where they'd been cut from someone's back.

In the most recent, Devin was pulling his blade from my stomach, and blood poured from the gaping wound. "Trust is for dreamers and fools," he said. "You think you can save the world, but how can you trust the people around you when you can't even trust yourself?" But it wasn't his voice that rang in my head, it was Astaroth's, and then he said something else, but I couldn't hear him as the blood rushed up past my nose and mouth, past my ears, and I woke screaming in a cold sweat to find Earth sitting at the foot of my bed.

She put her hand on my leg.

"It's him," she said, "isn't it? The one who can see into your mind."

"They're dreams," I said, struggling to catch my breath. "They're just dreams."

"No," she said, her calm, small voice comforting in the night. "It's him. It's easier when you're asleep. Don't let what he says scare you. It's not real."

Betrayal. Shattered trust. And if the dreams were right, I would die, soon, and violently. Possibly at the hands of someone I trusted. Gideon had only taught me how to protect my mind from infiltration when I was awake. I had no idea how to stop Astaroth from getting in while I was asleep. How would I protect my *dreams*?

The question plagued me: Were they visions of the future or just visions he was planting in my mind to rattle me?

Whatever it was, something was changing. Every day, the visions and dreams were getting worse. Order and Chaos were on the verge of colliding. A battle of some kind loomed even closer. I couldn't take it anymore. I had to find James, so we could stop the carnage from happening. Or before Astaroth drove me crazy in the process.

I only had a face to go on, and a name that didn't seem to match that face. It wasn't adding up, and we were running out of time.

Aunt Jo made dinner one night and invited the whole group over. She claimed it was safer when we were all together, and that she wanted to talk about our plan, but I had an inkling she had other reasons as well. Aunt Jo had been especially chipper lately. No, not chipper. *Glowing.* It was like I was seeing a side of her she'd never showed me before. She'd always loved having friends over to cook for, but this felt different. She wasn't doing it for herself this time, or even for me. She was doing it for someone else.

And he was sitting right next to her, watching adoringly as she passed the mashed ginger-and-carrot sweet potatoes.

"How are the prom plans coming, Cassie?" Aunt Jo asked.

"Fab," Cassie said. "You'll never guess what the theme is."

"Do we want to know?" asked Dan.

"It's the End of the World!" Cassie beamed.

An awkward silence fell over the table.

"Looks like I'm not the only one who eats their shoes," Raven snorted.

"That's the theme of prom?" I asked.

"You told me it was my job to bring the levity," Cassie said, trying not to look hurt as she glanced around the table. "It's based on disaster movies, Skye. *Titanic, The Day After Tomorrow, Poseidon, Twister.*" She paused and looked at me. "Your favorites. I thought you'd be happy."

My heart swelled for Cassie. She was helping, in her small way, the only way she could.

"It sounds awesome," I said.

"Yeah, if we make it to prom," Ian muttered.

"Ian!" Cassie cried. "That is, like, blasphemy. Of course we will." She turned to me. "We will, right, Skye?"

Would we? I wanted to say I didn't know, wanted so badly for them to comfort me. But I was this group's leader, and I had to give them hope—even if I was finding it harder and harder to believe.

"Of course we will," I said. Ian looked dubious.

"If we find my dad first." He pushed the broccoli around his plate and rested his chin in his other hand. "I just wish I could *ask* him where he is, you know?"

"Well, that would make things a lot easier," Aaron said. "Too bad we just have to rely on our own resources."

Or did we? Something about the conversation jogged a memory for me. *The letter from my mother!* She had said a time would come when I had questions. And I should *ask her*. I had no idea what it meant, but maybe it was worth a shot.

That night, while Aaron still slept behind closed doors in Aunt Jo's room, Raven occupied the couch in the den, and Earth snored softly in her sleeping bag, I took out the small wooden box. There was something magical about the way it was made, as if the etching of the key had glowed only for me.

"Okay, Mom," I whispered. "I have so many questions I still need answers to. You said I could ask, so . . . I'm asking." But what to ask first? "Are we going to win?" If she'd had the Sight, maybe she knew.

One of the four intertwining loops of the key's head glowed, bright and then brighter. My heart sped up. Maybe this would work.

But just as I began to have hope, it faded back to normal. And then it disappeared completely.

Nothing happened. The box sat in my hands, unchanged. Maybe she couldn't give me the answer to something that hadn't happened yet. Maybe that wasn't how this worked. I guess it was possible that even my mother's power had limitations. Or maybe it was me—blurring the future.

I decided to start with something more basic.

"Okay," I said. "How can you answer me, when you're . . . well . . . dead?"

Another loop on the key burned brightly, and suddenly I felt like I was going headfirst down one of those water slides at amusement parks, the tall ones that wind like snakes in spiral loops down to the bottom. But instead of splashing out into a pool below, I found myself standing in the bedroom of the cabin.

A man stood with his arms resting on the antique dresser, his back to me. He wore a blue checkered flannel and had dark brown hair that hung down his neck.

Dad.

"I just don't like that you're doing this to her," he said, his back rising and falling in a sigh.

"Sam," a woman's voice said from behind me. She walked right past me, and my breath stopped. My mother had honey blond hair, pinned up in a loose twist. Pieces fell down and framed her face, and when the light from the open window hit them, even I had to admit she looked like an angel. "We're doing it to protect her." Her voice was gentle, soft. "She's not ready yet. If we do this to her, it will be too much. She could die."

"I know," he said quietly. She wrapped her arms around him and leaned her head on his back.

"Turn around, Sam," she said, and he did. The sight of his face hit me with longing. Even now, all these years later, I still missed my parents acutely. Even now that I knew my memories of them were tampered with, weren't whole.

It made me angry to think about it. But I had a feeling my mother was showing me this for a reason.

"One day she's going to come into her powers, and she'll have a heavier weight on her shoulders than any one person before her. She's going to have questions. And what if we're not there for her?"

"Don't say that."

"It's possible, and you know it. Once the Order sets their minds to something . . ."

"I hate the idea of Skye growing up without us. Without knowing who she really is. We should be there to help her."

My mother paused, took his bearded face in her hands. "We can be."

He looked at her. "Well, sure, if the Order doesn't get their way, but—"

"No, Sam. Even then. *We can be.*" She looked into the mirror behind him, and her eyes met mine, as I watched.

I knew, in that moment, that she was talking to me. This—this was what she meant by giving me answers.

"When a Gifted One or a Guardian uses their powers to influence a person's mental energy," she said, still holding my gaze, "it changes a little bit of their makeup, and yours, forever. It creates a bond—a connection between the two minds. The more intense and prolonged the influence, the stronger the bond. It's not intentional—just a natural, accidental sort of side effect to mental influence. An accidental rift in the fabric of an angel's mind that lets the human see a little bit into their thoughts and feelings. If the influence is only for a short period of time, you might be able to make out snippets and inklings. If it's for longer, a kind of, well . . . portal is created." The look on my dad's face changed as he began to catch on. "You just look into their eyes. . . ."

"You've been doing this her whole childhood," my dad said. She nodded, excitedly.

"I've been preparing. We're going to die, Sam. I've seen it.

I know it's a sacrifice, but this will be worth it in the long run, when Skye finds herself caught in the middle of the two sides, without us to guide her, and she needs our help."

"But how . . . if you're not there . . . how will she . . . ?"

"Do you have the box you made for her?"

My dad nodded and reached into the top dresser drawer. *So Dad kept things in his sock drawer, too.* A smile tugged at my lips.

He took out the small wooden box, with the familiar etching of the key on it—the one I held in my hands at that very moment—and they held it between them.

"Give it your energy," she whispered. "Imbue it with your powers. Protect it, so that it can only be opened if someone has the key." She smiled at him.

"And only Skye will have the key."

I watched in awe as pale, twinkling light flowed through my mother's fingertips—and black smoke shot from my father's. When they met, the box glowed a bright silver between them. *Dark and light.*

You never lose your powers, Raven had said. *Even after you become human.*

I blinked, and I was back in my bedroom. Earth continued to snore, hidden away in her sleeping bag. The moon continued to shine through my window, and the stars continued to wink at me. I was exhausted, just completely drained from the connection to my mother's thoughts and the events of the past few weeks. Still clutching the box to my chest, I fell into a deep sleep.

I didn't sleep for long.

"Skye," the voice whispered, as if made of the darkness itself. "Let me in."

"No," I murmured, rolling over and shoving a pillow over my head.

"No?" he repeated. "No. What kind of attitude is that?"

"No!" I shut my eyes tight and began to build, brick by hurried brick, the wall that would protect my mind from Astaroth.

"Now, now, that seems awfully hasty," he said, his voice like honey. "Don't you want to hear what I have to say? Could be important, you never know."

"What could you possibly have to tell me," I said through gritted teeth, "that I would want to hear?"

"You might be surprised. You might say you'll find your mind somewhat . . . changed."

"I doubt it. I won't let your mind tricks work on me. I'm going to overthrow you. I'm going to make you wish you'd never tried to get me to choose."

"You don't understand, Skye," his voice was suddenly

hard-edged and brutal. "You were *lucky* that we let you choose. I could have taken you by force right at the start. But that wasn't the plan. It wasn't in the stars. No, you had to want us. Devin was as good a way to make that happen as any. I could have made him do much worse to you than he did. And he was easily disposable. The Rebellion can have him."

"Liar. You didn't need him. You could have gotten to me before I was strong, when you had the chance. But you didn't, because I don't think you *can*."

"Then you," he said, "are sorely misled. Others have tried to do what you're doing. Your mother tried. Look how well that turned out for her."

"Stop it," I said.

"She didn't get very far—the Order made sure of *that*."

"Leave my mother out of this."

"Your mother . . . she was so—*gifted* really is the right word for it, isn't it? Even for one of my most trusted. It hurt when she left me for your father, Skye. It really did. So good, so *talented* at controlling fate, influencing minds, manipulating the lives of paltry humans. It was such a betrayal when your father convinced her that this wasn't the life for her. Such a shame. It's not for everybody, I suppose. Many jump. And many . . . Well, many get their wings torn off in the night."

"Stop it!"

"Oh, you can handle hearing the truth. She was easily replaced. They all are. Your mother, Raven, Devin. As long as time beats on, as life begins and ends, the Order will persist. New Gifted will rise up, with new, stronger powers. New Guardians will carry out their bidding. It's so easy, really, Skye. Just like a machine. Tick tock. Tick tock. The great, beating tide of time draws in and out. Surf beating against the rocks of the beach at the end of the world."

The beach at the end of the world.

"You're wrong," I said. "I can change things."

"What makes you think you'll meet a luckier fate? What makes you think you'll beat us this time?"

"Because!" I shouted. "I'm stronger than my mother. I have powers that she never dreamed of having. I have her talents *AND* I believe in free will. Because of me, time stands still and destiny is unreadable. I can see the future and cause the earth to shake and trees to fall and mountains to move and the sky to come tumbling to the ground in great waves of hail and snow. I can do so much more than anything you've ever seen! And I won't stop until I beat you!"

"Perhaps," he said. His voice was too calm, unnerving. "You could be stronger. But you have a weakness. The same weakness that your mother had. And it's the reason that the Order will find a way to get you. It's the reason we'll win, every time."

I clenched my jaw. "What weakness?"

"Your heart," he said. "Your dogged need to see the best in everyone. Your belief in love. It's your great undoing."

"No, it isn't," I said. "It's what *makes* me strong."

"Is it really? It's what made you trust Devin, the very thing that made you vulnerable to his sword. It's what made you align with the Rebellion, despite the fact that you knew they didn't care about you—that they only wanted to use you."

"You don't know what you're talking about," I spat. "They were my friends."

"Were they? And what about your Rebel boyfriend? Where is he now? He was ordered to kill someone he knew you cared about. And what was he doing at that fire, Skye? Could it be that he was a part of the attack on your Aunt Jo?" I felt the blood drain from my face. "I don't foresee this ending very well for you, my dear."

"You don't know that," I said, panic rising in my throat like bile. "You can't see that. I've blurred out your ability to see how this will end. You don't know what Asher's capable of doing."

"Hmm, don't I?" He paused. "Either way." His voice was razors and sharp lines. "It's your love for him, it's your wish for him to be good, that will prevent you from seeing the truth about him. You want so badly to believe, to love him, all of them, to not be alone at the end of the world with the terrible burden you bear. But it's what's keeping you from staying safe. From fighting true and fierce. Your love will leave you ready for the taking." He laughed, a cold, hard laugh. "Everyone you love will leave you, eventually."

"That's not true," I whispered. Though I believed it less now.

"No," he said. "Even you know that's a lie."

A lie . . . a lie. Everyone you love will leave you. Maybe he was right. It was why I'd always worked so hard to keep people out, to not trust anyone more than I had to. You couldn't rely on people. There was no telling when they might leave you.

"See?" Astaroth said. "You're catching on. Don't you want to finally be free from worrying about all this? Isn't it better to cut Asher out—forever? He's probably plotting their next attack right now. He's still a Rebel. He hasn't changed."

Changed.

I blinked.

You might find your mind somewhat changed.

If my mother was right, my mind *was* changed. A portal was created between my mind and an angel's, every time they tried to influence my mental energy. Astaroth had been infiltrating my mind, trying to shake me up, make me question what I thought was right and true. Was it possible that a portal had been created between *us*? That his mind was changed, too?

Because if that was true . . . maybe there was a way I could see what he was planning.

Fighting with every inch of my energy to continue to push him out, I got up and started to leave.

"Where are you going?" he said. "Don't think you can end this just by walking away."

"I'm not walking away," I said calmly, opening the window and climbing out onto the moonlit roof.

"I'll always be able to get into your mind, Skye. You can't hide from me."

"So follow me, then."

Out on the roof, I spread my wings, just in case.

And what I'd hoped would happen did. Even though it pained me to do it, I steeled myself and felt my mind touch the cold, sickening steel of his—and slip through the rift.

It was dark, cold, like floating in space. There was an emptiness in him, and I felt it too, was swimming in it.

Images began to crystalize out of the void. Images I recognized. The small, twinkling lights I'd seen in another vision, blinking on and off. The sweep of a dress against the hardwood floor of a gymnasium. A dress that I recognized.

Because Aunt Jo gave it to me.

I'd seen it in my visions, stained with blood. And I saw it now against the backdrop of my school gym.

For prom.

I heard Astaroth's thoughts:

The battle will not end until one side has claimed her—or one side has killed her. It is the day of reckoning. The end of days—or the beginning.

I opened my eyes with a start. I was lying in bed, gasping. Sweat soaked through my T-shirt. The window was open, night air blowing the curtains back, and Earth was sitting up in her sleeping bag, staring at me curiously.

The battle we'd been waiting for. The battle over me.

It was going to take place on prom night.

16

"So." Cassie's eyes were sparkling. "I think I found a dress."

"Huh?" I said, blinking to focus. I had hardly slept the night before. Once I'd gotten what I needed from Astaroth and pushed him out of my head, I had tossed and turned for hours. I had tried all morning to forget the sound of Astaroth's voice, but his words wormed their way into the cracks of my brain, the empty spaces where before there had been only quiet. Could he be right? Would I always have to choose between love—and my life?

"For prom," Cassie said. "Are you even paying attention?"

"Stop the presses!" Dan cried.

"You might want to take note, Daniel," came the even

reply, "as you'll be wearing a matching boutonniere."

"A booty what?"

"What does it look like?" I asked.

"Light pink. Short. Body-hugging. I kept telling the salesgirls, short and tight doesn't have to be slutty, you know?"

"I know!" I agreed.

"I never know," said Dan. "What are you talking about?"

"It's all about proportions," I told him.

"And footwear," Cassie added. She whipped out her cell phone and produced a photograph of her modeling the dress in the store's three-way mirror.

It was beautiful—and couldn't be more perfect for Cassie if it had been made for her. A silky, satiny bandage dress in a pale pink, almost nude color that hit midthigh. It looked impossibly glamorous paired with her red shampoo-commercial waves.

"You look a little naked." Ian leaned over my shoulder, wide eyed.

"Thank you!" Cassie beamed.

"Let me see that," said Dan. He took the phone out of her hands and studied it. We were all silent while we waited for his response.

"Dan?" She prodded.

"Dan?" I nudged him in the shoulder. "The world? It still exists."

Dan looked up, dazed. "Can you send me this?"

Cassie blushed. "Let's talk later," she said under her breath.

"You're right, though. Your booty does look hot—"

"Bouton*niere*!" She smacked him on the arm. "It's a flower! You wear it in your lapel! Will you please take this seriously? Prom is in a few weeks and it might be our last dance ever and I want it to be perfect!" She sulked for a few seconds. "If you'll excuse me, I have to go finish painting the cows in the papier-mâché tornado before chem."

Ian and Dan burst out laughing.

As Cassie walked away, I felt my stomach sink. They were so excited for prom. How could I tell them that the big battle we'd all been preparing for—that we'd been fearing—was going to happen on prom night? How could I do that to Cassie? I knew I'd have to tell her eventually, but for now, I decided to keep what I'd discovered in Astaroth's mind to myself. It looked like I was back to keeping secrets.

"I have to go, too," I said. "I have a scholastic reputation to maintain. Gotta go meet with Ms. Manning before next period." I'd gotten a notice about it that morning. I almost wished I could go with Cassie to paint cows.

"Wuh-whoa," Dan said.

"If it's about those fireballs you threw in phys ed. . . ." Ian smirked.

"Can it, you guys. It's about something normal, for once."

"Let's talk about your GPA, Skye," Ms. Manning said, studying me over the top of her sleek wire-rimmed glasses. "Finals are coming up. I know you have your heart set on Columbia. So as your adviser, I just wanted to check in."

"Thanks," I said. "I think I'm doing okay."

Okay was a huge overstatement. What with visions of the future, connecting with my parents in the past, trying to find a missing Rogue, and plotting to save the world, studying hadn't exactly ranked high on my agenda.

What had happened to me? Were my priorities totally screwed up?

"Well . . ." Ms. Manning took out a calculator and did some number crunching. "You need to get at least a 98 on three of your exams if you want to keep your GPA where it needs to be," she said.

"Piece of cake." I laughed nervously to show I wasn't daunted by the task.

But I was, and now I had one more item I could add to the growing list I was worried that I'd really mess up.

I thought about it at length as I hurried down the hall to my next class. Grades, friends, prom—it was almost like the past six months had never happened. Except for the memory of Astaroth's cold steel voice whispering in my ear. Threatening me.

Devin was as good a way to make that happen as any. I could have made him do much worse to you than he did.

I wasn't sure it could really get any worse than stabbing me. But a lot had happened since then, while he was technically still under the Order's control. He had warned me, helped me, taught me about my powers of the light. There was the time at the party in the woods after Cassie's latest gig when I'd lost myself for just a moment and let him kiss me. Not just any kiss—the memory of it still made me shiver. Coming from Devin, someone who was normally so reserved, well—it had swept me up in its frenzy, and I'd been powerless.

Your dogged need to always see the best in everyone.

I did always want to think the best of the people in my life. I wanted to believe that Devin was good inside. That it was the Order that made him do and say all the things that made me not trust him.

I could have made him do much worse.

He had still been under the Order's control when he'd done all those things. Warning me. Kissing me. Telling me he loved me. I thought he'd been acting out, but now it occurred to me for the first time how impossible that would have been.

The Order *made* him do those things. They preyed on my weakness.

The Rebels thought he had been controlling the way I felt. They believed that was the reason why I felt so calm around him.

Why I trusted him.

We were interrupted before we'd had the chance to find out.

But now I had a way to know for sure. And it was all thanks to my mom.

I was determined to find out the truth and put that chapter of my life to rest, once and for all. It was what I needed, to fight.

It was hard to get Devin alone. He didn't go many places without Gideon and Ardith these days. I could feel the three of them watching me as they swept down the halls.

They had to be planning something new. Some attack of the elements on Aunt Jo or my friends. Or—I shuddered to think it—Earth and Aaron. They had come back to River Springs to help me. If I was the reason they got hurt, or worse, I would never be able to forgive myself.

The last vision I'd seen of the elements was the flash flood that trapped Cassie and Dan in Foster's Woods. But the weather had been beautiful—balmy and warm, not a cloud in the sky. How would I know when the flood was coming? I was determined to keep myself open to my powers of the dark, in addition to the light visions that had been helping me so much lately. I was a balance of both, if nothing else. I had to allow myself to be balanced, if I was going to succeed.

So I kept an eye out, and Ardith knew, and Gideon hid behind his dark sunglasses, and Devin—well, Devin was the only one who I couldn't quite get a handle on.

But that was about to change.

If he could lull me into a false sense of trust, I could do the same right back at him.

After school, I found him in a rare moment alone by his locker.

"Hey," I said, leaning against the locker next to his.

Devin looked at me, then glanced around to make sure he was really the one I was talking to. His face lit up when he realized he was.

"Hi."

"Where's the rest of your crew?"

"Why . . . ?" He looked wary, like it might be a trap.

I put my hand on his arm and smiled up at him. I could feel the warmth under his skin. "Don't worry," I said. "I just want to talk."

The locker door shut before I'd finished blinking, and soon we were sitting on the purple velvet couch in the back of Love the Bean—the one where I'd taught him how to make small talk all those months ago.

I sipped on my favorite—a chai latte—iced, now, for the warm weather.

"I'm confused," he said. "I thought we weren't speaking." He took a sip of his ginseng green tea. "That you were mad."

At the hurt and hesitation in his voice, I looked up—and suddenly, my script and everything I'd planned to say evaporated.

"We've been through a lot together," I said, letting the side of my knee touch his. "I guess I'm not ready to just say good-bye and never speak again." He let his knee linger near mine. "Even if we're fighting against each other now."

His voice dropped, low in my ear. "Skye, I meant what I said. About doing what I can to make it up to you."

I glanced at him, and my heart shuddered. I couldn't help it—my body still reacted to being this close to him, whether my heart and mind wanted to or not. I had always felt a magnetic pull toward Devin. It made it hard for me to stay away, even when he was yelling at me to do better, even when he was frustratingly impassive and hard to read. A montage of our stolen moments together flashed before me:

The snowball fight this winter that had ended in me falling on top of him, my hands on either side of his head, the steam of his breath against my cheek and his rare laughter in my ears—

Waking up next to him in his bed, the pull toward him strong even then, as he lay on his side, watching me, a shy smile playing on his lips—

That moment in the woods—

And then it was like the force of the world was at his wings, pulling him toward me. And his lips touched mine, and his hands were running through my hair, and his body was pushing me up against a tree that was hidden in shadows. And he kissed me.

"Skye?"

"Huh?" I blinked. Devin took a sip of his tea, and watched me.

I steeled myself. I had to put all that behind me now.

Because if I understood Astaroth correctly, none of it—not a single moment—was real.

"I'm sorry," I whispered. I put my hands on his shoulders and stared deep into his eyes. Devin cocked his head, just slightly, and that look of hope I'd seen in the woods returned.

"For what?" he asked, surprised.

"It's just that I have to know."

The blue pools of his irises suddenly opened up, expanding until the inky centers edged out everything else, and I was swallowed by them.

I was back in the tiny, cramped hallway outside the bathroom at Love the Bean.

And I was staring directly into Asher's fiery gaze.

My heart leaped. I knew I missed him, but I didn't realize how desperately until I found myself face-to-face with him again. I wanted to reach out to him, to wrap my arms around his neck, but I was trapped within the confines of Devin's memory.

This is the night of my birthday, I realized.

"You want to play by the rules? Fine. Be a good little Guardian. But I'm going to talk to her."

"Don't!" Devin said helplessly, grabbing his arm. "It's not time. She only just turned seventeen today. We have to wait."

Asher's eyebrow shot up, his eyes glinting. "Nothing interesting ever happened by waiting, Dev," he said. "I can't wait anymore. This girl is special. We've been waiting for too long, and I don't want to miss another minute of the fun."

He brushed past Devin, toward the door, and into the night, where I was about to meet Asher for the first time.

Devin turned to watch him go. In the memory, he clenched his fists at his side. *She's going to fall in love with him*, he thought. *And there's nothing I can do to stop it. I can't compete with that.* I didn't feel calm radiating from him—what I felt was frustration. That he couldn't be as bold as Asher. That he couldn't fight for what he wanted, too.

What I always took for shyness and cool reserve was his oath. He always wanted to talk to me. But he was bound by honor, too. I realized, strangely, that Devin and I had more in common than I'd ever realized.

The memory wrinkled and refolded, straightened itself out.

He was in a parking lot at dusk. I recognized it—it was the parking lot outside of school. And I was there, walking beside him, his jacket pulled tightly around my shoulders. Through Devin's eyes, I could feel him pulling back, his face a mask, allowing nothing in and nothing out.

I was crying. I felt something stir within him as he reached out and put his arm around me gently, pulling me in to his chest.

"It's all right, Skye," he said softly. "That's the reason I'm here. To watch over you, to protect you."

I remember this memory. It was right after he and Asher first told me the truth about my parents. That I was half Guardian, half Rebel, a human girl with powers of light and dark in her veins.

"The fight . . ." I heard myself say into his chest. "That night at the Bean . . . during my birthday . . . was that about me?"

"Yes. Asher made contact with you before we were supposed to. It upset the balance of things and has been causing chaos ever since. It's like I've tried to tell you. He's dangerous."

I felt myself flinch in his arms. I remembered exactly what I'd thought when he said those words. Was Asher dangerous because he made Devin so angry? Or because I didn't yet know who, or what, he really was? Or was he dangerous because he made me feel things I'd never felt before—not about anyone else?

In Devin's memory, I was sobbing quietly in his arms. I felt something spasm in his chest. And then I heard his thought.

If only I was allowed to break the rules—everything might be different now.

He touched my cheek. "You're so special. In ways . . . I wasn't expecting."

He told me I was going to have to meet my destiny. That it would be easier if I embraced it.

"For whom?" I asked.

"For everyone."

Through the memory, I could feel his frustration, and then, as we stood and faced each other, a curl of despair— a cold emptiness—entered his body like a sharp intake of breath.

What was that?

The memory faded, and I found myself sitting on the faded purple velvet couch at Love the Bean again, still looking into Devin's pool-blue eyes. I blinked.

The way he was looking at me, it was clear that he knew exactly what I'd seen. It was almost like he'd been transported back to the memory with me. But there was also something else in his eyes: regret.

My plan had worked. There was a connection between our minds—a rift, through which I'd found a portal to his memories. It wouldn't have been possible if Devin hadn't been influencing my mind and my emotions for as long as I'd known him.

And now, I knew for sure.

"I'm sorry you had to see that," he said, his voice low.

"Not you, too," I whispered.

"If I hadn't been bound to the rules of the Order, things would have turned out differently." He squeezed my hand tighter. "Your heart might belong to me now, of its own free will. Instead of him." I looked down at my hands.

"No," I said quietly. "No. I don't think it would."

"Skye—"

"It doesn't matter anyway, does it? We can't change the past."

"Listen to me, I can explain! It's not what you think."

"Isn't it?"

He didn't have an answer. He just sat there on the couch, his mouth slightly open, as if I'd just taken away the last precious thing he had. But I didn't feel bad. He had done it to me.

Now he knew how it felt.

On the drive home, I tried to see the road through the tears that had sprung to my eyes, blurring my world until I finally had to pull over. I leaned my head against the steering wheel and cried. And it wasn't just for Devin— though I felt torn up inside about it. It was for Asher too, still so far away, who loved me, and who I loved, but who I questioned, because that was the way my heart worked.

And I cried for me. Because I had committed to this path, and I would stick with it, but every day that passed it got harder, and I didn't know if it was the right one anymore.

17

The next morning was sunny and bright. My mood was the opposite.

I woke with a headache that must have been residual from my crying jag. When I looked in the mirror, my stomach sank. My face was blotchy and red, and my eyes looked like bees had attacked me in my sleep. Perfect.

I did the best I could with moisturizer and makeup and came stomping downstairs wearing black skinny jeans and my heavy boots. My life philosophy was something along the lines of, when life starts feeling out of control, put on a pair of motorcycle boots and kick it in the shins.

Sometimes it worked, sometimes all it did was make Aunt Jo give me the raised-eyebrow look she was giving me now.

"Tell the biker gang I need you home by ten tonight," she said drily.

I ignored the look and the comment and went to the fridge to forage for a cucumber. I took it out, cut a few slices, tilted my head back, and placed them over my eyes to wait for the de-puffing magic to work.

"Those are for eating," Earth pointed out from the kitchen table. "That's a waste of food."

"I'll eat them after," I muttered.

"I think Skye's having a bad day," Aunt Jo said to Earth. "Why don't you go upstairs for a bit so I can talk to her?"

"Fine. But I'm really good at talking." She sighed and mumbled something under her breath as I heard her patter to the doorway, then stop. "You should take an umbrella today. It's going to rain."

I didn't even bother removing the cucumbers or looking at her. "It's totally sunny out!" I yelled. "It's not going to rain!"

"I'm just saying—"

"And if it does I'll make it go away!"

The little girl said nothing, and I instantly felt bad for yelling at her.

"Take one anyway," she said quietly, and then I heard her patter out of the room.

"You okay?" Aunt Jo came up beside me. I felt a hand on my back. The fact that she wasn't making a funny comment about how hard it is to raise teenagers unnerved me. A few months ago, she would have made a joke, and I would have said something snarky and evasive, and I never would have thought to take actual advice from a grownup. But everything was so different now. Aunt Jo had gone from being someone I kept secrets from to someone who understood my secrets maybe better than anyone.

"No," I said, taking the cucumbers off my eyes. "I'm not okay. Look at me! I'm a mess! I'm hideous! No wonder Asher is fighting against me, he's probably decided to just give up looking for a way for us to be together, and is off right now gallivanting with some stunning Rebel and plotting my destruction. Astaroth is right. How the hell am I supposed to do this?" I could feel the tears coming again, hot and angry and frustrated, and there was nothing I could do to stop it. "I can't save the world! I'm just some stupid teenager with a crush and puffy eyes."

Aunt Jo took the cucumbers from me and put them on the counter. Then she took my hands in hers.

"Everyone has bad days, Skye," she said. "And no matter what anyone tells you, anyone who has ever done anything brave or risky or flat-out revolutionary has never *not* questioned if what they were doing was right." She smiled at me and sighed. "I'm not saying that you don't have a lot on your plate right now. But think of it this way. Today—right now? It's only puffy eyes. And the swelling will go down, I promise."

"I look like a Botox accident," I said.

"You look beautiful. Now get to school, and stop pouting. Maybe today will be the day we'll find James."

"We can only hope," I said. I sniffed and patted my face dry. "Okay. I think I'm ready to face . . ." I motioned toward the outside world. "That."

"That's my fighter." I walked to the hall and grabbed an umbrella from the bin by the door. "And Skye?" Aunt Jo followed me out.

"Yeah?"

"Remember what I said, about following your own star?" I nodded slowly, not sure what I was about to agree with. She hesitated. "You don't have to wait for him, you know."

"Aunt Jo," I said. "There's no one else I could ever want."

"That's not what I—"

"I have to go," I said. The last thing I wanted right now was to hear a lecture about how I should be dating other guys. "Out of everyone, I thought you would understand."

I rolled the windows down on my drive to school, hoping the spring air would be good for de-puffing my skin. What was Earth talking about? The sky was a cloudless blue, stretching and sparkling across the mountainous horizon. I squinted against the sun and flipped down the visor.

My talk with Aunt Jo had given me a renewed burst of strength. I just had to put my head down and keep going. That was the only way I would succeed. And the first thing I had to do, no matter how much it pained me to do it, was give my friends the bad news about prom. In the face of all this looming disaster, that was the one bright spot they'd been looking forward to. And I hated to ruin it for them.

Being prepared is way better than being excited, I rationalized. *Right?*

I didn't have to wait long. The gang was at my locker when I got there.

"How'd your talk with Manning go?" Ian asked.

"Oh, you know. Get a perfect score on all my finals or else burn in hell forever. No big deal."

"Yikes," said Dan.

"That is ridiculous." Raven tossed a sheet of glistening blond hair over her shoulder. "You don't have time to worry about stupid tests and meaningless grades. You have more important things to focus on, Skye."

"Yeah, like what shoes to wear for prom," Cassie said,

walking up. Cassie was really good at missing the first half of a conversation and continuing on with absolute confidence. "Skye, I got these black open-toed bootie cage heels. You're gonna freak."

Dan grinned at her. "Let's leave the freaking to you and me. I have a special date planned for us tonight."

"Ooh!" Cassie squealed, clapping. "Where?"

"It's a surprise," said Dan. "But I think you'll like it."

"What is happening to you, man?" Ian groaned. "Since when did you become a guy who plans special dates?"

"Since I rocked his world, Ian. Deal with it," Cassie snapped. "Now, about our special date . . ."

Dan grinned at Ian and shrugged.

"You are so whipped," Ian muttered. Then he added, "It wouldn't kill you to plan a special date for *me* every once in a while. . . ."

"Does somebody need some attention?" Raven said drily.

"And on that note," Cassie said, "what should I wear?"

Dan mulled this over. He wore the same jeans and navy blue zip-up hoodie every day. Outfits weren't his strong suit.

"Wear jeans," he said. "And no heels! Comfortable stuff that you don't mind getting dirty."

"This is sounding less and less like a date." Cassie scrunched up her nose. "The sacrifices I make for love."

"Anyway, you just focus on that, and let's let Skye worry about the upcoming battle, okay?"

"Speaking of battles . . ." I toyed with the end of my side braid. "I have some news, and I don't want to tell you—in fact, I almost didn't, but I figured, you know, better safe than sorry, and I don't want to keep things from you guys anymore." I took a breath.

They all looked at me expectantly.

"I found a way to see into Astaroth's mind," I said. Judging from their facial expressions, that might not have been the best opener. "I could see what he is planning. I was wearing this long flowy dress that Aunt Jo gave me, and there were twinkle lights—"

Cassie's eyes lit up.

"—and the hem of my gown was sweeping against the floor of the gym."

Cassie's expression turned from excited to skeptical.

"And I heard him say something. *The battle will not end until one side has claimed you—or killed you.*"

"Oh my god," Cassie whispered, grabbing Dan's bicep.

I paused and steadied myself. Talking about it out loud was making me anxious. Not just because it had been super freaky in Astaroth's mind—but because I didn't want anyone else to hear. "It's prom," I said. "The battle, the collision of Chaos and Order—it's going to happen on prom night."

I almost ducked, afraid Cassie was going to throw something at my head in rage. I closed my eyes. "I'm so sorry, guys. Please don't kill the messenger!"

But nothing hit me in the head. I opened my eyes.

"I was scarily spot-on with that prom theme," Cassie said darkly. "Maybe I can see the future, too."

"You saw into Astaroth's *mind*?" Raven looked stunned. "What . . . what was that like?"

"Um," I said. "It's pretty high in the running for creepiest place I've ever been."

The bell rang.

"Come over tonight," I said. "After the big date. We can talk more then."

The group began to scatter, and I grabbed Raven to see if she'd meet me after school to work on a few things. When I turned back around, the hall was empty. I had to slip into class late, making apologetic eyes at the teacher. Six months ago, before all this started, I never would have dreamed of being late for class. Now it was like a regular occurrence. But I was determined to ace my finals. I had changed over the course of the year, but let's face it, not that much.

After school, Raven came with me up to the roof, and I tried to make myself have a vision of James Harrison. I wasn't having any luck, and it was starting to scare me. I'd been trying to focus on the name *James* and picture the face of the man from the vision I'd had of the three Rogues. But so far, I kept coming up empty-handed.

"This sucks," I said. The afternoon sun was fading into a pinkish-gold dusk. "Why is it so hard? The visions are supposed to help me, not frustrate me."

"I hate to point out the obvious," said Raven, absently admiring the silver sheen of her wings in a window. "But what if you're looking for the wrong person?"

"What? Who should I be looking for?"

"I just mean," said Raven, "that maybe James Harrison isn't who you think he is. You have the clues, they're just not piecing together."

I exhaled loudly in exasperation. Raven shot me a pointed look.

"I'm calling it a day," I said. "I have hours of studying I still have to do, and then everyone is coming over. It is going to be a long night."

"What did I tell you? Stop worrying about finals. The fate of the universe, Skye." She pointed at me. "That's all I'm saying."

"Well, thank you for taking some of the pressure off. But college is something I've dreamed about since I was a little kid. And if there's any chance—even the smallest, slightest chance—that we can make it out of this and keep on living? I want to be able to live my dream." My voice cracked on the word *dream*, and I turned away so I didn't have to see the look on Raven's face. "I have to have something to believe in. Something I can control."

"I know this sounds unlikely," Raven said quietly. "But I know what you mean."

We walked down the fire staircase back to the main level of the school building. "Oh, man," I said. "Go ahead to my car. I forgot my umbrella in my locker."

"Your umbrella?" Raven balked. "It's a near-perfect day outside. Why on earth did you bring an *umbrella*?"

I shrugged. "Earth told me to. I know she's just a kid, but I don't know. She's freakishly right about a lot of things."

"Well, hurry up, then." Raven smirked at me. "If I'm out there without an umbrella, I don't want to get caught in the rain."

"I'll be five seconds. Promise." I wasn't aching to spend lots of alone time in the school after hours, either. Not with all the Guardians and Rebels. I grabbed the travel-size umbrella from my locker and sprinted out toward the parking lot. When I rounded the corner by the front steps of the school, I ran into something hard.

Not something. Some*one*.

It knocked the wind out of me and I fell backward. A pair of aviator sunglasses clattered to the sidewalk next to me, and in their reflective lenses, I could see the face of the person standing above me.

I looked up at him, my heart pounding.

"Give those back," Gideon said coldly, shielding his eyes with his hands as if the last rays of the sun were so bright they hurt. I grabbed the sunglasses and kept them out of reach.

"No," I said, thinking on my feet and not entirely sure what I was doing. "Look at me!"

"Give them back, Skye," he growled. The darkness inside Gideon rolled off him like smoke. "I'm not kidding around." At one time, Gideon and I had been friends. I had felt comfortable with him immediately, from the first moment Asher introduced us. His overall appearance made it hard not to like him—wild, dark curly hair, wire-rimmed glasses that made him look approachably brainy. Cassie even thought he was cute. As I stood there, holding his sunglasses out of reach, I couldn't help but be reminded that he'd agreed to teach me how to fight the Order's mental manipulation. Even though it was painful for him. Even though it brought the darkness rushing back.

I knew that feeling of emptiness now, the feeling that mental manipulation could cause. I knew that what he did for me wasn't easy. He'd done it because he cared about me. Because he was my friend.

And now we stood in the school parking lot, face-to-face, as enemies.

"You don't have to be like this, Gideon," I said. "It isn't you."

"And what do you know about me, really?" he asked, still keeping his eyes averted. "I've lived for thousands more years than you. My loyalties, my allegiances, my blood—you don't even know how deep they run. The sacrifices I've made," he said, "for love. For free will. You can't think I'd let those all be for nothing. I won't stop fighting until the Order has collapsed."

In a swift motion, Gideon reached out and swiped the glasses from my hand. And when he did, our eyes met, just for a second.

But that was all I needed.

The last time I'd looked into his eyes, they'd glowed as if

they were burning. Now, as the light of day faded around us, they swirled with clouds the color of wet asphalt. As we locked eyes, I could have sworn I saw a crack of lightning behind his pupils, and a cold, hard rain begin to fall.

He put the aviators on. "Don't stand in my way," he said, turning.

"Gideon, wait!" But he'd already made it clear he didn't care what I had to say.

Puzzled, I turned and walked, then jogged, then ran the rest of the way to my car, where Raven was waiting.

"Jeez, Skye," she said, looking pointedly at an imaginary watch. "Took you long enough."

"We have to go," I said, "*right now.*"

"Wait," she said, running around to the passenger side. "Go where? What's happening?"

My mom and I had a mental connection, because she'd manipulated my memories. I could see Devin's memories, because he'd made me feel calm and peaceful. Gideon had taught me how to shield my mind from that kind of manipulation. But in the process, he, too, had worked a kind of mental magic on me. He had opened a portal, and now I could see what the Rebellion was planning to do next.

The clouds, the lightning, the rain. I had seen it all in a vision: a flash flood that threatened to drown Cassie and pull Dan under with her.

Take an umbrella, Earth had warned me. *Just take one.*

I can hear the sky.

My two oldest friends in the world were in danger right this very moment, and it was because of me.

"We're going to Foster's Woods," I said.

18

The first drops of rain began to spatter against the windshield as I sped down the road—so fast it felt like we were flying above it. Light, at first, then heavier, harder. In seconds, the rain outside was torrential. I had seen it before. I knew what was coming.

A hard rain began to pelt the asphalt, immediately soaking me. Rain ran down my hair in rivulets, into my eyes and mouth. The ground beneath my feet felt wet and spongy, and when I looked down, I saw that I was on the bank of the river.

I could hear my friends' cries for help, still echoing in my mind from the vision, and I pressed my foot even harder on the gas.

As I drove us to Cassie's house, I kept my focus on the sky above, willing the rain back, the clouds to dissipate. But it wouldn't, they didn't. I was fighting against some strong powers of the dark. Likely it was more than one Rebel, working in unison to destroy my friends and defeat me.

The entrance to the woods wasn't far from Cassie's backyard, and this was where everyone parked when we had parties out there. Sure enough, Dan's car was in the driveway.

"Shit," I said. "Shit, shit." I threw the car into park, and jumped out. The rain immediately soaked through my T-shirt and made the black of my jeans even blacker. I pushed my soaking-wet hair out of my face with one hand as I ran in the direction of the woods and held the other to the sky, channeling my dark, elemental powers through my fingertips. I might not be able to stop the storm entirely, but with any luck, I could keep the flooding at bay.

"Skye!" Raven called, hurrying after me. "What's going on?"

"It's an attack!" I yelled back. "A flash flood!"

We ran down the hill to the woods. The rain beat down in huge, wet gulps, and the ground beneath us was slippery and saturated with water that continued to rise. I slipped several times before Raven grabbed my hand.

"Like this!" she cried. In the darkness I caught a flash

of silver and saw that she'd extended her wings. I let mine loose as well, and we took flight. But even that was difficult with the torrential rain. It beat against our feathers and pushed us back toward the ground. This was no ordinary rainstorm. It was powerful. *Otherworldly.* The water was so thick that I could hardly breathe. I swallowed mouthfuls of it. It ran down my face and into my eyes, blurring the dark woods. Trees rose up around me on all sides like lines on a map you're trying to follow in the dark.

"Cassie!" Dan's voice rang out through the trees. "Hold on to that branch!"

"This way!" I motioned for Raven to follow me as I traced the sound of Dan's voice.

"Dan!" Cassie cried, her own voice piercing the night. "I can't reach it!"

I stumbled as I landed on the bank of the creek, slipping through the mud, swimming, basically, with Raven right behind me. The water in the creek was rising, fast and furious, and a spot of red stood out amid the rushing tide. *Thank god for Cassie's hair.*

"Cassie!" I screamed. I couldn't lose my best friend again. I couldn't be the reason for it a second time. "Hang on!" *You're not going to die. You're not going to die.*

I kicked off from the ground again, swooping down, the

rain beating hard against my wings, soaking them. I let the silver wash through me and summoned my own powers of the dark, the heat, the fire I knew was within me. A ball of light radiated from my body, enveloping my wings and Raven's, keeping us dry.

"Skye!" Dan's voice rang out in the night. "Over here!" I sent another orb of fire out in front of me, and it lit a path straight to Dan, where it hovered around us, illuminating the churning waters of the river below.

"What happened?" I cried, expanding the protective bubble so that it included Dan. "Where is she?"

He struggled to catch his breath. "A branch snapped from that tree and knocked her in!" Before I could say another word, he dove into the rising waters of the creek, surfaced, and looked wildly around for Cassie. She'd disappeared.

"Cassie!" he yelled. The water rose over his head in waves and he beat it back.

"Hold on!" I cried. "Stay still!" I focused all of my energy on the river in front of me. *Come on*, I pushed myself. *You can do it*. I had never tried to work so many different powers at the same time before, and the strain of it pulled at my mind and body. I could feel myself ripping apart.

Then, some last reserve of power surged up in me,

pushing me onward, and the water where I was focusing my energy began to recede. As if a great wind was blowing on it, it curled back, and I spotted Cassie lying on the floor of the riverbed. Her red hair fanned out around her like a mermaid's.

"There!"

Dan ran down the path through the water and kneeled beside her.

"Bring her back to us," I struggled to say. "I can't hold on much longer!"

Gently, he picked Cassie up, her arms and legs dangling. "Hang on, babes," he panted as he stumbled to shore. Her red hair stuck to her neck, and it didn't look like she was breathing.

With the energy I had left, I raised my hands to the sky and beat back the rain. It felt like hours, days—but it was only seconds, I think, before the rain began to let up, and before I knew it, the downpour had been sucked back into the clouds. They rumbled discontentedly above us. A threat that they could burst open again at any moment.

And then through the trees, I saw something move. It was human-shaped, I was sure of it. With hair and eyes so dark, I knew in an instant who it was.

"Asher?" I whispered. My heart pounded, and not just from the effort it had taken to fight the Rebellion's powers. What was he doing here? First the fire—and now, this? I couldn't believe that Astaroth was right—*once a Rebel, always a Rebel*—but then, I didn't know what else could be going on.

I blinked, and the trees were still again. There was nothing there.

"Skye?" Dan nudged me. "Are you okay? Can you make it?"

"Yes," I said hoarsely. Dark spots swam into my vision, and I knew I was only barely hanging on, myself. I tried to cast a ball of fire to keep Cassie warm. It was small and weak—but it floated around her head, drying her pale and goose-bumped skin.

Dan quickly leaned over her, pumping her stomach and giving her mouth-to-mouth.

"Stop," I said faintly. "Let me."

I put both hands over my best friend's heart. "I couldn't save you last time, Cass," I said. "But I can now." And I let the silver powers I had left flow through my fingertips, into her blood. For the briefest of seconds, she glowed.

Then she coughed up a lungful of water and opened her

eyes. I pulled my hands away and fell back, exhausted to the point of tears.

"Skye?" She wheezed. "Did you save me?"

"We all did." I tried to smile. "It was a group effort."

"Babes?" she said, her eyes searching for Dan. He smoothed her hair back and kissed her. He couldn't say anything—I think because he was crying.

Cassie noticed Raven standing behind him.

"You!" She choked, struggling to sit up. "Did you do this?"

I put my hand on her shoulder. "It wasn't Raven. She's one of us now, remember?"

"Like hell!" Cassie's eyes rolled deliriously. Her face was flushed with fever and effort. "She tried to do it again! We can't trust her, Skye. None of us can. She's a total traitor!"

"I—I didn't." Raven looked shocked—and almost sad. "I wouldn't. Skye, you know that, right? Cassie? I'm on your side now."

"She knows," I said, trying to calm her. "I know, too. Cassie doesn't know what she's saying."

"It was so nice out," Cassie panted. "Dan took me down to the river, to practice for prom."

"Practice for prom?" I looked to Dan for an explanation.

"Yeah," Dan said sheepishly. "I felt like Cassie didn't think I was taking prom seriously. I wanted to do something nice for her—you know, since it might be our last dance and all." He took a breath and looked at her. She nodded and squeezed his hand. "I had the idea that we could do the dance from *Dirty Dancing*. You know, the one where he lifts her up?"

I was starting to catch on. "They practice in the lake," I said.

"So that if he drops her," Cassie explained, "there's a nice watery cushion. It was warm out, so we came down to the river." She beamed at him. "He thinks of everything."

"Yeah, but then it started to rain."

"It was flooding before we knew it," Cassie added. "It had to be angelic, there's just no way—" She looked fiercely at Raven.

"Cassie," I said, "it wasn't Raven. Or the Order. It was the Rebellion. Just like the fire."

She looked at me, then glanced in Raven's direction.

"Sorry," she mumbled.

Raven nodded uncomfortably. "It's okay," she said, her voice soft. "What I did to you back then was horrible. It was unforgiveable. You have every right to hate me." Cassie's eyes welled with tears.

"I don't hate you," she said. "I just don't understand you."

We were all exhausted as we trudged through the mud back to Cassie's house. I asked Raven to drive us over to my place. In Cassie's weakened state, there was no way I was letting her and Dan sleep at home tonight. I needed them under my roof, where I could keep everyone safe.

I had to find Ian's father soon. I knew it was only once I reunited the three most powerful Rogues that the fourth would finally be revealed to me. Secretly, I was hoping it was anyone but Earth. I felt a fierce need to protect her, and the idea of bringing her into this made me feel sick.

But she had known about the flood. Maybe not how or why, but somehow she knew. Especially after today, I had a feeling it was her destiny.

That night, I sat on the floor in the hall outside my room, my knees pulled up to my chest.

People I love are being attacked. My friends keep almost dying.

I knew in my heart that this was what I was *born* to do. But putting my friends in so much danger wasn't something I'd signed on for. Sure, they promised to stick by me and fight. They were my best friends. No, more than that— they were my family, and had been since I was five. I had been there for Cassie when Kim Mancuso called her tomato-head in middle school, and I had personally hand-delivered the Ben and Jerry's Kitchen Sink ice cream when her first boyfriend, Patrick, broke up with her because he wasn't ready to be "tied down." Cassie would expect nothing less than to be there for me, too—whatever I needed.

I leaned back against the wall and sighed. I wished that there was someone who could tell me what I should do, but every time I tried to think of what Cassie or Ian or Aunt Jo would say, they told me this was one I had to figure out for myself.

Cassie and Dan were talking in my room in low tones, their voices floating out into the hall. I tried to give them privacy by saying I had a headache and needed to be by myself for a while. But I could hear them anyway.

"I'm sorry," Dan said. "I'm just so worried about you. You're Skye's best friend in the whole world, her Achilles heel. You're an easy target for them. She'd do anything for you, Cass."

I felt my heart twist. Cassie whimpered, softly.

"Come here, babes," he said. "I love you. Life was totally sucky until you fell for me, don't you even know that?"

"It was?" She sniffled. "I never knew that. I thought we all had a pretty good life."

"Maybe you did." He laughed. "But dude, I was in love with my best friend. And I couldn't say or do anything about it. And I had to watch you frolicking around, swooning over other boys—"

"I didn't frolic—"

"And talking about how *foxy* they all were. And damn, Cass, you looked so hot up there onstage—"

"I did?"

"And it was like the whole universe was laughing at me, like, *dream on, buddy, she's so far out of your orbit you need a space shuttle to get to her.* . . ."

"Babes?" she said. "Dan?"

"Yeah?"

"I only said those things to make you jealous. I didn't think there was any way you were going to go out with a ditz like me. You're so smart. You could have any girl—"

He snorted. "Right."

"No, let me finish. Any girl in the math club, or the science club, or the comp sci club, or—"

"Okay, okay, I get it." He laughed. "Come here." There was some rustling as bodies were maneuvered. "You're not a ditz."

"I know." She sighed.

"You're a crazy talented musician."

"I know."

"Okay, *maybe* you act like a ditz sometimes."

"Dan!"

"But you know what? You make me laugh. And you make me take myself less seriously. And I need that. And that's why I love you."

I heard a soft sound, almost like laughter.

"I'm so lucky." No, not laughter. Cassie was crying. "I've almost died twice. I have *you* for a boyfriend. Skye hasn't ditched me yet. One of these days, my luck is going to run out."

"Well, if it does, it won't be in the form of me dumping you," said Dan. "Because I'm going to love you even after your luck runs out. You'll be the most loved unlucky girl in the world." I heard more rustling, and Cassie laughing through her tears. "You know, even if the world ends on prom night, I wouldn't want to take anyone else as my date for the last dance of my life."

"Shhh," Cassie whispered. "Stop talking."

And then it was quiet, except for the sound of them kissing. I got up and wandered down the hall to the bathroom to brush my teeth.

Raven was on her way out, carrying a towel. We paused in the doorway, facing each other.

"Oh," she said. "Look, about before, what Cassie said . . ."

"She didn't mean it. She was delirious."

Raven paused and looked at me, as if trying to decide whether to say something or not.

"You know I would never hurt you, right?" she said finally. Her voice was defiant, but I knew she was masking hurt. I reached out and hugged her tight. "Ah—ow—hey—what are you—"

"I know you wouldn't," I whispered fiercely in her ear. "I trust you with my life."

Raven broke away and straightened the T-shirt and pajama pants I'd lent her. She looked at me sideways.

"Don't ever do that again," she said. "I don't do hugs."

I shook my head and smiled, locking the bathroom door behind me, and flung the window open. The rain had stopped, and the night was damp, angry, vengeful. The Rebellion hadn't gotten what they were after, this time. But it didn't mean they were going to stop.

Cassie and Dan's conversation had filled me with an ache I'd been suppressing for so long. A deep, gaping chasm stretched open inside of me. And suddenly, I started crying.

I gazed out the window, staring at the wild mountains beyond. Moonlight struggled to push through the dense thicket of clouds that still churned restlessly above.

"Asher," I whispered. "Where are you? Tell me you're not a part of this. Please, just tell me you're working on a way to end this whole thing."

But there was no answer. Not from the moonlight. Not from the stars. Not from the shadows of the mountains, luminous against the night.

And not from Asher.

19

"You know," I said. "Finals really suck, but they suck even more when you're also preparing to stop a war."

"I think I have an ironic T-shirt with that very saying," Dan mumbled.

"They suck no matter how you slice it," Cassie said. "They're depressing. They're gloom and doom. They're the end of something."

"Yeah," said Dan. "Those happy carefree days before finals period began."

"Did I miss the part where those days were happy and carefree?" I asked.

Cassie paused, considering. "If they wanted finals to be inspiring, they would have called them 'beginnings.'"

She thought for another second. "Or, 'doorways to your future.'"

"Doesn't quite have the same fear-inducing ring to it," said Dan.

"But points for poeticism," Ian called from behind the counter.

"Thanks," she said brightly.

As if we weren't already tense enough, it was finals week. Love the Bean was crowded with students chugging coffee like it was the elixir of life and studying; they were curled up in the overstuffed armchairs and huddled in groups around the various low coffee tables.

Meanwhile, I was having an identity crisis.

As I looked at the kids around me terrified of balancing chem equations, flipping out over the answer to X, and losing sleep over that quarter of a point between a 97 and a 98, I realized just how far my life had come in only half a year. My classmates were worried about integers and the key dates in World War I. I was worried about whether or not my visions of the future had adequately prepared me to stand my ground against the rival forces of fate and free will who threatened to destroy the world with their ancient battle by turning me into the greatest human weapon who ever lived.

Suddenly, precalc wasn't looking so bad.

Yet even as I sat there, I knew that part of me was still clinging with all I had to my old life. Otherwise, why would I be sitting here with the rest of my friends, worried about keeping my GPA high enough so that I could get into the college of my dreams?

Because part of you doesn't want to face the reality of what's coming.

The stress was beginning to get to me.

Pete, the manager, had to hire another barista so that Ian could have some help. Ian divided his time into making double-shot, no-foam lattes; studying; and helping me figure out the answers to the final two pieces of the puzzle.

Where was James Harrison? Who was the shadowy fourth Rogue in my mother's vision? I had tried to ask the box the night of the flood, but I was so exhausted, my power so spent, that the etching of the key didn't even glow when I held it. It took me a few days to recover. But now I was ready.

Everything else seemed to be coming together. We had reunited Aunt Jo and Aaron Ward; Earth's special and quirky ability to touch the sky with her mind was proving to be super useful; Cassie and Raven were *finally* beginning to make peace, however tentatively; we knew that the Order was planning to kick-start this battle to end all battles on prom night; and I was the most powerful I had ever been.

That night, I took my little wooden box back up to the roof, where the sky was a velvety black and the moon was my guide. Only two of the four intertwined loops remained. Did that mean I only had two questions left? There were so many things I wanted to ask her, but I knew I didn't have enough time. I had to make them count.

So while the whole house slept below, I asked the question I hoped my mom could answer. The third loop lit up with a flash.

Again, I was pulled full-throttle down the waterslide, twisting and turning, until I found myself standing in the woods around the cabin that I'd grown so familiar with. There was my mother, standing with the third Rogue from my vision. The one I'd thought was James. He had short hair the color of hay and a smattering of freckles across his face that looked out of place on a grown man.

Rogues, always a little out of place.

"How do you do it?" he asked quietly.

The wind rustled through the pines, whipping my mother's honey blond hair around her face.

"It's different for me," she said solemnly. "This is my

family. My home. My baby is powerful, and I have to do what I can to protect her."

"So is mine," said James. "Ian is going to do great things. Important things. You saw it with your own eyes."

"James—" my mother said.

"I want him to know who he is. I want to tell him, to raise him knowing he's got a power in him that few have. I want to be proud of him."

"You know you can't," she said softly. "I want anything but that for Skye. It's too dangerous, for both of them. Don't you see that? The Order is always watching, yes. But they're too young for the things that fate is asking of them. We have to wait."

"I don't want to wait."

"You *have* to wait." My mother's jaw was a tense line. "What about Catherine? What will she say if you tell her who you really are? Who her son is?"

He looked grim.

"I want what you have. Sam, Skye—the three of you are a unit. I want to make Catherine and Ian a part of this life."

"It's not safe for them."

"Then I want to go back."

"We need you here." They were at a standstill. "You're doing Ian a favor by keeping him in the dark about this.

Catherine, too. These are dangerous times, James. The Order is getting restless. You've seen the flashes of white through the trees. I think they know."

She moved closer to him.

"James, I'm begging you. Don't tell them. Keep this secret. Just a little while longer. My daughter's life is more important to me than establishing this new faction, and I know you want the same for your son."

"But it's tearing me up inside."

"We all make sacrifices for our kids. This is yours. It's the sacrifice you'd be making for his safety. He'll grow up a normal boy. He and Skye will find each other. I've seen it."

And when I blinked again, I was back on the roof, holding the box, reeling, under a dome of stars.

James was jealous after all—but not because Aaron got Aunt Jo. Because my mother and father got to spend time with me, while he couldn't be the father he wanted to be for Ian.

What I'd seen must have happened right before my parents were killed, and James disappeared. Tensions were clearly running high. The Order was catching on to their plans, tracking them. Ian and I were old enough to understand what was happening, but young enough that we had to be kept safe. After the conversation I'd just witnessed ended, it probably was only a matter of time before the Order set the events in motion that caused the car accident that ended my parents' lives.

And yet, not mine. They wanted to save mine. Because they knew that the combination of my parents' blood was already beginning the process of making me special. They knew that, one day, my powers would explode with a vengeance that would shake the universe. And they knew that they would need me.

But that didn't tell me anything about where James actually was. Finals were here, prom was drawing closer by the day, and we still didn't have the final Rogues to complete our powerful circle. And if we didn't find them, we risked not being able to summon all the Rogues to join us in the fight. Without them, we didn't stand a chance.

"Hey, guys?" Ian's voice snapped me out of my thoughts the following afternoon, and back to the Bean and the task at hand: studying. He stood above me, holding a plate of cupcakes.

One day, Skye and Ian will find each other.

I'd always known he was important to me. But now I knew with certainty that he was vital to the fight.

"Don't tell Pete, but if there was ever a time to risk

getting fired for the sake of my friends, I think this might be it." Ian grinned. "On the house."

"Frosting!" Cassie yelped. "A girl's best friend." She chose a vanilla cupcake with yellow buttercream and a smattering of white sprinkles.

I can't do this without you, Ian, I thought, as Cassie and Dan dug into the sugary goodness. *I hope my mother was right.*

"Hey." I pulled him aside. "Do you have a second?"

"For you, I have many seconds." Ian narrowed his eyes. "Why?"

I grabbed his hand and led him outside, where it would be harder for anyone to overhear us. "How are you doing?" I asked him. "You know, since finding out about your dad being a Rogue, and you having . . ." I paused. "Angelic blood, I guess."

"I don't know," Ian said, his tone light. "I guess it hasn't really hit me yet."

"Have you . . . I mean, can you *do* anything? Powers, I mean?"

He scrunched his nose, thinking. "I don't think so. I'd know if I did, right?"

I couldn't help but laugh at that. "Yeah, you'd know."

Ian studied me. "Is that it, Skye? I gotta get back to work. . . ."

"Actually," I said. "There's something else sort of . . . related." I paused, and he looked at me expectantly. "I had a vision, a while ago. Back before we split into the Uprising. I'm walking on a huge, endless expanse of black-sand beach. Just miles and miles of sand, as far as the eye can see. On one side, cliffs loom, like, menacingly above me. On the other, the black waves of the ocean beat a steady rhythm. In and out. In perfect time."

Ian leaned forward, his eyebrows drawn together. "Go on," he said, his voice low.

"There's a figure, in the distance. He's advancing, but the closer he gets, the thicker the mist swirls around him. I can't see his face or who he is. All I know is that if I don't do something, he's going to kill me."

"Do you see what you do?" Ian asked quietly.

I nodded. "I have a sword. I raise it above my head. And I—" I swallowed hard. "I throw it."

"And?" The question was so quiet, so low a whisper, I almost didn't hear it above the sounds of the street.

"And as I do, I see another figure, running toward the first one. I think I know who it is, but I can never quite be sure. I'm always just about to figure it out when the mist swallows him, too. And I know I hit someone."

Ian's face was pale.

236

"I don't know who. I walk toward the mist. My dress is dragging me down, but I keep going, I have to keep moving. I have to find out. I draw closer. And as the mist clears, I know I'm about to see someone I love."

Ian grimaced. "Is it . . . me?" He drew a sharp breath. "Is that why you're telling me?"

"No!" I said quickly. "No, I know that at least."

"How do you know?"

"Because in the vision, you're right there beside me."

Ian studied me. Then he nodded.

"So that's it, then," he said. "My fate and yours, Skye. Intertwined."

I leaned closer and took his hands. "I know this is a lot to ask, but I'm telling you because it isn't just my fight anymore, Ian," I said. "It's yours too, now. It's your dad we're looking for. Your people we're fighting with. You'll be there, with me, in battle. This is your struggle just as much as mine." I took a deep breath. "I don't know where your dad is, but I know he left trying to protect you. You have to believe me on that. He's not a bad guy."

We stood there for a few seconds, in silence, while he thought.

Finally he said, "It makes so much sense."

"It does?"

"Being a Rogue. My dad working with your parents. Aunt Jo's story—how she always knew she was different but she didn't know why or how." He looked right into my eyes. "That night of your birthday party, I saw your eyes turn silver. I knew you were lying to me about it the next day, too. I had a feeling that something really strange was going on, but I didn't know what. I knew it this whole time, right up until the camping trip. I just thought I was crazy or . . . I don't know what I thought."

"I get it," I said.

"Every time I was in a room with Asher, I could feel my blood just boiling. Not just 'cause the guy's an arrogant ass, but like he'd done something to me, personally." He caught himself, and gave me a small, sheepish grin. "More than just steal you away from me, I mean."

"Ian—" I said gently. "He didn't steal—"

"I know, I know." He frowned. "I would get mad at you, too."

"It's okay," I said. "You don't have to—"

"No, I do. Those things I said about you to Ellie. They were terrible. I don't really think that. I just got so worked up, so angry. I didn't know why, I just knew that I was, and I had to take it out on you, because you had the silver eyes, and you also kind of knew what it was like to be different."

"Well," I said. "Maybe now you'll find some clarity."

He looked at me curiously.

"He was trying to protect me, huh? You're sure?"

"He wanted to be a part of your life. And he wanted to keep you safe. But he couldn't do both." He scratched his head thoughtfully then patted down his sandy hair.

"How do you know this?" he asked. "A vision?"

I smiled to myself. "Something like that."

"You know, Skye, you're amazing, the way you deal with all this. I wouldn't be able to."

"You would, Ian," I said. "If you didn't have a choice."

"I guess it would be a little inappropriate to ask you to prom right now, huh?"

"Honestly, right now I'm just worried about *surviving* prom. Literally."

He laughed, and soon I was laughing too. Hysterical, raucous, slightly delirious laughter.

"You can't blame a guy for trying," he said, wiping away a tear. Then he leaned in so suddenly it took me by surprise, and gave me a kiss on the cheek. "I'll save you a dance, though," he whispered in my ear.

Before I could say a word, he turned on his heels and went back inside. His step was a little springier than usual.

Ian and Skye will find each other.

I was so grateful that we did.

20

Finals began the following day, and we all met by my locker first thing in the morning. I had brought a big thermos of Aunt Jo's special, industrial strength coffee blend, milk, and lots of sugar. Cassie's tote bag contained at least three bottles of Mountain Dew. Ian wore his lucky Rockies hat, even though it was definitely too warm out for headgear of any kind. And Dan . . .

"Dan," I said. "Don't you have any rituals? You know, for luck?"

He nodded, grinning sheepishly. "You just can't see it."

Cassie made a face.

"Never mind," I said. "I don't want to know." I looked at my watch. "Well, I guess this is it. It's almost eight."

"I guess it's kind of an overstatement to say we're going into battle," Dan said. "Considering."

"Don't worry," Cassie said to me over her shoulder, already pushing him down the hall. "I'll smack him for you."

"That doesn't sound so bad. . . ." Dan's voice trailed off as they turned the corner.

Once again, Ian and I found ourselves alone in the hallway. "Well, Ian," I said, linking my arm through his. "I guess it's just you and me."

"Where's Raven?" he asked.

"She stayed home to prepare for prom—the battle—whatever—with Aaron and Aunt Jo. She's not going to take finals. She says after this is all over . . . well, she probably won't be sticking around."

"I don't blame her. I'm about ready to get out of here, too." It made me think of the conversation my mother had shown me. Something popped into my mind about the examples we set for our kids, but it popped out again before I'd fully formed a thought. Ian seemed nervous, and he took a deep breath. "Actually, I'm about ready to get out of here—*now*."

"Well, me too. But first we have finals, and then an epic battle. Or did you mean before eight o'clock?"

"Actually," he said, his voice serious. "I mean right now. I'm not going to take my American History final."

I felt all the blood drain from my face. "What do you mean?" I asked. "You're . . . you're *leaving* me? But where? Why? Where are you going?"

All the panic I'd been pushing down inside myself for the past few months began to fight its way to the surface. Was Astaroth right? Was this too much to be asking of them? Would everyone I loved just leave me, eventually?

"Skye," Ian said, "I'm not *leaving* leaving. I'm going to find my dad." He paused. "I know where he is."

"What!" The blood returned to my face, and with it, a rush of dizzy emotion. "Do you know what this means? Ian, if we find your dad, it means we actually have a fighting chance of beating the Order and the Rebellion once and for all! With all the Rogues on our side, we really could do this!" I jumped up and down, and threw my arms around his neck. "This is incredible!"

"Yeah." He grinned. "What you said yesterday, about him trying to protect me? Well, I decided to come clean and just tell my mom everything. Not about the Rogue angel stuff, but about how important it is for me to find him. It turns out she knew where he was this whole time. But she didn't want to tell me. She wanted to protect me, too."

I narrowed my eyes. This sounded familiar.

"What do you mean?" I asked.

Ian cocked his head, a puzzling array of emotions playing out on his face. "She said my dad didn't leave us, like she always told me he did. I guess the truth is she kicked him out."

"Really?" I asked. "But—" I stopped myself. There was no way my mom could have shown me that—or even *known* that. Her clues only took me so far, and we had to piece together the rest. "What happened?"

"She said he was gone all the time, keeping secrets, sneaking around. She was pretty sure he was having an affair. They argued about it a lot. Finally, she told him to get out. She said she told him if he wasn't going to be the father I needed, he could leave." Ian's jaw was set in a straight line. "He didn't fight. He just . . . did what she said."

I let the information fill in the blanks of what I already knew. He'd been spending all his time with the Rogues in the cabin in the woods. And my mother begged him to keep their secret from his family. He left his wife and son to keep it safe. And to keep *them* safe.

"So . . . where is he now?" My breath caught in my throat.

He dug around in his backpack, and held up an envelope. "My mom gave me this. Said this was where the last check he sent her came from." He pointed to the return address. "Apparently, he changed his name. See? Benjamin Sharpe. That must be why our online searches were pointless."

If he was a Rogue trying to escape his old life and leave that world behind, if he was trying to sever all ties and connections to his wife and son for their own protection—then it made so much sense to change his name.

"I wonder if that's why my visions didn't work either," I mused. "I was searching for James Harrison, along with the face I'd already seen. But together they wouldn't have added up to much."

"I guess it all makes sense now," Ian said. His voice was hard to read.

"Ian." I hesitated. "You know he wasn't having an affair, right?"

"Of course," he said. "Well, I do now. He was with your mom and dad, trying to overthrow the system." He looked out somewhere over my shoulder, his eyes unfocused. He was processing so much. "It's weird though, you know? My mom told me that she kept the truth from me because she wanted me to be mad at him for leaving—not her, for making him. Because he's the one who left, and she's the one who stayed. She knew it was selfish. But she did it anyway. To protect me."

"Yeah," I said, thinking of the conversation. "There's a lot of that going around."

"But I guess what she didn't know is that he was protecting her. He was protecting both of us. From . . ." He spread his arms out wide, then shrugged. "All this."

I knew what he meant.

"I don't know anything about him. All this time, I've been angry at him, hated him, for no reason. And now I find out he was doing it for *me*." He paused. "I'm so messed up."

I took his hand. "You know what, though?" I said. "They're the ones who are gone, and we're the ones who are here. And it's time for *us* to embrace the truth. We have powers, Ian—big ones—"

"I don't—"

"Yes, you do. You will. They'll manifest, like mine did, when they're ready. And you'll find your place in this world, because there's no other option. Our parents can't protect us from the future forever. We have to face this. Now is the time."

"I know, Skye," he said. "Which is why I have to go."

I looked longingly down the hall, in the direction of the final exam I was supposed to take in five minutes.

"Can you wait until after the test? We'll go together!"

"I can't." His eyes showed resolve, determination. "I know this is your Uprising, your battle. But this is my dad. My personal mission. I have to go now. And I have to go on my own."

"Ian, come on," I said, starting to feel the fire of frustration burning in me. "You can't go by yourself. It's not safe. And also, it's not fair. I've been searching for him, too!" I squeezed his hand. "This is a huge moment, for both of us. We have to go *together*."

"No," he said firmly, pulling his arm away. I could see the Rogue temper building in him—that part of him that was capable of saying things he'd later regret. "This is going to be a couple days' drive. I'm going now. If I leave in a few minutes, I can be back by prom." *Back by prom?* That would mean missing all his finals. "If you want to come with me, I guess that's up to you. But I'm leaving." He turned and walked toward the exit.

I stood there, stunned. Should I follow him? Should I stay?

You have to get at least a 98 on three of your exams if you want to keep your GPA where it needs to be. . . .

And I couldn't just disappear now, in the days leading up to prom. Not when my friends were counting on me.

Maybe I could let Ian do this. . . .

I glanced down at my watch. Two minutes.

Without another thought, I turned and ran down the hall, swinging open the classroom door and sliding into an empty seat just in time for my first final to begin.

21

The clock ticked out the seconds on the wall.

We know where James Harrison is.

Tick.

Ian is going to find him.

Tick.

We're going do this.

Tick.

I could hear the tension crackling just beneath the surface of my skin. Every cell in my body felt wired to explode.

I looked down at my test booklet and tried to focus on the words in front of me, but the ones in my head were too distracting.

Ian's dad. The third Rogue. James. The war.

"Skye," Mr. DeNardo said. "Eyes on your own test, please."

Right, I realized. I must have been spacing out, staring off into the distance. I looked back down at my own booklet.

Earth. Aunt Jo. Aaron. The fourth. Prom. So close.

"I'll be back in time for prom," Ian had said. Clearly I couldn't just up and leave for a few days, all because I wanted to go with him. Could I? Or what if . . .

The edges of the test in front of me were curling into darkness. And the classroom dissolved with it.

No, I begged. *Please, no. This is the worst time for a vision. EVER.*

I was moving. Wait—a car was moving, and I was inside of it.

Am I Ian? I wondered, my pulse quickening. *Is something about to happen to Ian?* I glanced around his dashboard for any sign, any clue, as to what was about to happen. It was surprisingly clean, clear of all the debris that usually cluttered his car.

As my vision crystalized and came into focus, it dawned on me that this definitely didn't look like Ian's car. So who the hell did it belong to? I felt it turn sharply, switching lanes suddenly. *Too* suddenly.

There's going to be an accident.

Out the windshield, I could see that I was almost

perpendicular now to the rest of the cars on the highway. I was barreling forward—on purpose—toward one car in particular. A hunter green Subaru. Ian's.

I happened to glance in the rearview mirror then. And found myself staring into a narrow face with an evil grin, framed by long blond hair. *Lucas.*

The Guardian who'd tried to pick a fight with us in the cafeteria when I was still a Rebel. The Guardian Devin warned me was now Astaroth's right-hand man. Raven's replacement.

"He's going to hit Ian!" I screamed.

"Excuse me?"

I blinked. The entire class was staring at me, pencils poised in midair, mouths hanging open.

"Ms. Parker, do you have something you'd like to share with the whole class or should we let you get back to that exciting dream?" Mr. DeNardo did not look as amused as my classmates.

"I have to go," I whispered. "I—I'm sorry." I gathered my books and my bag, and sprinted through the door and down the hall. Screw the test. Who was I kidding, anyway? I had given up any semblance of a normal life a long time ago. Right about the time Asher and Devin showed up in my life.

The night of my seventeenth birthday.

"Here goes nothing," I whispered to myself as I ran down the front steps. But instead of hitting the bottom, I spread my wings and took off.

Something broke painfully inside me as I left my dreams of a future behind.

I had to save Ian. I only hoped I wasn't too late.

I flew on silver wings along the highway.

Come on, I thought. *He can't have gotten too far.*

I narrowed in on the cars below. In the vision, Lucas had been about to cross three lanes of traffic to ram Ian's car. So Ian must be driving in the right lane, bordering the trees. I looked for any spot of green I could find.

And then I saw it—all unfolding before my eyes. A tan, inconspicuous sedan, its engine revving as I watched, veered sharply, too sharply, into the lane next to it. Right toward a hunter green wagon.

I swooped down, hoping to make it in time. The sedan's engine roared. I sped closer and saw Ian glance out the driver's side window. His eyes widened as he took in the scene that was about to unfold. I pounded on the window for him to open it. No—we didn't have time. I spun around.

The tan sedan was veering toward me, picking up speed. Heart pounding, I raised both hands out in front of me and summoned my powers. I had no idea if it was the power of the light or of the dark that I was calling—and I didn't care. All I knew was that a huge gust of wind burst from my hands and pushed the sedan backward. Lucas's eyes grew wide as the sedan narrowly missed a car speeding toward it, then rolled off the highway in the other direction.

Ian pulled his car onto the shoulder of the highway, and I came to a rest beside him. He opened the door and got out on shaky legs. Relief welled up in me as I flung my arms around him.

"Okay," he panted, struggling to catch his breath. "You win. I'm taking you with me next time."

"Next time?" I said, pulling away. "What about this time?" I extended my wings, and didn't care who on the highway saw me. "Come on. Let's go find your dad."

Ian grinned. He took my hand, and we left his car where it was on the side of the highway. I grasped him tight, and together we flew.

Turns out, Wyoming was a lot easier to get to when you had wings. The several-day journey Ian had planned took no time at all when I was carrying us through the air.

The landscape in the southern part of the state was unlike anything I'd ever seen before. Vast green brush swept across the land, and every now and then huge burnt sienna buttes jutted out at odd angles, like some giant had dropped his toys and forgotten to pick them up.

I remembered Asher telling me that angels—particularly Rebels and those with Rebel blood—gravitated toward wild beauty and natural landscapes. I could see why James would want to escape to somewhere like Sunset Peaks, Wyoming.

We followed the return address on the envelope and found ourselves in a community of small, rustic houses that bordered a lake so big, we couldn't see the other side.

I glanced at Ian. "Do you want to knock?"

There was no answer. The lights weren't on, and there was no car parked in the drive.

I nodded at the lake.

"Down there," I said.

We rounded the path, and the wide, blue water stretched out before us. The clouds above were reflected in the glassy surface. "Skye," said Ian. "Look." The lake fed into a wide, flat river that ran down along the houses we'd passed. And dotting the river was a group of fly fishermen—maybe twenty or so, at first glance.

"Do you see him?" Ian whispered. I looked around for

a tall man with hair the color of hay and a smattering of sun-faded freckles. But we were too far to really see what any of them looked like.

"Wait—there," I said excitedly. I pointed to a man in a navy blue fly-fishing vest with bright orange piping. A khaki fishing hat shielded his face from the afternoon sun. But it wasn't his taste in fishing gear that caught my attention. It was the way the water moved around him—not just rippling, but swelling, breathing. Like he was moving it with his mind, or—

"Rogue powers?" Ian said.

"I think so."

Ian looked at me and raised his eyebrows.

"Well," he said. "There's only one way to find out."

"What are you going to—"

"Dad!!!" He shouted, standing on his tiptoes and waving his arm at the man.

"Stealthy," I said.

The man's head turned, quickly, to look at us. He seemed to squint against the sun.

"What if he doesn't recognize me?" Ian asked. "I'm older and manlier now."

"That's true." I rolled my eyes. "Maybe yell, *Dad, it's me, Ian!*"

I didn't expect him to take me seriously, but he did exactly what I suggested.

"Ian!" I hissed. "Well, I think it's safe to say our cover's blown."

But at Ian's words, the man froze. His fishing rod dropped into the river and was swept away by the current.

"Do you think he saw us?" Ian asked.

Ian's question was answered when the man began to make his way toward us. When he got close enough that I could see his face, I gasped. Short, sandy hair. Freckles scattered across his nose from being out in the sun. Like Aaron Ward, he was easy to recognize from my vision— the same, but older.

Like us . . . but older.

He regarded Ian with a mix of fascination, wonder—and caution. Like Aaron, he, too, seemed on edge at the mention of something that could tie him to the Rogues.

He opened his mouth, then closed it again.

"Ian?"

"Dad." Now that we were here, face-to-face with him, Ian seemed unsure of what to say. For a minute, the two men stood there, silently, regarding each other.

And then in a flash, they embraced each other tightly.

"Son," said James, his voice cracking slightly. "How did

you—did your mother—what do you—"

"Know?" Ian asked. "Everything, Dad. I know every-thing."

"I wanted to tell you," James whispered into his ear. "But I knew I had to protect you. And that meant leaving. When your mom told me to get out, I didn't argue. But I couldn't stay with those Rogues. It was just too hard, and being around that little girl of theirs, well, it reminded me too much of you."

I smiled. I could feel tears springing to my own eyes. All this searching, all this waiting, wondering if and when we would find James Harrison—Ian's dad, the third Rogue my parents had gathered together—had paid off in the best possible way.

"That little girl?" Ian said. "She's right here."

James stared at me. "You're Skye?" He turned to Ian. "Mer and Sam's daughter?"

"That's the one." I grinned.

"God, you're so grown-up! Both of you are." He wiped his eye with the back of his hand. He had the same open, earnest energy as Ian, and I couldn't help but immediately like him. "Do you kids have time to stay? Because—" He saw the look in our eyes, and his face fell. "I guess there's a reason why you know all about me now."

Ian looked at me for support, and I nodded.

"There's a lot we have to tell you, Mr. Harrison—er, Sharpe," I said.

"It's James, Skye. I guess it's time I go by James again."

I nodded. "James. Ian and I have to fill you in on what's going on."

We did exactly that.

James didn't seem quite as resistant to the idea of coming back with us as Aaron had—but then, Aaron had reasons to be nervous about his return to River Springs. James had left because of his secret, but now that he didn't have to hide it from his son anymore, he had nothing to fear in returning. His biggest concern was helping us.

And that was how I gathered the whole group back together again—with some new additions, of course. James flew back with us to River Springs, helping me along with boosts of power when I needed it. He decided to stay with us at Aunt Jo's, not quite ready to face Ian's mom, the one person who still didn't know his secret. He, Aunt Jo, and Aaron began to practice combining their powers, preparing for what was to come.

I learned more about the Rogues and the kind of power they harnessed every day. They drew from the Rebels, but as only half angelic, they couldn't harness the full power of the elements. Instead, each Rogue, I learned, had some small spark of talent or skill. Aunt Jo was able to manipulate the earth in small ways, which apparently was the reason she had started running excursions out of Into the Woods Outdoor Co. in the first place. Aaron had some power over the wind and sky. James, as we'd seen in Wyoming, was handy with water. When the three of them combined their powers, they could do some serious damage. One afternoon, they actually forged a river through the field behind our house.

And now that the three of them were back together, we were one step closer to calling a Rogue army.

In the middle of all this, final exams ended. And I didn't go back to school after the very first final I ran out on. Aunt Jo called to tell them I was out due to a family crisis, which wasn't even a lie, and that I would have to take an incomplete. I could finish the credits in summer school. Of course, none of us knew if we would make it till then. But wasn't that kind of the point?

I could see into the future—see flashes and signs of things to come. But my visions only took me so far. I couldn't see how it would end. I didn't know who would win. Just like the dream I'd had over and over, I was hovering on the edge of a great precipice. The biggest, steepest, most challenging ski slope of my life. And I knew that now, the time had come for me to strap on my skis, pull down my goggles, and take the plunge into the unknown.

I couldn't control everything in my life anymore. I had to just let go.

Junior year was almost over—the weirdest, hardest year of my life—and senior year stretched out before us. But while everyone else was preparing for prom and summer vacation, my friends and I prepared for some kind of epic battle. And none of us knew if we would survive.

We gathered every night during finals week, in the days leading up to prom. Our house was fuller than ever before—and I loved it. It had been me and Aunt Jo, just the two of us, for so long. But now, I didn't ever want to go back to those cold winter days where the house was empty and I stared out my window at the moon, alone. I wanted a full house, and everything that came with it.

My mind kept coming back to Earth. She had become like a sister to me, and I still had a persistent, lingering feeling that she was the fourth Rogue in my mother's original vision. Shadowy, hard to see, because she hadn't been born yet. It made sense. But the idea of having her play such a crucial role in all this made me ache. She was just a little kid. How could I throw her in harm's way? How could I take her into battle with me?

Our parents had tried to protect us, too. They hid the truth from us all our lives. But we found our way to it anyway.

I couldn't put it off any longer. I had to ask my mom. One last piece of advice, before it was time to put the past behind me and face the future on my own.

I had one loop of the key left. One more question.

So one night, while Aunt Jo and Aaron took Earth upstairs for a private talk (no doubt to explain the full extent of what was about to take place), and Cassie and Dan went over their color coordination for the zillionth time, and Ian and his dad caught up, and Raven snuck off for some much needed alone time—I went upstairs and took the wooden box from my sock drawer. As I asked my mother one last question, the final loop glowed brightly.

"Who is the fourth Rogue you were never able to see?"

It glowed even brighter, searing the wood until all four swooping arcs of the engraved clover burst into flames that illuminated the darkness.

I heard my mother's voice answer:

My little clover.

Four leaves.

I had to protect you. You weren't ready yet. Wait. Was she talking about Earth or—

You are the key to all this.

Four intertwined loops.

It was the last thing I expected to hear, but it had been in her letter from the beginning. The clues had been there all along.

The fourth—was me.

The fire went out. The key had disappeared. And the box was sealed forever.

I had the answers now.

22

"Okay, everyone, listen up! Skye's about to speak! We are now entering . . . planning mode." Cassie beamed at me. "Take it away, Skye."

"Thanks, Cassie," I said, stepping before the group. Raven sat on a kitchen stool to my right, and Ian on one to my left. Dan sat cross-legged on the tile countertop of the island, and Cassie leaned back in his arms. James, Aaron, and Aunt Jo sat in chairs around the kitchen table. Aunt Jo had Earth in her lap.

Earth watched me with a grave expression. I guessed Aunt Jo and Aaron had talked to her about the battle, because she looked like she was taking the whole thing very seriously. I could almost see the cogs and wheels in her head turning.

"Here's what's going on," I said. It was so funny—I used to hate being the center of attention. That was Cassie's obsession, not mine. I loathed the "surprise" parties my friends threw for me every year, and whenever I was in a big crowd, I longed to escape for fresh air. That was how I met Asher.

But somehow, I'd become used to commanding the attention of a room. It wasn't so bad, really, once you got past all the eyes boring into you.

"All of you—every last one—have helped lead us to this moment. We all know that tension between the Order and the Rebellion has been brewing for a long time. What once began as an ancient rivalry over fate versus free will has now become a battle—over me and my powers.

"The Rebellion has been waging a war against you guys—my friends and family—the people I love most in this world, with their power over the elements. "The Order has been trying to manipulate my life, my mind— to make me question what I now know I'd be stupid to believe. That I am alone and always will be. That those I love will only leave me. That you all might not stick this out, that you would abandon me to fight the final battle on my own. An impossible task, one I definitely wouldn't survive." I looked around the room at the faces of my friends and family. "Cassie, you've almost died for me, twice. I know you have a flair for the dramatic—but even you know that's a little much. You could have left me so many times, found a new best friend, stayed safe. But you didn't."

Cassie's face flushed, and she beamed at me.

"Please," she said with mock humility. "High school would be so boring without you."

"Dan," I continued. "I know you'd rather be a track sensation and a Mysterious Ellipses groupie—but you stuck by me when I needed you. You're a true friend."

"I wouldn't say groupie, exactly," Dan muttered as Cassie patted his knee.

"Ian, you could have bolted the minute you realized that you played a bigger role in this than you'd ever imagined, or were prepared for. But I need you. We need each other. We're supposed to do this together . . . and, well, I've never gotten to use this excuse before, but my mother said so."

"It brought me back together with my dad," he said. "That alone is worth it. Besides"—he turned pink under his freckles—"you know I can't say no to you."

"Raven." I sought out her ice-blue eyes. "You were an enemy, but now I trust you with my life. I couldn't have done any of this without you."

Raven shrugged. "Don't let this go to your head, Skye," she said. "But saving your life may have been the best thing I've ever done."

"*May have been?*"

"Hey there, Miss Ego," Raven snapped. "I've done quite a few things I'm proud of!"

"Aaron, James," I continued, shaking her off. "You didn't have to come back to River Springs. You didn't have to confront your difficult past. But you did, and with your help, we actually stand a chance at changing the entire course of destiny. Thank you."

Aaron huffed in response, and James slapped him on the back with an enthusiastic grin.

"Earth," I said. "I think you and I were supposed to find each other. Earth and Skye. We balance each other out in so many ways. You're the little sister I always wanted. The freakishly smart one who can show me messages in the stars."

Earth giggled. "Thank Milo!" she said.

"And Milo! Our attack dog, of course. Thank you, Milo." Milo yawned and rolled onto his back.

There was only one person left to thank. My eyes found Aunt Jo's. There was so much I wanted to thank her for. But when the time came to speak, I didn't know what to say or how to say it. "I love you," I whispered.

"I love you, too, Hurricane," she answered, her own voice cracking.

I took a deep breath.

"We've all spent a lot of time in our lives protecting each other in one way or another. We've helped each other get this far. What Astaroth said was my greatest weakness has actually been what's made us so strong. Love. It may be known as the great destroyer of worlds, but I'd rather believe that more often than not it brings them together. We have the opportunity to free our world from forces that have oppressed us for too long. And I say—let's do this."

A huge cheer echoed across the kitchen. I smiled grimly.

"This battle is going to take place on prom night, and I know we're all ready to face it. There's just one last thing I can't figure out. I've seen myself fighting on a beach."

"A beach?" Aunt Jo's eyes went wide. "Like a lake?"

"An ocean," I said. "With cliffs jutting up on one side. And I have no idea where it is, or how to get there. Only that that's where I end up." I looked at Ian. "That's where *we* end up."

The room fell silent with thought. Then Raven opened her mouth.

"I know how you get there."

We all turned to look at her. "You do? How?"

"I mean, it's obvious, isn't it? Do you remember the night, Skye, when Cassie was in the hospital—"

"Hey . . ." said Cassie. "Where are you going with this?"

"—and you and I had a little, let's call it a polite disagreement—"

"I can think of a few other things to call it," I said.

"—outside in the parking lot? You were overtaken by a vision. Do you remember?"

"Actually, yes," I said. "It was all white and misty, and—"

"It wasn't just a vision. Skye, you *went somewhere*."

"I—what?"

"You disappeared. You weren't on the ground in the parking lot anymore. That's why I freaked out and told Astaroth. That was the moment we knew you were even more of a threat than we thought you were. If you could transport yourself to the places you envisioned—what was to stop you from getting into the Order's realm?"

"So you're saying if I can make myself have a vision of this beach at prom, I'll be able to get there?"

"Well, no. There's no way I could know that for sure. I'm not the one with visions of the future. What I *am* saying," Raven said, "is that it's worth a shot. I mean, I don't see us all lining up with options, right?"

"She has a point," said Ian.

Raven nodded. "Look at it this way. I may be a bitch sometimes, but at least you never have to wonder if I'm telling the truth."

I couldn't argue with that.

"But once we're at prom," said Ian, "how do we know it's time to leave?"

"I'll tell you," Earth piped up.

"Earth." Aaron's face had turned red. "This is serious."

"I know," she said. "The sky will tell me." She winked at me, and I grinned.

"Okay," I said. "So our plan is this. We go to prom. Earth watches the sky for a sign. And then . . . I make myself envision this beach. If I succeed, I take the Rogues with me. When we get there, Aunt Jo, Aaron, and James—form the circle. And"—I paused—"leave room for me. Because I'm the fourth Rogue."

"Skye," Aunt Jo said. "How did you figure that out . . . ?"

I smiled enigmatically. "Let's just say I had some help."

"Wait a minute," Cassie pouted. "Dan and I don't get to come?"

"You seriously think I'm taking you with me? I've almost gotten you killed, twice. There's no way I could live with myself if it happened a third time. Besides," I said. "Some-one has to watch Earth."

"I don't need to be watched," Earth piped up. "I am *almost* in third grade. I'm not a little kid anymore."

"Good point, Earth," I said, kneeling by her. "You're more grown up than half the people I know."

"True story," said Dan.

"But you're so special that I need someone whose *only* job in this whole world is to keep an eye on you. To make sure you're safe so that when we get back, you and I? We can have a day of fun, just the two of us."

Earth looked up at me, smiling devilishly. "You mean like a sister day?"

I patted her on the head. "We can work out the seman-tics when we cross that bridge, Trouble." Aunt Jo and Aaron had turned red, but they were grinning.

This instinct I had to protect Earth made me think of my parents. My mother and father's mission had failed because they would sooner let that happen than put me in danger. They knew that I would be the one to complete the circle, and they took that secret to the grave to pro-tect me. It was what I'd worried about with Earth. And what Ian's dad had worried about with him. We all tried to protect the ones we loved. But we couldn't do it forever.

Eventually we had to let them go. So they could fight their own battles.

I wasn't a little kid anymore, and I had to face the future, no matter what it held.

23

Clouds obscured the moon that night, shrouding my room in darkness. I lay in bed for hours, but I couldn't sleep. Earth tossed and turned in her sleeping bag, and the house seemed to creak and groan more than usual. I had a feeling I wasn't the only one having trouble quieting their mind.

Everything was in place for prom—but it wasn't the battle I was thinking about. Weirdly, it was something Ian had said. *I guess now would be an inappropriate time to ask you to prom, huh?*

If I went to prom at all, I always pictured myself going with Asher. But the next time I saw him, we were going to be fighting against each other. I never thought it would get this far.

Before I knew it, dawn was casting its wide net of light across my room.

There was a knock at my window.

At first I thought I was dreaming. Earth turned over and mumbled something in her sleep. I pulled my jersey comforter up over my head to block out the light and the noise, and burrowed under the covers. I only had a few hours left before everyone else in the house woke up. And the day of the battle would begin.

Then I heard it again, and my heart leaped into my throat. Because there was only one person I could think of who ever appeared at my window like that.

An inky black feather danced across the floorboards. . . .

I threw the covers back and vaulted out of bed. I didn't care that I was in boxers and my old River Springs Community College sweatshirt that was faded and pilled and had holes in the wrists from sticking my thumbs through. I didn't care that my hair was a mess, and my eyes were bleary and red from lack of sleep, or that I wasn't wearing any makeup. I had been waiting for this. He had come back. Maybe we wouldn't have to fight against each other after all.

Maybe, finally, this was all over.

I flung the window open wide, and let the spring air rush into my lungs. I couldn't wait to see his face, to feel his hands on my cheeks, his thumb brush across the freckles on the bridge of my nose. I couldn't wait to see his devious grin.

But the face that met me was kissed by the sun, his hair golden and his eyes serious. He wasn't grinning. Because it wasn't Asher.

It was Devin.

I must have looked confused, because he smiled sheepishly. "You were expecting someone else." It wasn't a question. I was too baffled to even respond. I half expected him to offer me a hand to pull me up to the roof, like Asher always did, but instead he said, "May I come in?"

"What are you doing here?" I demanded. "Shouldn't you be with the Rebels, buffing your swords or whatever?"

"Buffing our swords?"

"You know what I mean. You're consorting with the enemy. The half-asleep enemy."

"Um."

"Sorry," I muttered. "I haven't had my coffee yet." Devin raised his eyebrows. He looked a little bit amused. With a sigh, I stepped aside and motioned for him to climb through the window.

"Look," he said once he had maneuvered his way between Earth's sleeping bag and Cassie's fortress of blankets and pillows. "I know I'm probably the last person you want to see right now. And I don't blame you. But since you left so upset the other night I haven't been able to think about anything else. I told you I would make it up to you. I made a promise to you, a promise I'm going to keep."

"Devin. Slow down. What are you talking about?"

"You told me to put my money where my mouth is. I couldn't stand the thought of us going into battle against each other, and you thinking I'm some horrible monster."

"Aren't you?"

"Do you know why you never felt the coldness or the emptiness when you were with me, before—only the good feelings? Have you figured it out?"

"I . . . I don't know," I stammered.

He looked up at me. Pain flashed in his eyes. Something about it reminded me of Gideon. The darkness behind the crystal blue, the trauma that lingered and tortured him still.

"I found a way to take it away from you."

For a second, I was so shocked I was sure I'd heard him wrong. When I didn't say anything right away, he continued.

"I knew that Gideon was teaching you and that you knew how to tell if you were being influenced. When Astaroth realized that the plan didn't work—that I didn't kill you after all—he commanded me to keep you close, to find a way to win your affection back. I had to find a way to make you want to spend time with me, to trust me, when I knew you didn't. Skye, I know this is going to sound weird, but if they hadn't forced me to, I don't know if I ever would have spoken to you again."

"It's not weird," I said, shaking my head. "I'm . . . I'm grateful for it."

His mouth twisted in a painful smile. "I found a way to do it without you knowing. But it meant I had to sacrifice something for you. I was able to pull away your emptiness, to take it out of you, so all you felt when you were with me was good. *I'm* the one who felt cold and empty. I took your pain as my own. And you never knew."

All I could do was stand there quietly, letting his words sink in. Earth turned over in her sleeping bag, and Cassie snored loudly.

"Can I ask you something?" I said finally. "The early days? The ones before you—" I paused, and he nodded uncomfortably before I had to say more. "Everything between us then—that was all real?"

"Every minute of it," he said. "But so much has happened since then. I know those moments are lost now, forever."

My eyes began to fill with unexplainable tears.

"I know," I said. "It wasn't always easy, but—I'll always keep those memories someplace safe." He had been looking at the ground, but now he looked up at me. Those blue eyes of his always had a way of piercing right to my heart. When our eyes met, I knew it was true. I would always hold them close.

"So will I," he said.

"I guess I'll see you next in battle."

"What?" He frowned. "Skye, I'm here because I'm leaving the Rebellion."

"Where are you going?" I gasped. "You mean you're not going to fight?"

"Oh, I'm still going to fight. But I'm going to fight with you."

For a second, I was sure I hadn't heard him right. But as the words sunk in, I thought I understood.

"You really are a Rebel now, aren't you?"

"It would appear so, yes." He grinned at me, almost shyly. His eyes were so impossibly blue. "Who'd have thought that I would finally become a real rebel, just as I'm leaving them?"

The floorboards creaked behind me, and Devin looked up sharply. I whipped around to see Raven, hovering in the doorway.

"Devin?" she said softly, standing there self-consciously in her borrowed T-shirt and pajama pants. Her lower lip trembled. When I turned back around to Devin, his eyes looked glassy.

"Hey," he said. He moved toward her quickly and they stood facing each other.

"You came."

"I had to. Raven, I—I've been so confused. I didn't know what love, real love, was until I jumped from the Order. For so long, I confused love and longing. For what I couldn't have. And who I couldn't be. But Skye was right—I didn't know what it meant to love, not really. I thought it was winning. But love is falling, isn't it? It's giving up what you've fought so hard to control—and being okay with that. Since being free, I've realized something, Raven. We're a team. We always have been. And I—I need you." She crossed her arms and snorted. "I know, you probably never want to see me again after what I did to you," Devin continued. "But if there's a chance . . . even a small one . . ."

Raven looked up at him, a bewildered expression on her face.

"What do you want, Devin?" she asked.

"We were forced together by fate. But somewhere along the way, I fell for you, Raven. I want to be able to choose you."

She put her hand on her hip.

"Do you mean it?"

Devin's eyes lit up and a smile tugged tentatively at his lips.

"Do you forgive me?"

She opened her mouth to argue, but suddenly seemed to change her mind. Instead, she grabbed his face and pulled him toward her, and he wove his fingers through her glossy blond hair, and they kissed. And when they pulled away, they were both smiling.

"I'll think about it," Raven said. "But only because we're about to go to war."

My heart filled with an ache I couldn't control. It was both happy and sad, full of contentment and a deep, gaping emptiness. *Love doesn't have to destroy worlds. It can bring them together.*

Something tugged at my sweatshirt, and I looked down to see a pair of messy brown pigtails. And then, Earth's innocent face tilted up at me.

"You don't have to wait for him," she said.

"Wait for Devin? I think it's safe to say that's over, Earth."

She rolled her eyes at me. "Not *him.* Asher. You don't have to wait for him to come back."

That sounded familiar. Hadn't Aunt Jo said almost the exact same thing?

Remember what I said, Skye? About following your own star? You don't have to wait for him.

I'd thought she'd been telling me to forget about Asher, to move on with my life. But now I understood that she had meant the exact opposite. She was telling me to go get him. Devin had done it, even though the odds were stacked against him. Couldn't I? There was a chance that Asher had turned, that he believed in the Rebellion more than he believed in us. There was a chance that he had hurt me and that he might do it again.

But if there was a chance for us—even a small one—it was a chance I had to take.

And suddenly, I couldn't stand there another second. I could make my own destiny.

"Devin." It was painful for me to say it. "I need your help. One last thing, while you're still kind of a Rebel."

"Of course," he said. "Anything."

I took a deep breath. I didn't know what was coming. I didn't know if the past was real or what the future held. But right then, in my heart, I knew what I needed to do.

I needed to find him. I needed to fight for him. In the time I had left, I had to show him how much I cared.

I needed to prove it.

"Help me find Asher."

Devin and Raven looked at each other and squeezed hands. Then Devin turned to me and grinned.

"Let's go get him, Skye," he said.

•24•

"We stood together in the middle of the field. "The way to find a Rebel," Devin said, "is to follow your heart."

I paused, waiting for more. "Like, literally?"

"Yes. Rebels are guided by emotion, so the way into the Rebel realm is different for each person. You're tied to it by what's meaningful for you. And what's meaningful to you is Asher."

"Uh, I don't get it." Once again, we had fallen back into our same old roles as student and teacher. I grinned at Devin, to see if he remembered, and surprisingly, he grinned back.

"You have to follow a treasure map of all the places that mean something to you. The places you made special, because you were there together and for no other reason. You have to retrace the story of you and Asher. From beginning to end."

"That's practical," I said.

"Well, it's the Rebellion. They're a faction that was founded on the guiding principle that you should let emotion guide your decisions."

Because war forces you to make choices. And so does love. Maybe Ardith had it right all along when she said, *Love can drive an angel mad.*

We should have listened to her then, but it was too late now. And if I could go back to the beginning, to the night I'd turned seventeen, I'd make all the same choices. I'd fall in love with Asher all over again.

My heart was pounding out a manic rhythm in my chest. It vibrated through me, thrumming in my bones.

"Okay," I said. "Okay. The very first time I saw Asher was on the night of my seventeenth birthday party. I went outside to get some air, and there he was." I smiled to myself. "Standing in the shadows."

Devin grabbed my hand.

"What are you—"

"Just trust me," he said.

Flash, we were standing outside of Love the Bean,

shielding our eyes against the morning sun. I looked questioningly at Devin.

"You have to picture it. Bring yourself back."

"Okay," I said, closing my eyes. I let myself remember. "It was night . . ."

He stepped into the light.

Our eyes met, and something in the way he looked at me made me pause. The blackness of his eyes was magnetic, and something strange flickered through my own in response. I had the weirdest feeling of déjà vu.

It was dark where we stood on the street, but what moonlight there was shone on his face, exaggerating the definition of his cheekbones and illuminating his smooth olive skin. His short hair was so black that it was hard to tell where he ended and the night began. "You're Skye, right?"

"I remember everything about it," I said to Devin, still with my eyes shut. "It was the night that changed my life."

"So do you make a habit of ducking out of your own parties?" Asher asked.

"Only when they're thrown for me against my will. Do you make a habit of lurking outside of other people's parties?" I shot back.

"Without question." He grinned, showing off an adorable dimple. "You never know who you'll meet."

"This isn't the place," I said suddenly, opening my eyes.

Devin studied me. "No?"

"No. This is only where we met. It's only the beginning. I wasn't in love with him, here." I paused, thinking about it. "It's only a memory."

"Okay then." Devin grabbed my hand again.

Flash, we were on the front steps of school. I closed my eyes, and thought back to that morning. . . .

"I'm Asher."

He held out a hand. I eyed him suspiciously. Slowly I reached my hand out as well. He met me halfway. When our hands touched, a tiny wave of goose bumps trailed up my arm. I quickly pulled away.

My eyes shot open. "Not here," I said, beginning to feel the urgency.

"Ready to try the next place?" Devin asked.

"Yes, I'm ready."

Flash, my fingers and toes were freezing, numb, and I was surrounded by iridescent ice. We had fallen beneath the snow in the side of the mountain. We were in the ice cave.

I could feel his chest against my back, his breath trace across my neck.

"Don't freak out."

I stared at our hands, resting on top of each other. How could I possibly feel more freaked out than I already was?

And then.

A small flame bloomed between my palms.

I was holding fire in the palm of my hand.

Slowly, I opened my eyes to face Devin. He looked at me questioningly.

I had realized something. I wasn't just revisiting the story of me and Asher. It was also the story of how I came to be the version of myself who was standing here today, on the edge of a battle whose consequences were unfathomable. I had begun this journey as an uncertain teenager. I was ending it confident in who I was, a powerful angel ready to face my future.

Devin grabbed my hand.

Flash, the spring breeze skirted around us. There were mountains as far as the eye could see, and below us, the field where we'd spent so many days after school, practicing. We were on my roof.

I held my arms steady on either side for balance. Asher and I had sat up here together, looked out across an inky velvet sky, scattered with stars, as we watched our breath plume out into the bitter cold night. Now, I stared out at the early summer sky.

"Come on," I challenged. "What are you, afraid of heights?" I kept climbing.

Soon I crested the roof ledge and crawled several feet across the sloping surface. Asher was right behind me. I pulled my knees to my chest and stared out at the stars. He sat down next to me. Our breath made clouds of steam in the freezing night air.

"Is that where angels are from?" I nodded at the stars.

He chuckled. "Nah. It's really more of an alternate realm than a city in the sky. I've never even been there." He looked up. "Anyway, the Rebellion camp is somewhere else."

"Where?"

He looked pensive. "On earth, actually."

"Where?" I asked.

"Far, far away."

"This isn't it," I said, opening my eyes and turning to Devin. The sun was rising high in the sky, and I knew we didn't have much time. Prom was that night—and I had to find Asher first. "I know where we have to go next. The closest I've ever been to my angelic history. The place where I learned about the Uprising, and my parents, and the Rogues—and who I was destined to become. It was also the place where everything changed between me and Asher."

The sun reached the very center of the sky, a golden orb. It held hope for the future, but it also held a reminder that there are some things you can never escape, no matter how hard you try. Your past is what makes you who you are—no matter what your future holds.

"Where?" Devin asked.

"The cabin."

Flash.

The woods around the cabin were silent and still, save for the chirping of a few birds, the rustling of the breeze in the dry, cracking branches of the trees. The cabin was there, just as we'd left it.

The weathered wooden door swung open easily when I pushed it. I stood there, in the threshold, but something kept me from going inside. We must have left a window open, somewhere in the house, when we left. The cool mountain air blew through it, creaking across the stairs like a ghost.

In some ways, the house was filled with ghosts. This was where the Uprising began, but it wouldn't be where it ended. We'd moved so far beyond it.

The past didn't have to be my future.

Devin held the door open for me, and we walked inside.

I closed my eyes and remembered it like it was yesterday.

Snuggled into Asher on the threadbare couch, while a fire that we'd lit using our powers crackled reassuringly in the hearth.

"I missed you so much," Asher whispered into my hair, stopping my thoughts. "I thought I was going to lose you."

I brought my hand up to his face and smoothed a stray hair. "But you didn't," I said. "I'm here. I'm yours."

He took my hand in his. "Can I . . . can I ask you something?" His voice shook slightly.

"Of course," I said. "Anything."

He paused and took a breath. "Join the Rebellion," he said. His voice was barely a whisper. "We'll fight the Order side by side. Whatever's coming, we'll face it together. We'll be unstoppable. Fierce."

I opened my eyes and looked around the room. Everything was where we had left it, the morning my friends and I left to start our own faction. The spring breeze blew through the open window, a reminder that the window was still open, and I went to close it. I glanced outside, remembered walking with Asher in the snow, an orb of fire to guide us through the Rebellion's elemental charms, the snow and the fog. It was out there beyond the cabin that he'd first asked if he could show me something special to him, that he took me to see—

I turned so suddenly to Devin that his eyes grew panicked.

"What?" he said. "What is it?"

"The waterfall. We have to go to the waterfall. That's it. That's the place where I'll find Asher. I know it."

"Where is it?" Devin asked slowly, as if he could sense that this last place was different from all the others.

"I—I don't know."

On earth, actually. Far, far away.

Asher had deliberately not told me where. He thought I might go looking for it. Well, he was right. That's what I was about to do.

On earth—but where? Someplace hidden away from human eyes, someplace special and powerful. A small corner carved out of the natural world, humming with magic. I just had to follow my heart.

"Can I just show you one thing?"

"Of course," I said.

We were at the top of a huge cliff. Water spilled down over the side in huge, driving waves, pounding into a whirlpool below.

"Do you like it?" Asher asked.

I squeezed his hand. "You made this for me?"

"I made it because I didn't know what to do with myself."

I tried to remember how we'd gotten there. We were inside, on the couch, and then he asked if he could show me something. And then suddenly, there was this cold mist, and we were standing on a cliff overlooking the waterfall. I'd thought it was in these woods, but now I realized exactly where he'd taken me. He showed me something only he could reveal, that was accessible only through the depths of my emotions for Asher. A place that exists in the placeless, and a time in the timeless.

"The Rebellion camp," I said out loud.

"So follow your heart," Devin urged me. "That's the only way." He took my hand. "I'll be there with you."

There was something I wasn't remembering. My heart sank as Ardith's words from the first time I woke up in the cabin flooded my brain.

"If she does wake up, her powers will be much too unstable. They'll collide with so much chaos. It could destroy us. Or her."

"Devin," I said. "It's not safe for me to go there. My powers mixed with the Rebel chaos—it's too volatile."

He shook his head. "You're more controlled now. You can do this."

"Wait." Panic began to rise up in my throat. "What if I'm not? What if it kills me?"

Devin looked at me sternly. I should have known that as a teacher, he never took no for an answer. "If you can't do this," he said sharply, "then you're certainly not ready to fight a war." His blue eyes sparkled. "Now." Daring me to be great. "Are you ready?"

I had lived for so long by staying in perfect control, keeping my feelings in check, closing myself off, not allowing myself to fall. And my life was planned down to the smallest detail. I knew exactly where I wanted to go to college, and what I needed to do to get myself there. Everything was perfect. But in perfection, I didn't feel alive. The only time I truly felt my blood pulsing through my veins was the time I spent on the slopes with the wind in my hair.

That was true, anyway, until I realized who I really was.

Until the first time I kissed Asher.

Now, I knew how it felt to let someone in, to really live. The only way to do that was exactly what I'd been avoiding—to fall and let it happen. I had to find him, and then, I had to let go of everything that held me back. This was one thing I couldn't control.

Astaroth said that love was my weakness. It would get me killed.

If I had to choose between love and life, I knew I would

choose love. I would choose love every time, even if it killed me. If it meant finding a way to be with Asher again.

I slipped my hand into Devin's. "I'm ready," I said.

25

The wind picked up around us, whipping my hair into my face. I could feel the sun grow brighter, hotter, and the scent of pine trees grow so strong, so intense, that I felt almost faint from the overwhelming sharpness of it.

"What's happening?" I whispered out loud.

It was blinding, sweltering, and I was dizzy, weakening, falling to my knees.

And then suddenly everything was still. The air was cool and dry. The scent of pine gave way to something earthy: rocks and dirt and sand.

I opened my eyes.

I was in the desert. The air was arid, the sky a faded violet, as if the sun had just finished setting but was still throwing off light from below. The moon rose in the distance. A coyote howled somewhere, far away or very close by. It was impossible to tell. For a second, I felt an intense pang of vertigo, and the desert pitched before me. The rocks turned to sand, and then rocks again. The plants sprouted shoots, bloomed, and withered, went through an entire life cycle all in the span of seconds.

The landscape was changing before my eyes, every second—all I had to do was blink.

Where am I? I breathed deeply, trying to catch my balance. My blood felt slow and fast at the same time, cold and hot. I put a hand to my neck. My skin was feverish but cool, slick with sweat but dry.

As I stood there, the night sky fell around me like a veil, dark and velvety. Stars scattered across the dome of space, cosmic glitter.

I took it all in. *It was late afternoon just minutes ago. Time moves differently here.*

As I walked, signs of the desert materialized around me. Sand dusted up beneath my feet, scattering on the wind. Fuchsia night blooms opened like secrets. Invisible insects chirped and whirred. A snake uncoiled from underneath the low, dry brush, rattling its tail at us as we passed.

I reached a spot where a syringa tree twisted up from

the earth before my eyes, roots churning and rolling, and just past it, a flat, smooth rock stretched out under the night sky. I looked up at the blanket of stars.

"You made it," Devin whispered beside me. "Welcome to the Rebellion. A pocket of time and space that's folded in on itself. Ever-changing, ever-evolving—pure chaos. Impossible to describe, or pin down on a map." He looked around, as if he'd been a Rebel all his life. "Impressive, isn't it?"

The darkness in me began to stir, the chaos outside me pulled at the chaos within. I felt strange and lightheaded.

"I don't care," I said. "I just have to find him."

Silver liquid thrummed through me, fast and light, then slow and thick, then quick again. The night air around us rustled, and suddenly I felt my wings burst from my back, catching the moonlight in folds of silvery feathers and throwing it onto the sand before us.

Something was changing. Tiny pinpricks of light winked across the nightscape, growing bigger as the light shifted. Despite the desert heat, a chill ran through me as I realized something. They weren't growing bigger. They were getting *closer*.

I covered my head and ducked as meteors hurtled down around us, the rushing of burning rocks almost unbearable in my ears. Amid the flashes of light and dust and fire and rocks I shielded my face. I faltered.

Trust yourself.

It was so much easier said than done. But if I was going to find Asher, if I was going to keep my friends safe and my mind calm and clear, if I was going to be a leader, I had to trust myself.

And so, I looked up again at the sky, shielding my eyes from the falling debris. The silver flowed through me, pulsing, alive. It had a mind of its own, as if the energy around me was controlling my powers. I closed my eyes and tried to harness it somehow, to keep the power at bay.

I thought of Asher. The two of us in the mountains, causing the rain to fall hard, wash away the fiery trees.

Asher reaching for my hand.

Asher's fingers on my neck.

His voice whispering to me. "You got this, Skye."

Something shifted within me, and I opened my eyes. The fiery rocks were floating in midair. They glowed like burning coal against the backdrop of the night, as if lit from within. A fine gold dust sparkled in the air around us. Fireflies ducked and twinkled between the embers.

It was beautiful. A beautiful dark. A dangerous night.

Devin stared at me. "That was amazing," he said. "You're

more powerful, more controlled than I've ever seen you."

I grinned. "I've been practicing." But even as I said it, dizziness pushed at my temples and the backs of my eyes. No matter how in control I was of my own powers, I could still feel them colliding with the chaos in the air of the Rebellion. I couldn't stay here—I had to find Asher and leave.

Devin seemed to feel it, too. "We have to hurry," he said gravely.

The landscape changed again even as we stood there, pitching me into another wave of dizziness. The desert sands gave way to the tall, pale grass of an alpine field, ghostly against the backdrop of night. The moon was high and bright above us.

"I feel so strange," I said as the alpine grass morphed into a desert oasis, and then into the slick black rocks of the Mediterranean coast. The air had an energy to it; it seemed to vibrate with change. "So dizzy." A great pressure was pushing down against my lungs. Breath came fast and shallow, almost not at all.

Amorphous shapes moved past me in a blur, nothing I could describe or define. The manifestation of pure chaos. I realized with a start that the blurred shapes were the Rebels. Something Asher had told me back when I'd first learned the truth about who I was came rushing back to me.

When we're on earth, we take on human form, human desires, human needs.

Could it be that when he appeared to me, he appeared the way he did on purpose? Because I was a seventeen-year-old girl? But when I was gone, was he just a blurred shape like the rest of them, moving so fast that it was impossible to pick him out from the crowd? Was he near me right now, and I just couldn't tell? I couldn't understand how anyone could live like this—it would drive any sane person mad. *But they're not people*, I reminded myself. No matter how much they seemed like it when they were around me.

Colors and shapes swished past on either side of me. I kept my eyes on the constantly moving ground. The dirt beneath me writhed with growing roots, twisting out of the earth, shooting up into plants and trees, green stems and massive trunks. Branches spindled out, wilting, dying. Struggling to keep my footing, I looked up, hoping the sky would be a constant. But the sky, too, shifted and moved.

My head was spinning. It was too much. It made me ache for home, for the clean mountain air. I couldn't stand it anymore.

"Asher!" I called. My voice echoed across the unbound sky.

"What are you doing?" Devin grabbed my arm.

"He can hear me, I know he can. Asher!"

"That's not the point! It's dangerous to yell like that. Your powers are colliding with the chaos. You won't make it."

"Asher!" I yelled again. I didn't care. I had to find him, and time was running out.

"If the Rebels hear you, they'll come. Skye, listen to me. It's not safe."

"I don't care about safe." I ripped my arm away. "We came this far. I have to try." I called his name just one more time.

The ground beneath us began to shake. But instead of the rumbling beginning in the ground, moving up through the bottoms of my feet and through my bones, somehow it worked in reverse. The great movement began in me. I could feel it in my heart, pumping out like blood, radiating from my fingertips and toes down into the earth itself, where it spread through the ground, traveling through roots, shaking the trees. The air itself was humming.

"Skye," Devin yelled. "What did you *do*?"

A cold, wet mist moved in between us, so heavy that I couldn't see more than a few inches in front of me. Devin had disappeared completely.

"Skye! Where are you? Are you okay?" The frantic note

in his voice was clear. He was afraid my powers were com-
busting, consuming me in a swirl of mist. He thought I
was dying.

I wish I could have called to him to tell him I wasn't, but
even I wasn't totally sure. What *was* happening? And just
as I was about to shout his name, the mist began to clear,
and I knew exactly where I was.

I stood on a rocky path, slick with moisture. My breath
came in short, uneven gasps. My heart was pounding.
Water crashed in my ears. And when I looked up, I saw it.
The waterfall.

It stretched before me, looming up into the clouds. I
began to climb the path that curved around the side, to
the top. With each step, my lungs burned, and my vision
swam. But I kept myself focused.

Finally the path opened up onto the flat expanse of rock.
It was higher up than I remembered. Too high for trees
to grow. Too rocky for grass. The mist was so dense that
I could see actual droplets of water suspended in the air.
And then, as I let out the breath I'd been holding in, the
tiny droplets of water pulled back like a curtain, and I
saw him standing with his back to me, facing out over the
waterfall.

His wild dark hair was curling up from the mist, and

he was hunched over, hands shoved deep into his jacket pockets.

My heart leaped at the sight of him. He was in human form—maybe he wanted to be found. I took a deep breath. "Planning on jumping?"

He whipped around. His eyes grew in surprise.

Time seemed to stop, just for that one moment. The water stopped rushing. The earth stopped spinning. And all I could hear was the sound of my own heartbeat. *Please*, I thought. *Just smile.*

And then, he broke into a wide, wicked grin, like all his life he had been waiting for this one moment.

I wasn't in control anymore, didn't stop to think about what I was doing or where I was. Something inside of me took over. And I ran to him.

He reached out his arms to catch me, and I struggled to keep my footing on the slippery rocks. But the minute my sneaker hit a wet patch, I knew it was all over. I grasped his arms and pulled him with me.

And suddenly we were falling sideways with nothing but air beneath us and rolling clouds in the sky above.

We unfurled our wings at the same time. The massive feathers caught the air, and we clung to each other as we plummeted toward the waves crashing against the rocks below. We went under, plunging through the surface of the freezing water. I felt it go up my nose and burn my lungs. Asher's grip tightened around my arms. We burst through the surface at the same time, both of us gasping.

For what felt like a whole minute we just stood there, staring at each other. I couldn't believe I was standing there with him, the whirlpool of our waterfall rushing in rivulets around us. I coughed and pushed my soaking hair out of my face. The water slicked his short hair in all directions, and he wiped his eyes. They were as dark, as bottomless as I remembered them, brimming over with so much emotion that I couldn't hold myself back anymore. I burst into tears, the hot saltwater running down my cheeks and mixing with the freezing freshwater, and he was crying too, and then we were both laughing.

"I wasn't actually going to jump, you know." Asher grinned.

"Shhh." I put my finger to his lips. "No jokes. Just for a second. Until I understand." Asher opened his mouth in protest, but I stopped him. "Please."

He nodded.

"Astaroth said you'd turned your back on me, were fighting against me. But it isn't true, is it? I—I believe in you. In *us*. I'm so sorry I pushed you away. I didn't know how much I believed until now." I struggled to catch my breath. He just stood there, watching me. "Feel free to jump in anytime."

"Actually, I kind of like seeing you squirm a little." He winked.

"Asher!" I hit him in the arm—hard.

"Ow! Hey! I thought you believed in us! This doesn't feel like believing."

"Then just answer me this, okay? The fire? The flood? I saw you there. What were you doing?"

His eyes grew serious. "You saw me, huh?"

"You know I did."

He sighed and raked his hair back from his face.

"Look, Skye," he began. "I went back to the Rebellion out of duty and loyalty. And—this is hard to admit, okay?—once I was there, you were all I could think about. I had to find a way to keep you safe, to end this. I realized something. Ardith and Gideon, they're only loyal to the Rebellion because they're loyal to each *other*. They're fighting for revenge out of love, not ideology. I don't have anything like that tying me to the Rebels." His dark eyes met mine. "Not since you left."

I held his gaze, my heart beating faster. "So what are you saying, exactly?"

"I'm saying," he said, breaking out into an adorable grin, "that . . ." He took my face in both his hands. "In a shocking turn of events, I've been rebelling against the Rebellion."

I stared. "You . . . *what*?"

"I've been trying to bridge communication with the Guardians, to make peace—to help you. But neither side would listen, they only ramped up their plans to attack. So I had to work in more covert ways. The fire, the flood; all I could do was show up and try to keep the damage from growing however I could with my powers. I kept Aunt Jo from getting engulfed in flames during that fire. I gave you the extra boost of elemental power you needed to part the waters of the river and save Cassie. Only I had to do it in secret, in the shadows—if the Rebellion found out I was helping you, they'd have killed me."

I knew I should say something, but all I could think was, *You didn't betray me.* My mouth hung open. "That—that was you? You did that? For me?"

Suddenly, it all made so much sense. *Of course,* I realized. During the fire at Into the Woods, I'd felt the definite presence of powers at work. And I'd been on the brink of collapse in Foster's Woods during the flood when *something* had given me a surge of energy. Asher hadn't been there to attack me—he'd been there to *help* me. "I knew you wouldn't hurt me." I smiled. "I *knew* it."

"I never could. I was trying so hard to put an end to this, so I could find a way for us to be together. It was just taking a really"—he paused, and took a breath, and grinned at me—"*really* long time. But there *is* no way, Skye. There's no end. The only way to see this through is to fight."

My heart fell. But when I looked up into his eyes, I didn't feel hopeless. Instead, I felt a surge of confidence. "Asher, will you fight with me?"

He slid his arms around my waist and pulled me toward him. Our bodies pressed together, a bloom of heat in the freezing waterfall. "Skye," he said. "My Skye. I wouldn't fight alongside anyone else."

And then he kissed me like I'd never been kissed in my life. As far as I was concerned, all those other kisses were just practice. This was the one that mattered. The first kiss of the rest of my life.

"I can't believe I found you," I shouted above the din of the crashing waterfall.

He smoothed the sopping hair out of my eyes. "I knew we'd find a way." He pulled me to his chest, wrapping his arms around me and tucking the top of my head under his chin. "I love you," he whispered. And even though water crashed in our ears, I heard him perfectly.

"I love you, too," I said fiercely. "I am never letting you go again."

"Why did you the first time?" he asked, raising an eyebrow.

"I got scared."

"You?"

"I was afraid that if I let myself fall for you, I wouldn't be able to stop."

Once the words left my lips, I knew that they were true, and always had been. That was everything I'd felt since turning seventeen, wrapped up in the tiniest of nutshells. Chaos versus control. If I let myself fall, I would keep falling. And what if there was no one to catch me?

Asher cupped his hands under my face gently.

"I wouldn't let you fall alone," he whispered.

But as he said it, my vision swam with light and color and sound and my lungs burned bright and my hands and arms shook violently, and then my legs gave out and I fell into him. The chaos, the emotion—it was too much.

"I—I have to go," I said.

"I'm coming with you." His voice sounded far away. I felt myself going under the water, darkness creeping along the edges of my vision. "Skye!" Asher shook me. "Stay with me! Come on, stay awake. Without you, none of this is worth fighting for."

Light flashed around me. For a brief second, everything went still, and we were back in the snow cave, Asher surrounding me in warmth and light as I was about to pass out from pain. "Asher," I whispered. I knew I sounded delirious. "Will you go with me to prom tonight?"

He laughed. "That's tonight? Hm, I think I have plans but lemme see if I can move some things around."

"Shut up," I mumbled. My tongue was growing heavy in my mouth.

"Shh," he said. He lifted me up in his arms, freezing water streaming from my clothes. I could hardly feel my body anymore.

"If you move any slower, I'm not going to make it to prom, and then you'll have to go by yourself," I said hoarsely. He laughed. The world was spinning into chaos, and I was spinning with it.

"Come on, Skye Parker. Daughter of dark and light. Let's get you home."

He held me in his arms, and the sky grew brighter, too bright, blinding, and I felt myself pass into darkness as he said, "This time I really can save your life. Because you saved mine."

26

ist swirled around us. I opened my eyes, felt the floor beneath us, saw my bed, my dresser, the window that looked out over the mountains. Asher had brought me home. We were kneeling, facing each other. "I'm sorry it took me this long to realize that fighting for you was just as important as fighting for the universe."

He grinned, but his eyes were serious. "I'll always fight for you, Skye," he said. "We'll fight for each other now. No matter what. Promise?"

"Promise."

I smoothed his hair back, and something changed in his eyes. He opened his mouth to speak, but I stopped it with my own.

This time when we kissed I knew it was different. With hands that trembled slightly, he peeled off my soaking wet tank top. My hair got caught, but he laughed and gently untangled it. I slid off his jacket and pulled the faded black T-shirt, still damp, over his head. I pressed myself against the smooth, olive brown skin of his chest, and he traced his fingers up my back. My breath caught, and when I hesitated, he pulled me closer.

"Come here," he whispered. He wrapped his arms around my waist and lowered me gently to the floor, spreading his old army jacket beneath us. "Is this okay?"

I nodded, laughing softly.

"What?" he asked, smiling back. "Tell me what you're thinking."

I took a deep breath. "I was thinking," I said. "That I hope we don't burn the whole house down this time."

"Well," Asher said, that infuriating, mischievous grin spreading across his face. "Damned if that won't stop me from trying."

I laughed. "I think I can control myself now."

"We'll see about that."

And there, in my bedroom, where I'd first caused the heat between us to grow and where we'd played checkers all those months ago with the snow falling softly against the windowpane, there, we found each other's arms, and the heat grew hotter still, and I kissed him, and he kissed me, and we made a promise right then and there never to leave each other's side again. Not in war. Not in peace. Not if we lived or—and we didn't say it outright, but I knew we were both thinking it—if we didn't survive the night. Because I knew he was the one. For the first time in my entire life, as we lay beside each under the darkening, radiant sky, I didn't have to think about it. I just knew.

"Skye! Come on, let's go, we're going to be late!"

I pinned a tiny purple flower in my hair and took a step back to stare at myself in the full-length mirror. The dress Aunt Jo had given me fell in soft, ethereal folds, fading from white to a dark, dusky blue where it grazed the floor. It was the color of the sky just after sunset—or just before dawn.

It's always darkest before the dawn.

And it was going to get dark tonight. Before we could move on.

I'd pulled my hair in a loose, low side bun, but black tendrils escaped around my face. I wished so badly that my mom was here to see this, that she could have a chance to see who I'd become.

As I looked in the full-length mirror, my eyes flashed back at me, silver, mercurial. I was ready for this. Whatever would come, whatever was going to happen—I had never been more ready.

I walked to the top of the staircase and peeked over the side. Asher stood in the downstairs hall, looking good as always in his jeans and boots and beat-up army jacket, trying to flatten his messed-up hair in the mirror by the door.

"No tux?" I asked, smiling. I knew full well that he didn't have a tux.

Asher turned around, and his mouth hung open a little. He put a hand to his heart. "God," he said, looking a little bit at a loss. "You are so beautiful."

"Stop," I replied, blushing. I walked down the stairs slowly, careful not to step on my dress.

"No, really," Asher said. He took my hand and spun me around. "For once I don't know what to say."

"Maybe this will help." I stood on my tiptoes to kiss him. He wrapped his arms around me, pulling me closer.

"Skye!" Earth came bounding out of the living room, wearing an elaborate tutu and ballet slippers. "We're going to a dance!" She threw her arms around my legs and squinted up at me. "You look like a princess."

"You look," Aunt Jo said from behind her, "like an angel."

Aaron came in too, followed by James. He put his arm around Aunt Jo. "I'm a lucky man," he said. "Not only am I going to prom with three beautiful women—"

"Dad!" Earth rolled her eyes. "I'm just a *girl*."

"—but I'm going to prom with three kick-ass heroines as well. I want you three to know that whatever happens tonight, I am honored to fight beside you."

Asher coughed from over by the door, looking awkward.

"Asher," Aunt Jo said, extending her hands to him. "I know we haven't always been allies in the past, but if Skye loves you, well, then so do I."

He blushed scarlet. "Nah, I mean I—" Then he seemed to think better of himself. He straightened, and his face grew serious. "I would never let anything happen to her. Not as long as I'm alive."

A car honked from the driveway.

"That's the others," I said. I looked nervously at the group in front of me. "Ready?"

Aunt Jo glanced at Aaron, who squeezed Earth to his side. Asher took my hand.

"Okay," I said. "Let's go."

A white stretch limo was parked in our driveway.

"You have *got* to be kidding me," I muttered.

"Bonjour!" Cassie popped her head out of the sunroof. "Your ride, *messieurs et mesdemoiselles*."

"Cassie, what the—"

"I know, I know," she said. "At first I sort of wondered, is this excessive? And then I was like, I *am* excessive." She grinned. "Besides, I figured, you know, not to be all grim or whatever, but if this is our last night on earth, we should kind of live it up while we can, right?"

I couldn't help but smile.

"You're crazy," I said.

"But you love me."

"If I could go back to when I was five and pick a new best friend, I wouldn't change a *thing*."

"Okay then," she said. "Now that we got that yearbook message out of the way, let's blow this popsicle stand." Her eyes slid past me and landed on Asher. She grinned. "Skye," she whispered. "I really hope you win so you can tell me that story later."

"I'll do what I can."

"We're going to take the car," Aunt Jo said, coming up behind me. "We'll see you there."

I kissed her on the cheek. "See you there," I said, and I was surprised when she wrapped her arms around me and squeezed tight.

"Be safe," she whispered fiercely into my ear. "Be so, so safe."

"I'm going to make it through this alive," I promised. "We all are."

"Well." She tucked a tendril of hair behind my ear. "Just in case."

Asher and I climbed into the limo and squeezed in between Dan and Ian. Across from us, Raven and Devin held hands and grinned at each other. She looked luminous in a simple black column dress, her blonde hair pulled back in a chic knot. Devin practically glowed in his tux. He nodded at Asher, who squeezed my hand and nodded back.

"Promward bound!" Cassie yelled, and the driver stepped on the gas. As we pulled out onto the road, the stars twinkling above us, I tried to suppress the feeling that our lives would never be the same after tonight.

Even without the war, I knew mine wouldn't.

Once we were on the road, Cassie's eyes glinted mischievously. I looked at Dan for reassurance.

"Don't look at me," he said. "I have no idea what she has planned."

"Just a little surprise." Cassie winked. From behind her, she pulled a bottle of champagne.

"Dude," said Ian. "Really?"

"It's nonalcoholic," she said. "So we can toast. I'm not actually encouraging us to all get tipsy right before we try to stop an ancient war from happening. Seriously."

She pulled a stack of plastic champagne flutes from a bag by her feet and popped the bottle. Sparkling apple juice spritzed everywhere.

"Cassie!" I cried.

"Sorry! Sorry. Okay, here's one for Ian . . ." She handed one to Ian. "And Dan. And one for you, Skye. And for Asher—yay, by the way! Welcome back—"

"Cassie . . ."

"Okay, okay. Devin, you get one too, of course. And lastly . . ." She caught Raven's eye, and Raven stiffened. "But certainly not least, one for Raven." She handed Raven a flute, and they shared a look. "The newest member of our group, with the best hair. I was wrong about you. You've more than made it up to us. I'm sorry."

Against all odds, Raven's face broke out into a genuine smile.

"I'm sorry, too," she said. "Thank you, Cassie. You have, er . . ." She paused. "Very nice hair, too."

I laughed and held up my glass. "Even if this is the last night of our lives," I said, "and it's *not* going to be, believe me—let's make it the best." Cassie, Dan, Ian, Raven, Devin, and Asher held up their glasses to clink mine.

"To seventeen," Cassie said, her eyes misty. It was the toast we had made at my birthday party six months ago, before any of this had started. Just me, Cassie, and Dan. My two best friends from childhood. Dan caught my eye and grinned.

"The year it all falls into place," he finished.

The gym had been transformed. The entrance was strung up with hundreds of paper lanterns, forming a tunnel of light that we had to walk through on our way inside. Asher grabbed my hand and squeezed it. Just ahead of us, Cassie walked next to Dan, the soft light blurring her red-blond hair like a vintage photograph. Dan looked at her, and for one really beautiful moment, he just smiled. There was no worry in his eyes. He leaned in close to whisper something in my best friend's ear, and I think I actually saw her blush. She pushed him lightly.

On the other side, the tunnel opened up into the End of the World.

Someone—I glanced at Cassie—had gone crazy with the papier-mâché, creating a giant chasm in the gymnasium floor to simulate an earthquake. A smaller version of the Statue of Liberty leaned off-kilter in the corner, surrounded by a deep snowdrift of cotton balls. By the half-court line, the stern of the *Titanic* rose into the air. Tiny plastic LEGO people clung for dear life, some suspended by strings to show them plummeting to their icy fate. "Check it out!" Cassie spun in a circle. "It's the end of the world!"

I couldn't help glancing at Asher. He didn't seem to find the theme very funny.

"Well, guys," said Cassie. "Who knows what's going to happen tonight, but I think we better get in a dance or two, right?"

"For once," Dan said, "I'm with this one. M'lady?" He held out his hand, and she took it proudly.

"You guys," she said, walking backward so she could talk to us as Dan led her out onto the dance floor. "I have the studliest prom date!"

Devin guided Raven onto the dance floor, and Ian wandered off to the punch.

"How about it?" Asher held out his hand to me. "One dance before it all goes down?"

I hesitated. "I don't know. Shouldn't we find Aunt Jo, Aaron, and James, and go over the strategy one more time?"

"Skye," Asher leaned in close, and I felt that familiar shiver up my arms. "If I know you, you know that plan cold. Let yourself have five minutes of fun." He pulled back and flashed me a grin, then gestured to the dance floor.

I glanced at Dan, who was twirling Cassie in circles around us. She laughed and laughed, as if she didn't have a care in the world. How did she let everything just roll off her shoulders like that?

I took a deep breath.

"All right," I said, and placed my hand in his. "But no fancy stuff."

Asher laughed. "I'm *all* fancy stuff. Come on, let me show you my moves." I rolled my eyes and let him lead me onto the dance floor. Asher wrapped his arms around me, and I leaned my cheek against his T-shirt. As we turned slowly, I knew that being here with him was giving me strength.

"I don't know what you've done to me, Skye," Asher whispered in my ear. "But I've never felt this way about anyone before." I pulled back to look at him. Now that I had him back, was this the last time we'd ever dance together? I had finally found him only to face the thought of losing him. There was so much I wanted to say, but I was afraid if I opened my mouth, I would cry.

Instead, I stood up on my tiptoes to kiss him.

Over his shoulder, I spotted Devin, standing alone as Raven walked off to scout for Guardians and Rebels. He caught my eye.

"Asher," I said softly. "Can you give me a minute?" Asher turned around and caught Devin's gaze. Something passed between them, something I wasn't sure I was supposed to see. The hatred of those early days was gone. It was replaced with a tense agreement. An understanding.

After everything we'd been through, who could have predicted that Asher and Devin would find themselves on the same side, voluntarily? That they would take the same risk, at the same time, without even knowing? At the end of it all, they had so much more in common than they ever realized.

Asher nodded and said in a low voice, "I'll be waiting."

I made my way across the dance floor to where Devin stood. He watched me approach with a look on his face that was hard to read.

"You look . . . wow." He shook his head, and I blushed.

"Would you dance with me, Devin?" He looked surprised, but he reached out, tentatively, for my hand.

"Just one more memory," I said, and led him onto the dance floor.

Around us, the paper lanterns glowed, like fireflies, in the dark gym.

"Devin," I said slowly. "I just wanted to say thank you, for helping me find Asher. It meant the world to me."

He swallowed sharply.

"You showed me how to have the happiness I never thought was possible for me. I owed you the same."

We danced in silence as the music wrapped around us like the softest blanket. Whatever happened, I would never forget him.

I'd realized something then. I'd had this vision before, seen this moment—but it had been different. Somehow, somewhere along the line, I had changed my own fate, along with the world's.

The song ended, and I looked up at him.

"You and I," he said, "we were never meant to be. It's true, right? It was always an uphill battle. There was always an obstacle."

"I know."

"Thanks for this memory." He pulled away. Weirdly, I felt tears stinging my eyes, and bit the inside of my cheek. I looked over to see that Raven was hovering on the edge of the dance floor, watching us. Her expression was part anxious, part hopeful.

When I turned back to Devin, he was gone, and I had lost him in the crowd.

27

I stood alone on the surging dance floor.

I felt at peace. I'd tied up all my loose ends.

I was ready to face the future.

I scanned the room and spotted Asher talking to Aunt Jo, Aaron, and James. Earth was very intently staring out the window, a serious expression on her face.

They all looked up when I approached.

"Where are Cassie, Dan, and Ian?" I asked, just as Cassie bounded up next to me.

"Well, I lost my boyfriend. Have you seen him?"

We heard laughing and followed the sound to where Dan and Ian were standing by the giant papier-mâché *Titanic*. They each held a LEGO figurine in their hands and looked like they were acting something out.

"Seriously?" I muttered.

"You know," said Cassie, "people have broken up for less."

I cleared my throat and Ian and Dan whipped around. "We were . . . uh . . ." Dan fumbled.

"This is why we're not allowed to go on missions, Daniel," Cassie hissed.

"Entertaining as this is," I said, "come on. I want to get everyone together." Earth was signaling to me frantically.

Just as we all reconvened, the DJ's voice rang out in the background.

"Ladies and gentleman of Northwood, it's time to announce your prom court."

"Ooh!" cried Cassie.

"Are you sure it's *my* fault?" Dan asked.

"A shooting star!" Earth cried breathlessly. "And Skye, it has your *name on it*!"

"It's now," I said. "That was it." Asher moved to my side.

"NOW?" cried Cassie. "But what about the prom court?!"

"Tell me how it turns out." And then I closed my eyes, and I let go of high school.

322

An image began to take shape in my mind.

A vast white space. Slowly, through the mist, I began to pick out shapes and patterns. The slope of an archway, the geometric zigzag of steps. Was it a city? A palace of some kind? Figures moved like shadows against the blank white background, like the ghostly image that's left on your eyelids when you close your eyes. I couldn't tell if they were human—or something else.

My eyes still closed, my skin stippling with goose bumps, I watched as the mist faded away, and the shapes that had begun to materialize formed fully before my eyes. They weren't the glistening arches and steps of a city somewhere in the sky, where I'd always imagined the Order to be. As I watched, I realized they were cliffs and rocks, looming above a wide, endless beach.

I trudged across a great expanse of black sand, the ocean tide lapping at the shore, as if calling my name, rising to meet me. It soaked the bottom of my dress, already smudged with sand, and washed away something dark and sticky that left behind the echoes of a deep red stain. Blood.

This was it. I'd seen this beach before in my visions. I'd carried a sword, wearing the very dress I was wearing now.

But this time was different. This time, when I moved, I was actually moving. When I spoke, my voice echoed out over the sea. *Whatever I'm seeing, I'm already here.*

I kept my eyes closed, focused on the beach around me. But I knew, on the other side of my eyelids, the entire group was watching me, waiting. The lights around us dimmed and glowed, the disco ball casting sparkles and shadows on the walls and glimmering across our faces and hair. The music played on.

"Are you guys ready?" I asked, and was met with a solemn chorus of agreement. "I see it, in front of me. Give me your hands. I'll take us there."

The events of my life had brought me to this moment— but my visions had, too. Because they foretold the event that was supposed to take place tonight, of all nights— the cataclysmic clashing of the celestial factions. Timed perfectly to coincide with prom. There was about to be a battle. Someone I loved was going to die.

With eyes still closed, someone took my left hand, and someone else my right one—completing the circle.

"Bye!" Earth's voice rose above the music.

"Be safe!" Cassie called.

"Are you guys ready?" I asked. "Because we're about to leave River Springs, and I can't promise that we're all going to make it back."

When the mist cleared, we were standing on the beach, still holding hands. Asher, Ian, Raven, Devin, the three Rogues—and me.

The beach was deserted. The only sound was the lapping of the waves. Gray clouds hung low, blocking out the sun and allowing only the dimmest light to filter through. Black sand stretched out before us, as far as the eye could see. On one side of us, a massive, rocky cliffside towered up into the sky, so that I had to shield my eyes and squint to see the top. On the other side, the gray ocean churned, restless, coming in and out with the tide.

The wind whistled through the endless expanse.

"Where are we?" I asked Raven. "Is this the Order's realm?"

"No," said Raven slowly. "This is no place *I've* ever been."

"It's the Cradle of Time," a voice boomed, echoing around us. We all looked up. I realized that the cliff face stretching out to our left wasn't just a cliff face. It was an intricate maze of steps and arches, carved into the sea-ravaged, weather-beaten rock.

Standing in the center of each arch—and there must have been a hundred of them, carved into the side of the cliff—stood a Gifted One. They were easy to spot, older and grayer, with aged, yellowing wings. At the same time, each lit a single candle. Collectively, the flames cast an eerie glow over the beach.

Standing at the top of the cliff, I could just make out Astaroth.

"Time is born here and dies here. It passes and returns, like the tide of the ocean lapping at the sand beneath our feet. This place is where the Sight begins and ends. It's where all destiny originates."

"We're in the Before Place," said Raven, her voice breathy and full of awe. "Astaroth told me about this. It existed long before there was even an Order, or a Rebellion to break away from it. It's where the first angel was born with the Sight. It's the place where destiny began."

"Very good, Raven," Astaroth's voice echoed down at us. "You were always my star pupil. I thought you were going to go far—not abandon me for some futile Uprising."

"I didn't abandon you, sir," Raven said boldly. "By the ancient laws of the Order, I was no longer allowed to return home. So I found a new home."

"And how is that working out for you?" Astaroth said mildly. "Your . . . *new home*." I saw what he was doing—he was a master at manipulation, and he was trying to plant seeds of doubt in Raven's mind. "Have they accepted you? Welcomed you into their fold with open arms?" He laughed ruthlessly. "Or were they more skeptical? Will they always think of you as a Guardian?"

In the distance, farther down the beach, I thought I could make out a body drawing closer. And another. And another.

"And Devin," Astaroth continued. "My, how the mighty have fallen. From Guardian to Rebel to nothing."

Devin lifted his chin defiantly.

A sea of dark figures materialized at the edge of the beach. Coming toward us. Or coming *for* us.

The Rebellion.

My group huddled together, achingly small compared to the two armies facing us down.

"We can't control your powers, Skye," Astaroth said. "And we haven't been able to claim you for our own. Or, for that matter, kill you."

"Nor have we," a voice spoke up. Ardith was at the front of the group on the beach before us, a sword strapped to her back, her hair in a long, glossy chestnut braid. Gideon stood close to her side.

She drew the sword, at the ready. She and Asher made eye contact, and a storm of fury charged between them.

He stepped closer to me. She barely even paused on Devin.

"Just tell me again," I whispered to Asher, "what side you're on."

"Whatever side you're on, Skye." He squeezed my hand.

"You've had the opportunity to choose for yourself," Astaroth said. "And we've all tried to choose *for* you—to force you to pick a side. But you are untamed. Unbound by the laws of the Order and the Rebellion. If neither side can kill you, and neither has claimed you, there's only one thing left to do." A sinister smile tugged the edges of his lips. "We'll just have to fight for you."

"I can fight for myself," I said.

"We all know you can control your powers. But it's when you are panicked, when you are under attack, that your control weakens. And powerful, unexpected things happen."

He cocked his head at me.

"Do you know why you are here, Skye?"

I swallowed.

"No," I said.

"If I may," he said, taking a candle from one of his Gifted, "allow me to tell you a legend:

"It began with a vision. Many, many millennia ago. Before your parents were even conceived. Before they were born, fell in love, were cast to earth, and before you were created, their flesh and blood—and something else, some magical essence we still do not understand. Nor do I think we ever will." The candles that the Gifted held aloft flickered, casting light across the Rebellion, below. "I was not the one who had this vision—though I was alive at the time. It was my father who saw it."

I stepped forward. "What did he see?"

"Chaos," Astaroth said. "Cities burning. Flooding. Death. The Order unable to control it, to stop it. Because the Order could not have seen it coming. For they had lost the ability to see along the lines of fate. They had lost the Sight. It was," he said, "an End of Days."

"But," said Ardith, "another angel had the same vision. He didn't see destruction. He saw renewal. He saw a Beginning of Days. The dawn of a new era."

"The two angels argued. One was convinced that if we lived according to free will, that day would be a day of hope and light. While the other was bound to his belief in fate, and was convinced the day would be the destruction of the world. So one angel left the Order. And he was the first Rebel."

"What does this have to do with me?" I asked. "Why I'm here?"

"Because in the vision it was you—your powers—who brought this day to come. The daughter of dark and light caused the End—or the Beginning—of days. But nobody knew which would happen. It's why we tried to prevent you from ever being born. And it's why we watched you so carefully when you wouldn't die."

"And it's why we tried so hard to fight them, Skye!" Ardith said, raising her voice above the wind as it began to howl, blowing sand into the air around us. "Because we knew you would bring a day that would change the world—and make it better! It's why we wanted you to side with us."

"So you could destroy the Order," Astaroth said.

"No—so we could use her for good—and prevent you from destroying *her*."

"But neither side succeeded. And so we have only one option left."

A shiver ran down my spine.

"That day is today." Astaroth's voice was grave. "We'll let your powers take over. And the rest . . . is what they'll base new legends on."

Something Asher had once told me came roaring back,

filled every inch of me.

"I know you're stuck between two choices, and you don't exactly have a conscious say in the matter. Your powers will take over when it really counts."

Ian stepped up beside me on one side, Asher and Devin on the other. Their hands tensed by their sides.

"So," I said. "What happens now, Astaroth?"

"Now," he said. "We fight. And we see just what you're made of. Will it be the end of the world or the beginning? Will the Rebellion plunge the world into darkness—or will the Order rule forever?"

I turned toward my small team. Hopefully we wouldn't be small for long.

"It's time to call the Rogues!" I said, strangely calm now that the time had finally come. Aunt Jo, James, and Aaron formed a circle, taking hands. They left one spot empty.

"For you," Aunt Jo said. If she was nervous, she didn't show it. "Let's call our army."

I ran to her, grasped her hand and Aaron's. Power surged between the four of us, so strong and quick it almost broke our hands apart. But we held on tighter.

I called out to the Rogues. I willed them to come and fight with me. I summoned them. The balance of power in my blood shifted and changed, now light, now dark, now both. There was a rushing in my ears, so enormous that it blocked out all other sound.

And when I opened my eyes, they were coming. Stretching out down the beach in the other direction were hundreds of people. Their eyes were angry, their faces, determined. They were dressed in normal clothes, like they'd been pulled from normal lives. They swarmed the beach, coming from all sides.

The closer they drew, the angrier they looked. I had a sudden panicked thought. What if they didn't want me for their leader? What if they didn't want to fight with me?

What if they wanted to fight against me?

When they reached us, they came to a stop and turned, as one, in my direction. Trying to keep my hands from shaking, I took a deep breath.

"Rogues," I said. "You may feel that there's no place for you in this world. But that ends now. I'm like you—I've had to find my own place. But your place can be here, with me. Please"—my voice sounded so strong across the beach—"fight with me. Fight for a world that isn't so divided. Fight for someplace to call home."

Their eyes flashed. For one sickening moment, my heart leaped to my throat. And then—they began to cheer.

Their voices rose above the howling wind, and lightning cracked across the sky.

I had found my people.

"Astaroth!" I called into the wind, whipping around. "You think you can fight over us? You think one side is going to beat the other? Well, guess what! There won't be an End of Days today. Or a Beginning of Days, either. I have the Rogues on my side, and there's power in numbers. We're going to keep the balance between dark and light. The world will keep spinning, and neither of you will take control of the universe if I can help it!"

Astaroth looked panicked, for the first time, as the Rogues continued to storm the beach. He hadn't been expecting the force of the Uprising. My ability to blur destiny had made sure of that.

"I guess there are many more people in this world who are mixed up, who believe in gray areas, than you could have imagined. We are the people who don't believe the world exists in your black-and-white terms," I said, sweeping my arms wide at the children of angels and humans who, like me, belonged to no true place but their own. "And we're going to change the way of things," I said. "Once and for all."

I let my wings expand from my back, massive, catching

the gleam of the fire in their silvery feathers. Reaching behind me, I plucked one bright, shiny feather and held it aloft.

When I brought it down to my side, I was holding my own angelic sword.

28

The sword gleamed in the firelight. I held it at the ready, in a fighting stance.

"Guardians!" Astaroth yelled. "Attack!" The sky grew dark with clouds. The Gifted let their arrows rain down around us, and Guardians swarmed from the steps of the cliff, storming the beach. Immediately, I felt my optimism fade, and a sense of gloom and dread seep into my heart.

They're manipulating us, I realized with horror. *Making us weak*. I turned wildly to look for Asher and Ian, Raven and the Rogues. They'd all brought hands to their ears, as if somehow they could block out the Gifteds' sickening voices.

You will never beat us.

"Rebels!" Ardith shouted with a grimace, and the dark army of Rebels raised their hands in the air to create fire.

The Rogues spanned out around us on all sides. They had a range of powers to draw from—they called upon their different holds over each small part of the natural world. Birds swooped from the sky and fish darted from the ocean. Plants and roots sprang up across the beach, tripping people as they fought. Aunt Jo, James, and Aaron grabbed one another's hands once again, and with their powers combined, they created a series of watery fissures that zigzagged across the beach.

"Skye," Ian grabbed my arm. He spoke quickly, as the fighting swarmed around us. "I know our friendship wasn't ever meant to be anything more. I really see that now. I think the reason I always felt so close to you is because you were supposed to help me figure out who I really am, and lead me to my true calling."

"Don't tell me you believe in fate now!" I yelled above the wind, above the shouting voices. "It's a little late for that!"

"Honestly? I don't know what I believe," Ian said. "But I do know that we were supposed to find each other. We were meant to help each other, Skye. I'm a Rogue, and my father is a Rogue, and one thing I have to do is fight by your side for all the Rogues until the bitter end. For all of us who don't know exactly who we are yet—and don't want to decide. Call it fate. Call it free will. But it's a choice I'd make again and again."

"Ian," I said, grabbing him with both hands. "Thank you. I couldn't have done this without you."

"Don't," he said. "Don't thank me. Just win."

Asher was by my side then, the wind whipping at his dark hair, a wild, determined look in his eyes. He held out a hand to Ian. And Ian took it without hesitation.

"Let's do this," Asher said.

And together, we ran into the fray.

My beautiful, diaphanous dress blew in the wind. I kicked off my heels and fixed my sword to one of the straps of my dress. I would try to fight using my powers first. I'd only use my sword if I needed to. If it came down to life—or death.

All around me, I watched angels throwing fireballs, blowing wind, casting those force fields that Devin had once used against Asher. My blood began to simmer and then to rise to a boil, and I knew, though I hated to admit it, that Astaroth was right—I could control my powers, but when I felt out of control, it was out of my hands. The blackening clouds above us opened up, and rain began to pour down.

"Careful, Skye," Asher called.

Through the rain, I could make out Devin and Raven fighting, side by side. A Rebel's fireball zinged toward Raven's face—but Devin pulled her out of harm's way at the last minute. *So he really is fighting on his own terms*, I thought happily. Ian had taken my sword from me and was fighting off Guardians. I turned around and saw Asher going head-to-head with Ardith. It broke my heart, but I lobbed a ball of fire in her direction. She ducked, and Asher looked at me, fierce and proud.

The battle raged on. I don't know how long it lasted. We might have been there for hours, or it could have been days. The beach thinned out. But I managed to keep my powers under control. The waves churned, lapped angrily against the shore. The rain turned to hail, pelting down hard.

"Traitor!"

I spun around at the voice, but it wasn't meant for me. Gideon was crouched on the black sand, panting. Devin stood above him, his sword raised above his head. Behind him was Raven. Her hair whipped in the wind and she gazed at him gratefully.

"Don't you touch her." Devin's voice was low and dangerous.

Gideon's face, which had once been so open and friendly to me, was twisted in a sneer.

"How easily you turn your back on your supposed side! First the Order, and now you're fighting against *us*? Does honor mean nothing to you? Is loyalty just an empty word?" He pushed his glasses up on his nose.

"No." Devin's voice was scary calm. "It meant too much to me, for too long. It ruled my life. But now, all of this is meaningless. The Order, the Rebellion. The Rogues. At the end of the day, what does any of it mean? They're all just empty words for something I don't believe in anymore." He tensed, about to strike. "I just know I have to fight for the only people who have ever cared about me." His eyes found Raven's. And then mine.

Gideon looked unsure. He opened his mouth and paused. The two of them stood there, and for a minute I wondered if Gideon was about to come fight with us. But before he could speak, a dark figure hurtled itself at Devin.

Ardith took him from behind, her arms wrapped tightly around his chest and a sword at his neck.

"Stop!" Raven screamed. Gideon scrambled to his feet

and held her back. She struggled frantically against him.

"Never hesitate when it comes to love," Ardith spat. "Never stop fighting for a second."

"Ardith!" Asher yelled, appearing beside me. He held an arm aloft, a cluster of embers burning and smoldering in his cupped palm. "Don't you dare hurt him. Put the sword down and *join us*."

Ardith glared at him, tightening her grip on Devin. The fallen Guardian and former Rebel looked strangely serene—at peace, almost. Was I hallucinating, or was Asher trying to save him?

"Surrender!" Ardith cried. "I'll kill him—I'll do it! And if you don't, it just goes to show you how meaningless your words are."

"Don't do it," Devin said, his voice barely rising above the wind. "The rules, the sides—none of it matters, anymore. You were right, Asher. You were right all along."

"No!" Asher and I cried at the same time. The embers whizzed from his hand—but Ardith ducked, and they missed her by a hair.

"It does matter!" I yelled. A fog, thick and heavy and white, was beginning to descend on the beach. I tried beating it back, but it was the work of many Rebels' powers combined. Instead, it surged forward. I could hardly see what was happening. "Keep fighting, Devin! We're going to win! You and Raven will be free to be together. You just have to believe that this is going to end well."

Ian drew up beside me, panting. "What's going on?"

Through the fog, I could just make out Devin's face, Ardith's arms circled tightly around his chest. The sword's blade glinted at his throat.

Devin looked between me and Asher. But I was done trying to figure out what all of it meant. I had a fight to win.

"Give me my sword," I said to Ian. He placed it in my hands. My heart was pounding. I had to trust that love would guide my aim. Like it had for me throughout my whole life. Astaroth was wrong. Love would make me strong this time.

And so, I raised my sword above my head and threw it into the mist with all my strength—aiming straight at where I could just see Ardith's silhouette. The sword disappeared into the mist.

Ian gripped my arm. "Where's Asher?" I whipped around to see him hurl himself into the mist at Ardith at the same time. Straight at where I'd thrown my sword. And then the mist was so thick I couldn't see anything anymore.

A strange silence settled across the beach. I was aware of Ian standing at my side, saying something that I couldn't hear. There was a scream, and then a sob. A vague understanding dawned on me. I had hit someone. The world bottomed out from under me as I realized it. But who?

As if in a dream, I began to move. I tripped on something and fell to my knees. Panic tore at me blindly, but it was only the hem of my dress, dirty and soaked, that had gotten tangled beneath my feet. I stood up. I kept moving, collecting the folds of the beautiful dress in my arms to keep from stumbling again. And then my feet hit something solid.

Feet, I realized. *Those are feet.*

The fog drew out with the tide, and now that I could see again, dread descended on me.

Asher was kneeling on the sand. He looked up at me, helplessly.

Lying on the ground at my feet, his blood seeping out around him, was Devin.

Raven let out a strangled cry and fell to the ground. Sheets of blond hair came loose from her bun and covered her face.

I killed him. The panicked thought tore through me. But

then I looked closer. His eyes fluttered open, his chest rose and fell with shallow breaths. My sword was nowhere to be seen. Instead, a deep slice of blood arced across his chest. From a sword, it seemed, that had been held to his neck—but had missed its mark. *No*, I realized. *I didn't do this. Ardith did.*

Devin's breath came in short gasps. He met my eyes sadly.

"Over there," Asher said somberly. And I followed his gaze. Ardith lay several feet away—where the force of my sword had thrown her back. Her eyes were closed, her mouth still. The sand around her was a deepening red.

A choking sob forced its way from my throat as Asher ran to me, and I dropped to my knees. Devin's breathing was weak. He looked up into my eyes, and I was struck, again and again, by how deep they could pierce me. I grasped his hands in mine.

"I really do care," Devin said, his voice barely a whisper. "I always have. Everything I did, I did for you."

I knew I was crying, and my tears mixed with the wet air until I couldn't tell where they ended and the elements began.

"No," my voice cracked. "Please don't die."

Tears slid down my cheeks and I pushed them away

with the back of my hand. "I'm so, so sorry. I wish it didn't have to end this way."

"Shhh," he whispered, with effort. "It's okay. Maybe it's better that it end like this. Now. While you and I— we're okay. While Raven knows how I feel about her. Happiness can't last forever, right? At least I got to be happy at all."

"I'll always care about you." I smoothed the hair back from his forehead. His eyelids fluttered.

"No!" Raven came running over, collapsed at Devin's side, across from me. His eyes met hers.

"We would have been happy," he said.

"I know," she said, her voice trembling. She pushed the hair out of his face. "It's all I ever wanted."

And he held her hand in his and closed his eyes, and soon his body and Ardith's disappeared with the mist and floated away on the wind. Gideon looked up at us help-lessly.

Raven was sobbing into her hands. "I think I get it now," she said. "I think I understand."

Asher wrapped his arm around me. And, a second later, he wrapped his other arm around Raven. I let my head fall onto his shoulder.

I couldn't think. I couldn't stand. I couldn't believe what

this was coming to. Devin was dead, and the world was already unraveling. Chaos, Order, everything was falling apart. Maybe this was the End of Days. Maybe this is what it looked like. Losing someone you cared about. Knowing you were to blame.

The rest of the world came rushing back. The sounds of fighting, farther down the beach. The angry roars. The battle cries. Aunt Jo and Aaron and James—and hundreds of thousands of Rogues—were fighting. For me. And I had to finish this. I couldn't let anything happen to them, either.

I stood up.

"Skye," Asher said quietly. "Are you okay?"

I turned to him. "I love you," I said.

"What are you—"

"It's the only way, Asher," I said. "I have to."

"No." He grabbed my arm. "Whatever you're about to do, don't do it. We can end this a different way." I pulled away from him. "Skye, listen to me. We can end it together. We have to keep fighting."

"All I want is to keep the two sides in balance." The wind whipped and howled, and I had to yell to make my voice heard. "There's only one way to do that. I see it now."

Asher's eyes turned dark and stormy. "If you're thinking what I think you're thinking—"

"It's the only way."

"No," he said. "I'm not letting you sacrifice yourself. You're too special, you mean too much. To the world." He swallowed hard. "To me."

"Asher, please, let me—"

"We can do this another way! If we talked to them—"

"You think we'll end this fight by talking? They won't listen to reason."

I stood up and wiped my eyes, grabbed my sword from the ground.

"Skye, don't!"

"Astaroth!" I yelled.

Maybe he was right, the night he visited my mind. Maybe in the end, you did have to choose between life and love.

I looked up. He stood on the top of the cliff, commanding his army. He met my gaze.

"Come down here and fight!" I screamed. "You and me. One-on-one."

Astaroth's face twisted into an evil smirk. He took a step and jumped off the cliff, descending on huge, ancient wings.

"Skye!" Asher called.

I stopped. To my right, my whole group was lined up. Asher and Raven, Ian, his dad, Aunt Jo and Aaron. Each held a weapon. Each was deadly serious. Behind them, the Rogues covered the beach.

"If you're going to fight him," Ian said. "We're going to be behind you. And we're going to finish him."

Asher met my gaze, and his look said it all. *I'm not going to let you die.*

But all I could think of was Devin's good-bye: *Happiness can't last forever, right?* I had been happy for a moment. But I couldn't let anyone else I loved die.

Astaroth had his sword outstretched. And as I ran toward it, I was surprised to hear a new voice bloom in my mind. Earth's.

Save him, it said.

"Are you going to listen to me, Skye?" Astaroth sneered. "Here's my sword. It's now or never. You could end this. You could end this whole thing."

Save him.

Earth's message in the stars. Was it possible there was another way? She was sent to me for a reason. *Help Skye.*

Out of the corner of my eye, I saw a Rebel's fireball soaring across the clouds—heading right for us. Before I could think twice, instinct took over. I veered to the left, grabbing Astaroth and pushing him to the ground with me. The fireball arced over our heads, leaving a trail of smoke and ember in its wake.

I sat up, gasping. Astaroth wrapped his arm around my neck and we struggled on the ground.

I knew then that Astaroth didn't have power over my mind anymore. He didn't have power over me. And I would end this my way. I grabbed him and struggled to my feet.

"You—you saved my life," he growled. "Why would you do that?"

A group began to gather around us, Guardians and Rebels, swords and bows falling softly to their sides as they watched.

"Because now you owe me."

Gideon limped to the front of the group. His face was pale, his eyes wild.

"That's fair," he said. "You know the laws of the heavens." He stepped closer. "Cause and effect. For every action, there is an equal and opposite reaction. It's the guiding principle of the Order and the Rebellion. The *rules* you fight so hard to maintain."

"So what would you have me do?" Astaroth spat. He

gnashed his teeth like a caged animal.

"Let us establish an Uprising," I said. "A third group of Rogues, who will forever keep the balance between chaos and control."

"And what about you?"

I'd thought about this moment for a long time.

"Let me go," I said. "This isn't the life I want. I don't want to cause any more destruction, or fighting, or death. I don't want to bring about an End of Days— or a Beginning of Days. I just want to go to college, and follow my dreams, and lead a normal life." I took a deep breath. "I want to end this war. And I want to be human."

"But Skye!" Aunt Jo cried out. "What about your parents? Everything they fought and died for? What about everything you've been working toward?"

"This *is* what I've been working toward," I replied. "They had their fight, and this is mine. I can write my own ending."

Astaroth considered this. "That may be a solution," he said. "For now. You'll keep the peace, perhaps. Your friends, your Rogue army. You may keep the balance of the heavens in check. It may be true that I owe you—that the rules dictate I cannot harm you. But that's for now, only now. The universe exists in cycles, Skye. It ebbs and flows, like time, like the great ocean behind you. Nothing is ever truly over, not really."

I thought about Earth, so young and innocent but with an incredible power. Would it be her job one day to lead the Rogues in another Uprising? Would she be the next chosen one, whose job it would be to keep the peace between the two sides? Would she rise too, to be a leader?

I didn't want to leave her that kind of life, either.

"No," I said. "You don't understand. There will be no more Sight. No more Order and no more Rebellion. You won't meddle in people's lives anymore. There will be no such thing as destiny, no chaos, no cause and effect. They'll live their own lives, as they want to. You, Astaroth—I'm ousting you from your position of power."

"You can't do that!"

"She can," said Ian, stepping up beside me. "Watch her."

"I'm establishing a new council, to govern the celestial laws fairly and honestly. Gideon." The bereft angel nodded at me grimly. "Raven. Ian. Can each of you step forward? The three of you all have a mix of blood, of powers. Your allegiance was never to a side, but to your heart. I trust the three of you to keep peace and balance in the world. Will you accept?"

"It's all I have now," said Gideon simply.

Raven raised an eyebrow, and a small, sad smile spread across her face. "I'll do it for Devin," she said. She held out her hand. I took it, gripped it tightly in mine. Our hands buzzed with the power that flowed between us, connecting us. "You know, you really surprised me, Skye."

"Thank you," I said. "I know I can never make it up to you, but—"

"Stop," she interrupted. "You're changing the way of things. So that it won't ever happen again. And that's enough."

I turned to Ian. "What do you say?" I asked. "You can be the council's liaison to earth—the Rogues and humans need someone like you to look out for them." I smiled. "Like you've always looked out for me. This is what you were meant to do—remember?"

Ian grinned, his freckles stretching across his face.

"I told you, you helped me find my place," he said. "I would be honored to do this."

Astaroth fell back, helpless, as I held my sword aloft.

Silver flashed through me as the wind blew around us, the sun broke through the clouds, and night became day. The whole beach flooded with light.

"It's done," I said, tears in my eyes. "It's over."

Across the beach, Asher and I found each other. I began to run at the same time he did, and we met in the middle, pulling each other close and holding on tight. The wind still howled around us, and we pressed together, my dress and hair blowing in all directions at once.

"Are you sure this is what you want?" He yelled over the wind. "To give up your wings—and be human?"

"Yes!" I cried. "But only if you come with me. I promise we'll be a team from now on. I'll fight for you over and over. I'll never stop fighting for you."

"I may be a Rebel," Asher said, his voice cracking. "I may be free to think and feel what I want. To choose what I want. But I didn't know what love was until I met you. I didn't have anything worth fighting for until I fought for you. I've never had a choice about how I feel. Wherever you go—I'm going, too."

I remembered sitting, curled up with Asher in the big Adirondack chair on our deck, as the moon rose above us in the sky, and he kissed the top of my head and said:

"I have a choice, Skye. I have the power to choose whatever I want. And there is nothing that I've ever wanted more."

If I had understood then what was going to happen, I would never have let him go. I would have said the same thing. I would have meant it.

And it wasn't too late.

"I choose you, Asher. I want so much more than just memories. I want more than just one moment of happiness. I want to live and not know what the future holds."

We leaned into each other, and the wind and light raged around us, blinding us, and we kissed in the middle of that vast expanse of beach as if we were the only two people in the world. Suddenly, a searing pain sliced through my back. Asher's face contorted in a grimace. Silver liquid pooled with blood in the sand at our feet. And then, our wings were gone.

I held out my hand to him. He took it.

"Partners," he said.

"For always."

I looked into his eyes. We both knew that Astaroth was right. In the course of time, war would break out again, cities would fall and be rebuilt, and people would be born and live and die, and we would always fight for the balance, and that's life. It existed in cycles, ebbing and flowing, and this might not be the end. But maybe it was a new beginning.

And I couldn't wait to find out what would happen next.

We held hands and looked at each other.

"Are you ready?" I said. "To jump?"

"I've been ready for a long time," said Asher.

And together we closed our eyes and let ourselves fall.

29

I opened my eyes.

The tiny, glowing lights, the click of high heels against the gymnasium floor.

The taste of punch and the sound of laughter.

My boyfriend's dark brown eyes, smiling as they realized I was awake.

It all came rushing back to me.

"We're back," I said. "We're at prom. We made it."

"I knew we would," said Asher. He offered me his hand and pulled me to my feet. The hem of my ethereal dress swept across the floor. There was not a trace of the battle on it—the sand, the surf, the blood, all of it, gone. Left back in the other world.

"How did it—"

"I don't know." He smiled. "But we're lucky, Skye. We're so, so lucky." He pulled me into his arms, and I pressed my face into his chest. The familiar gray T-shirt. The beat-up army jacket. The scent of cinnamon and pine, the woods, my home, washing over me.

It was over. It was all over.

Somehow, incredibly, and against all odds, I had saved the world.

"Get a room, lovebirds!" Cassie came bounding up to me, her pale pink dress shimmering in the light and a prom princess tiara perched on her head. I grinned. "You did it, Skye! You really did it! Dan, come here! They're back!"

"Babes," Dan yelled from across the floor. "Leave them alone. They're having a moment."

Cassie pouted. "But I want to be part of it."

"Come here, Cass," I said, pulling her into our hug. "Dan, you can be part of it too!" Dan came sprinting over and pounced on us.

"Dad!" A little voice cried. I turned my head, and Earth was running full-speed across the dance floor. I followed her path to where Aaron stood by the door to the gym. Beside him was Aunt Jo, her hand in his, her head resting on his shoulder.

"Hey, Trouble!" he cried, kneeling down so Earth could jump into his arms. "Were you good for Cassie?"

"Duh," she said. "You were only gone for, like, a minute."

She caught my eye and winked at me. *"Thank you,"* I mouthed.

Behind them, James Harrison looked around. Suddenly, his face lit up. Ian was standing by the punch bowl, grinning at his dad.

"Ian!" Cassie cried, waving him over.

"Ian, what are you doing here?" I asked. "I thought—"

"Rogues live on earth, right?" He said with a wink. "Maybe I'll be the first Rogue in my family to graduate high school, stick around. Besides," he said. "Can't I keep the peace from homeroom?" We laughed.

"We made it through the battle, *and* junior year, guys," I said. "Can you believe it?"

"It didn't seem so daunting back in September," said Ian.

"Senior year is looking pretty good, huh?" I grinned at him.

"Ooh," Cassie cried, "this is our song. Daniel, shall we show them what we've been practicing?"

"I believe," he said, extending his hand, "we shall." Cassie put her hand in his, and he twirled her out onto the dance floor. And then, before my very eyes, Cassie ran toward Dan and he lifted her up into the air. She squealed, the light from the disco ball reflecting off her pale pink dress, as she spread her arms wide like she was flying.

"We did it! We did it! We—" Dan's footing faltered beneath her. "Ah! Put me down! There's no river to catch us this time!"

I watched them tumble to the ground with the biggest smile on my face. Asher was right. We were so, so lucky.

"Hey, Skye?" Ian put his hand on my back and smiled. "I knew you could do it," he said. "Even when you didn't. I always believed."

I watched him make his way across the gym to where James was waiting for him. And when I turned around, I realized someone was waiting for me. He stood on the edge of the dance floor, in the shadows.

And then he stepped into the light. His eyes were dark and dizzying. His hair was as black as the Colorado sky at night. He grinned and raised an eyebrow as he held out his hand.

"Skye," Asher said. "Will you dance with me?"

But the screech of an amp feeding back made us turn suddenly to the stage. Cassie stood up there with an acoustic guitar, the rest of the Mysterious Ellipses behind her.

"Girls and boys, for the last dance of the night, I have a surprise for my best friend. This is a song about being brave."

She began to sing, her voice high and clear as a bell. The band strummed softly, filling the gym with slow, beautiful music.

Asher and I grinned at each other. I took his hand without a word, and everything I'd ever felt for him came rushing up inside me. He pulled me close, and I rested my forehead against his chest as he guided us across the floor.

"This is what I would wish for," I whispered, "if I could go back to that night we met. I may not have known it then, but I do now."

We'd already had our last dance before the battle, but now, this felt like our first. We had a whole life ahead of us, one that was messy and beautiful and entirely up to us.

As we turned, I saw Aunt Jo, Aaron, and Earth smiling at me. My family. Maybe now that the store was gone, Aaron and Aunt Jo could build a new life—something from scratch, together. Dan stood by the stage, nodding his head to the music and beaming at Cassie. Ian and James stood in the corner by the punch bowl, talking. Everything seemed right with the world. I knew it might not last, I knew it couldn't be perfect forever. But right now, this? This was a perfect moment. And I never could have seen it coming, not with all my visions of the future.

Asher twirled me, and the world glowed. I would always have a trace of my powers—I would never really lose them. But I had a chance at a real life, and I was going to take it.

We would make mistakes, we would argue, we would make up. We would lose the people we love and find new ones, and hold our memories close. We would fight for each other, again and again. We would keep living. We were in love.

And we were only human, after all.